To Teresa

PENCIL

LEAD

FRAN HEATH

Facebook/Instagram/Twitter:
@franheathwriter

For my parents who employed me
when I didn't know what else to do

PART 1

MISSING A POINT

1

The day Holly turned up at the shop, I'd been mostly passing the time by looking out of the windows. It was early spring and the weather was changing; some people were no longer wearing coats and leaves were returning to the trees which lined the opposite side of the street. The high clouds formed closely-fitting chevrons giving the sky the appearance of filleted cod.

I saw the man in the camouflage gear on the other side of the road, his face inclined towards the ground, concentrating as he drove his radio-controlled car along the pavement. He sped it up, slowed it down and circled a tree. He waited for a break in traffic and manoeuvred the car down onto the road where the kerb dropped. I could see him smile as he did that.

The girl-with-the-arse was there again, standing with her back to me just a few metres away beyond the glass. In the tight, black and white dress she wore for work, she began to cross the road, moving with a swing of the hips which seemed a little exaggerated, unnatural. It made me wonder if she knew I was there and put it on for me.

Ha! Don't be stupid, Lyle. You already fucked that up.

With an unexpected burst of speed, the camouflage man drove his car into the same space on the tarmac the girl was about to step. Stumbling, she yelled at him, but his focus on the vehicle didn't waver. Understanding there'd be no apology, she continued on, and I watched her sashay along Market Street until she was out of sight. It really was a great arse.

Turning my head away, on the far wall I noticed a gilt-framed picture that was new to the shop. I went over for a closer view. It was a smallish oil painting of a lighthouse and a ship in a storm. After running my fingers over the painted relief of the waves, I lifted the picture down from its hook, and flipped it over to see the back. In one corner there was a tiny part of the brown paper coming away. I picked at it with my nail and carefully peeled it back further with the tips of my finger and thumb. Thinking about it for a minute, I took out the short pencil from my pocket and wrote under the paper:

AFTER THE STORM, CALM

AFTER THE WINTER, SPRING

It could've been a fortune cookie aphorism or a motivational slogan. I wanted to rub it out, but left it there. People liked that kind of crap. Sometimes *I* liked that kind of crap. Sometimes it actually helped.

I worked in an antiques shop on the corner of a crossroads. It had large, plate glass windows on two sides (practically from floor to ceiling) allowing broad views in all four directions and as far as the church and park at the end of the street. Beyond the park was the city centre, but there it was like a scaled-down version, a distinct and separate community with almost all of the shops you could want.

I'd spend hours sitting at the desk, watching through the windows. I saw shoppers, dog walkers, joggers, people getting on and off the bus, going to and from work, coming home from school. I saw them but they didn't see me and I got to know their routes and their routines. There was the man in the orange hi-vis who cycled past several times a day, the brother and sister with the red hair who bought sweets from the newsagent's after school, and the fat man who went to The White Horse pub at eleven and left again at four.

I liked to see Mr and Mrs Stephenson – an old couple who held hands as they walked together. They were both short and

7

exactly the same height; he dressed in a grey suit and trilby hat and she wore a mustard-yellow coat whatever the weather.

Mr and Mrs Stephenson bought daily papers and went to the café to drink cups of tea. I couldn't see the café from where I sat as it was a few doors down on the same side of the street, but I often saw them there when I went in to buy my lunch, and I knew their names because I'd heard them being addressed by the older waitress. The girl-with-the-arse also worked there and I wouldn't go in unless I was sure she was out. On the days I didn't see her leave I'd go elsewhere. But I liked the filled baguettes from the café best.

I didn't know much about the antiques: I didn't know how old they were, where they were from, or what they were used for. Customers often asked me for things I'd never heard of – like corbels, or a credenza, or carnival glass. I'd tell them we didn't have any, then once they'd moved away from the desk, I'd go through the index of one of the Miller's reference books to find out what it was.

Not that it mattered anyway because if someone came in looking for an item I *had* heard of – like a door knocker, or a boot scraper, or a nutcracker – I'd show them the ones in stock and they'd never be right. Even if we had the exact thing they'd described, for some reason it wouldn't be quite what they wanted.

A bald man passed the window and came up to the door. I knew what *he* was going to ask for. I waited for it.

"Thimbles."

I hated that – people saying one word. It happened a lot. It was never, "Excuse me, do you have any thimbles please?" It was just, "Thimbles."

I wanted to say, "What about them? Are you looking for some? Do you have some to sell? Do you have one lodged in your arsehole? Do you know how to form a sentence?"

But, as usual, I went with, "Sorry, none in at the moment."

On his way out, the thimble man held the door open for Louisa on her way in. That wasn't her name – I didn't know her name. She was an old lady with white hair tied in a neat bun, and I could tell she was quite tall even though she stooped over the stick she walked with. Her movements around the shop were slow and her breathing difficult. At intervals she'd unload a wet cough into a tissue (which she apologised for), and frequently cautioned me not to take up smoking. To myself, I called her Lou-wheezer.

Despite her coughing and breathing I liked Louisa. She came in often to look at the small items on sale. The first time I saw her I'd been having a good day so happily spoke to her. She thought that was who I was, and so that *became* who I was – for her – and somehow I didn't find it an effort to pretend.

After she'd been around the shop, Louisa always sat on the chair near me for a rest and a chat. She had interesting stories to tell. Mostly she talked about the things she'd done and the places she'd travelled with her husband who'd worked in films. She talked about him a lot given he'd been dead for over thirty years.

It seemed to me the old people were always looking back. There were plenty who came in for the sake of nostalgia and treated the shop like some kind of museum. They would say, "I remember my mother had one of those," and, "You used to get these for sixpence in Woolworths." Then they'd recall other things from their childhood and tell me about them while I nodded and smiled and willed them to leave.

People my age tend to look towards the future, so is there a time in the middle – perhaps forty or fifty – when we're all content with where we are? Or maybe there are moments of contentment throughout our lives that come from the satisfaction of completing goals, but if so, do they only last until the next goal is identified and strived for? The old people that I saw in the shop probably had nothing else significant left to achieve in their lives. They'd already done it ... or not done it. Either way, the time had passed.

"So you've met Sean Connery?" I asked Louisa.

"Oh yes, many times. He was so handsome – but I only had eyes for my Jack." She smiled warmly. "I was on the set of quite a few of the Bond films."

"Did you get to see any stunts?"

"Yes, and explosions ... from a safe distance. They were spectacular."

"I bet they were." I was impressed – I liked Bond.

As we talked, Mrs Valensis came in with her skull-like, unsmiling face, and string of pearls around her long, corded neck.

On her approach to the desk she glanced at everything but me, and asked, "Is the man here?"

Mrs Valensis was a regular customer and had spent some good money, so for the sake of 'the man' I answered with more pleasantness in my voice than I felt, or she deserved.

"No, Keith's not in on Mondays I'm afraid. He'll be here tomorrow."

"Oh," she tutted, "that's inconvenient. I was hoping to do a deal with him on some furniture." She looked at me for the first time. "I suppose I'll have to come back tomorrow if I want to see him?"

Yeah, that's what I said. And maybe you should've listened to me LAST Monday when I told you he wasn't in on Mondays.

"Yeah," I said, "He'll be here then."

She placed her tan leather bag on the floor behind my chair, informing me I'd keep an eye on it while she took another look around.

As Mrs Valensis ascended the stairs to the first floor, Louisa raised her eyebrows. "I'll think I'll leave you to it. We can continue our conversation next time." She struggled to stand from the chair, but managed without the help I offered.

After Louisa had gone, Mrs Valensis came back down.

"I'd like the mahogany chest of drawers and the marble-top washstand that you have upstairs ... but I'd need his best price. Reserve them for me."

It's always the ones with money who knock the price down while the normal people generally pay what's on the ticket.

"OK," I said.

And how about saying "please" for a change you fucking rude bitch?

She stared at me as if she'd heard what I'd thought, and for a second I worried I'd said it out loud.

"You will do that for me won't you? Do you want me to show you the pieces I mean?"

Pieces! I hated that.

I didn't like getting out of the chair for customers, and I certainly wasn't going to for *her*. "I know the ones," I said, "I'll reserve them." I did know them – they were heavy. I'd helped carry them upstairs and didn't want to shift them again.

Mrs Valensis's time was important and she was rushing off to the next place she had to be. Her bag was still behind my chair. I very nearly called after her ... but didn't. Before long she would no doubt realise where she'd left it. But there was a chance that she wouldn't remember, have to cancel all her cards, and have an even more inconvenient day.

A few minutes passed and she hadn't returned. Glancing around at her bag, I reached down and hesitatingly pulled the zip a little way. Then I thought better of it – I didn't want to be caught going through her stuff.

Over at the front door, I pushed the catch down and put up the 'Back in 5 Minutes' sign. Picking up the bag, I took it into the back room and closed the door.

I set it down on the draining board next to the sink and unzipped it all the way. The lining was a floral-patterned silk, and in it was a folded umbrella, keys to her house and car (a BMW), sanitary towels and tampons in a case, two lipsticks, and a box of mints. I shook out one of the mints and put it in my mouth. There was a cheque book in a leather cover, and a gold fountain pen. In her purse were some credit cards (all platinum), shop loyalty cards, and her driving licence – her first name was Caroline, her birthday was on New Year's Day and she was only forty-six (I'd have guessed she was older). There were two photos behind the licence – a young girl on a horse, and a fat man by a pool with a glass of red wine in his hand. Neither of the people were smiling and I assumed they were her daughter and husband. I counted the money: eighty pounds in notes and some small change. Did she know how much she had in there? Would she miss a ten or a twenty?

Loud, rapid knocks sounded on the glass of the front door. I returned the purse and closed the bag, having first taken the lid off the pen – a small thing, yet satisfying. When I came out from the back room, Caroline Valensis was peering impatiently through the door. Hastily swallowing her mint, I took the bag to her. There was no gratitude and no smile.

When I eventually went upstairs to put 'Sold' stickers on the washstand and chest of drawers, I carefully took out one of the smallest drawers and on the unvarnished wood of the underside wrote:

REMEMBER YOUR MANNERS

In the afternoon, I sold a butter dish from the area in the window where nothing ever remained for long. Scanning the shop for a similarly-sized item to take its place, I settled on a little wooden house.

It was a music box in the style of a Swiss chalet, with an overhanging roof, and shutters and flowers around the window. Winding the small key on the base, I lifted the roof (which was the lid of the box), and the music began. I tipped out the rectangular piece of wood that covered the mechanism underneath, and watched a revolving, studded cylinder pluck the teeth of a metal comb to create the notes.

As I hadn't wound it far, the tune played slowly. It was familiar but slightly off-key, making it sound menacing, like something you'd hear in a child's bedroom in a horror film. I replaced the wood, closed the lid, and the music ended abruptly. As I positioned the box in the empty space, Amy from next door passed by in her red and black school uniform.

Amy must've been around fourteen or fifteen, but unlike some other girls of her age, still presented herself as a child; there was nothing provocative in how she acted or dressed (she didn't wear make-up, her skirts were knee-length), and I certainly didn't look at her in the way I did those other girls of her age. I can't help noticing curves on a woman whether they're on a fifty or a fifteen year old, especially the ones who show off what they've got with tight clothes, short skirts, or low-cut tops. It's entirely natural – all men must do it – but, of course, looking is all I'd do, and it's best not to be obvious about it.

It was getting late in the day. Along with watching through the windows, I started watching the clock, waiting for it to reach five so I could finish and go back up to the flat.

It slowly made it to ten to.

Near enough.

As I rose from the chair to begin closing up, the shop door opened and someone came in. Cursing inwardly, I started to sit back down. I stopped when I saw it was Holly.

It'd been about a year and a half since we'd last seen each other, and she seemed unsure how to react – as unsure as I was. But then she smiled and asked me the question I'd been asking myself for a long time: "Lyle! What are you doing here?"

2

I'd left university with a low-graded degree in English and a large debt. Neither concerned me – the grade was a reflection of the work I'd been prepared to do, and the debt could be ignored until I earned a wage high enough for it to become payable.

I stayed in the city where I'd studied. It was as good a place as any. Better, even. I knew it well – the shops, the pubs, the bus routes and the train line. I hadn't known where else to go but I was sure it wouldn't be to my parents'; after three years of living away it would have felt like a step backwards.

Marcus stayed too. We searched for a flat to rent and found one in Oldchurch – a place unfamiliar to us as it was on the other side of the city from the university campus.

It was above an antiques shop, with access through a wooden gate in the wall to the side of the shop, across a yard, and up an external metal staircase to the front door. The antiques dealer – who was also the landlord – had a workshop that opened onto the yard. He sometimes used the space to restore furniture, and on the day we had our viewing, there was an iron bedstead leaning against the wall, and sawdust and off-cuts of wood on the ground.

Inside the flat it was the 1970s, mostly in brown: the textured wallpaper, the barkcloth curtains, the kitchen tiles above the woodgrain-effect worktops, and the lino resembling parquet flooring. Even the bathroom suite was the colour of shit. The one thing which stood out for not being brown was the green and furry living room carpet. It was as if Oscar the Grouch from *Sesame Street* had been skinned.

The landlord waited in the kitchen while we stood in the living room, discussing what we'd do.

"I dunno, man," Marcus said, staring down at the Muppet pelt. "Let's find something else."

"Yeah, where?"

We were two young, unemployed men. Most wouldn't consider us as tenants, and of the properties we'd already seen, one stank of a combination of cat's piss and damp, and the other was in the middle of a ghetto. Although there some of the wallpaper was faded, the perishing lino in the hallway patched up with duct tape, and a tap dripped in the bathroom, something about it made me like the place.

I tried convincing him. "We're out of options. We're not going to find better than this. It's furnished … and cheap …" There were technically two bedrooms, but as the second was small, the rent was the same as some one-bedroom places.

I followed Marcus through to the bigger bedroom for a second look. More bold-patterned paper covered the walls. He opened the door of the dark-wood wardrobe, then closed it.

"Don't look in there," I said, "it's Narnia business."

"Huh?"

"Don't worry." If they don't get it, I don't bother to explain.

Marcus sat on the double bed and bounced experimentally. "OK, I s'pose we'll take it … but only if I get *this* room."

Reluctantly, I agreed, and we moved in just as everyone we knew moved away.

The first part of the summer was like a holiday. I felt I'd earned a break, I deserved it. There'd be plenty of time later to look for a job, but in those first few weeks I wanted to not have to be anywhere or do anything. In the meantime I had the dole and housing benefit to just about get me by.

It was a proper summer – nearly every day was sunny and hot. Marcus and I would get up late in the mornings, buy cans of cheap beer and take them to the park. We'd lie on the grass and see girls sunbathing in their bikini tops and going past in their short skirts. A couple of times we ventured down to the pub by the river where we always used to go, sitting at the tables outside until the sun set, and then moving inside to play pool and the quiz machine. We watched films and talked and drank into the early hours. It was a good time.

Then Marcus got a job. It was in London and he had to be out by quarter past seven to make it into work for nine. I meant to get up early and have breakfast with him on his first day, but found it too difficult to get out of bed and fell asleep again, waking long after he'd gone. On other mornings, if I heard him moving around the flat getting ready to leave for work, it gave me a great deal of satisfaction to know I didn't have to get up at that time ... or at all if I didn't want to.

Marcus wore a suit to work and had shiny black shoes. He was encouraged to have his hair short and keep his face clean-shaven; it made him look different and older. I didn't want to work for a company that expected those things from me. I wanted to be able to wear jeans and T-shirts – I liked my own clothes – and I liked not shaving if I didn't want to. Although I wouldn't have thought it, Marcus didn't seem to care. His transition from student to besuited man was smooth. He focused on the salary.

I had the daytimes to myself. There was no one I could hang around with: there was no one I knew. But I could watch porn through the TV in the living room (an improvement on my laptop's small screen), and for the first few days after Marcus started work, that was pretty much all I did.

Then I didn't know what to do. I didn't want to go out to the park – it wouldn't have been the same on my own – so for the most part, I stayed in and watched TV. From the mid-afternoons (although too early to do so), I began to anticipate Marcus getting back from work. From the late-afternoons, I'd turn the volume down so I could listen out for him coming through the gate. But usually Marcus didn't get in until after seven, and then he'd be tired after his long day. He complained about the "fucktards" he worked with, and his tedious commute. He ate dinner, showered, and zoned out in front of the TV until he went to bed no later than eleven.

So, I was on my own during the day, and I may as well have been most evenings too … but there were still weekends. The weekends were the same as they'd been before Marcus got his job. And I looked forward to them.

In mid-August it turned seriously hot; it was the main story on the news and some people had died because of it. I wasn't sure if it was too hot to stay in or too hot to go out, but it had become almost unbearable to be indoors (even with every window open), so I was forced to find relief outside.

In the street, the air felt static and oppressive. My shirt was sticking to the sweat on my back so I crossed the road to the shady side. As I stepped onto the pavement, I spotted a pound coin on the ground and bent to get it. But the coin wouldn't move: it had been glued down. Embarrassed for having been fooled, I checked no one had seen, then, in an attempt to dislodge the coin, kicked at the side of it with the tip of my shoe. But it was stuck fast. Giving up, I headed to the Co-op for beers.

The artificially cool climate of the supermarket was welcome. I grabbed a four-pack from the fridge and explored the aisles for special offers. But soon it felt *too* cold in there, so I paid and left.

Back through the door, the temporarily forgotten heat wrapped around me like a dry towel from a radiator. It was suffocating for an instant, and I nearly went back in, but wanting to drink, turned away towards the church.

Although not religious, I like churches – the architecture, the stained glass and the history. This one had been around since the eleventh century and had eventually given the area its name. Entering the churchyard through open gates, I walked the path paved with old gravestones; the shapes of the stones could be clearly seen, but after being eroded by feet and weather, many words were impossible to decipher. A pencil lay on the ground there. It was short – around ten centimetres long – painted yellow, with a stub of pink rubber on the end. I picked it up, this time with no trouble.

Leaving the path, I made my way across the grass to the shade of a large oak tree near the perimeter wall, and sat in a shallow indentation on top of a low, rectangular tomb (perhaps someone else had had the same idea for a seat). I took off my shirt and opened the first can. Between the tree trunk and the wall I was hidden from view, and I was glad no one could see me … drinking on a grave, with my shirt off, in the middle of the day, when everyone should be at work.

It was quiet in the churchyard. There was no breeze and it didn't seem any cooler than it had been in the flat. A wagtail momentarily landed on top of the rough stone wall, its tail bobbing vertically three times before the bird flew off again.

If this heat was going to last the weekend, I thought Marcus and I could do something air-conditioned like bowling or the cinema. I was well into my overdraft and it would be a stretch to afford it, but maybe I could ask Marcus to lend me a twenty.

Yeah, ask.

I read the inscription on the headstone nearest to me:

IN MEMORY OF

ROBERT HIX

BORN 7th JUNE 1786

WHO FELL IN A DUEL

IN OLDCHURCH PARK

25th SEPTEMBER 1809

AGED 23

It was disappointing not to see details of the circumstances of the duel. I always liked to find epitaphs that said something beyond names, dates, who someone was married to, or were the parent/child of. It was good if they mentioned a person's character or profession, or how they'd lived or died. But the space (and money to the stonemason) was usually wasted on God or Jesus, and euphemisms for death.

I read the words on the grave next to the duellist:

BENEATH
THIS STONE
lie the mortal remains of
SYLVIA AVERY
Died 30th March 1847
AGED 18 YEARS

Why did you die so young, Sylvia?

She'd been a 'beloved daughter' and was 'not lost but gone before'. I briefly mourned her, then wondered if she'd been good-looking or if she'd ever had sex. If I'd lived then, I'm sure I'd have enjoyed the challenge of getting past petticoats, corsets and Victorian values.

I'd finished two of the cans and decided to save the rest for later. Before leaving the churchyard, I crouched at the base of Sylvia's headstone, moved the long grass to one side and, using the pencil I'd found, wrote:

LYLE McNORTON

AGED 21

LIVING NOT DEAD

I hadn't known if pencil on stone would work, but in fact it wrote easily.

I helped the grass settle back to cover my words; if anyone saw them they might think I'd been disrespectful. But it wasn't like that to me. It felt like I was connecting myself to her, someone who'd been dead for well over a hundred years, who no one alive would remember.

Fuck what you'd think anyway. After all, they'd made memorials into a path.

Sitting on the sofa with my feet on the brown, tile-top coffee table and my plate resting on my lap, I ate the dinner I'd made from what little I had in the cupboard and fridge. The meal was good; sometimes it turned out better if you had to get creative with the only ingredients to hand. I watched game shows and waited for Marcus to get in from work.

Past nine o'clock he still wasn't back, so I called him. It rang and rang and went to the answer message. I hung up.

Five minutes later he returned my call, but it was difficult to hear him at first with all the background noise of music and talking. I heard him say he was with Nina.

"You're with Nina?" I said. "What, *Nina*?!"

"Yeah, *Nina.*"

"Where are you?"

"In a pub. Shepherd's Bush."

"When did you arrange that?"

"She texted this morning."

"Oh." People were cheering and I strained to hear. "For fuck's sake Marcus, can't you go outside?!"

He spoke louder. "I won't be back tonight."

"OK. When *will* you be back?"

"Dunno. Maybe tomorrow. Prob'ly Sunday."

"Uh … are you and Nina back together then?" I questioned.

"Yeah," he confirmed, "we're back together."

3

Some weekends, Marcus stayed at Nina's place in London, and others she stayed with him at our flat. Whichever it was, I hardly ever saw Marcus. If they were both at the flat they were usually out or in his room. They had a lot of sex in his room. She was noisy and alternated between a loud whimpering and a strange kind of squealing. Mostly I didn't want to hear it, but sometimes I liked hearing it. Then I'd imagine putting my hand over her mouth to shut her up as I fucked her hard.

That was the way it had always been with them. The times when they were seeing each other, they were no longer two separate people; they were one entity who we'd referred to as 'Nincus'. I'd never allowed myself to be part of 'Lolly' or 'Hole' or anything else.

Marcus wasn't just with Nina at weekends. She lived nearer to his work so he was often there in the week too. I was alone in the flat a lot of the time, not knowing if he was coming back.

I didn't feel like doing much and was finding it difficult to remember what I used to enjoy. One afternoon I wrote a list to remind me of things I could do, things that would make the time pass more easily:

WATCH TV

WATCH A FILM

WATCH PORN

LISTEN TO MUSIC

READ A BOOK

GET DRUNK

EAT

SLEEP

GO FOR A WALK

HAVE A BATH

WRITE

I referred to the list many times. Often I went with 'watch porn'. When I had the money it was 'get drunk'.

The last weekend that Nina stayed at the flat, I spent much of it in my room keeping out of their way. Outside of sleeping I didn't like being in that room. It was so small that there was only space for a single bed and a narrow chest of drawers, and the door couldn't be opened fully as it hit the end of the bed. The wallpaper was a poor-quality William Morris-type print of flowers and leaves. I tried to see the flowers and leaves, but once I'd noticed that together they resembled eyes, a nose, grinning lips and a hat on top, all I could see were clown faces. The walls were thin and through them I could hear the next door neighbour – a girl. She played crap music and sang along. She spoke on her phone, coughed and closed a lot of drawers.

I was sitting on the bed with newspapers, copies of my old CV, and some handwritten notes spread out in front of me. But I wasn't doing anything with it all – I was listing the American states, and had reached thirty-seven before my memory stalled.

A knocking on the window startled me and I turned to see a large fly crashing against the outside of the pane, struggling to free itself from a web. The spider, half its size, appeared from a corner and crawled towards its prey.

I stood and took the two paces to cross the floor. My intention was to open the window and free the fly, but I hesitated – it was nature's way, why should I choose sides? So I watched. But when the fly got away before the spider could reach it, I was glad; I *had* chosen sides and would've regretted not helping. The spider returned to its corner.

Remaining by the window, I leaned against the frame with my head resting on my forearm, and peered down at the street below and the people walking there. It was a windy day and women were holding down their skirts. I watched to see if any would be lifted up but, disappointingly, none were.

Another knock, this time on the door. Quickly seating myself back on the bed, I picked up my notebook and pen.

"Yeah?"

Marcus opened the door as far as it would go and put his head around it. "Hey man, we're off out." He didn't say where.

"OK." I didn't ask.

He noticed the papers. "How's it going?"

"Good, thanks."

"Good. Uh ... see you later."

"Yeah, bye."

Prick.

He left the room and I put the notebook down. I'd made sure he hadn't seen what was on it.

After hearing the front door shut behind them, I moved into the living room. There was no point in pretending to write job applications if there was no one to appreciate the pretence. And *I* didn't appreciate it – I wasn't kidding *myself*; I knew I wasn't going to do anything, no matter how long I sat there.

From my position on the sofa, my gaze rested as often on the wallpaper as it did the TV. The design there a repeating scene of hills and trees and a river, all in brown. I liked the pattern, but thought it could be improved with some extra details. Remembering the pencil I'd found in the churchyard, I retrieved it from the depths of my back pocket where it had lain ever since.

I drew lightly on the paper, but I'm no artist. Firstly I added a simple boat to the river, and then a man to the boat – a crude, stick-like figure. I tried to sketch a few animals, but they didn't turn out the way they were supposed to: the fox was more like a horse, and the squirrel like some kind of dinosaur clinging to a tree.

It was early evening when Marcus and Nina returned. Nina went straight to his room, but I was surprised when Marcus came into the living room, handed me a beer and sat down.

"Lyle, I need to talk to you." By his tone it didn't sound like anything I'd want to hear.

Opening the can, I said, "Yeah?"

He cleared his throat. "I'm moving in with Nina."

I drank.

"In London," he added.

"Right." I drank some more.

Marcus narrowed his eyes and tentatively asked, "OK?"

"No, not OK." I placed the beer on the table. "We've got a six month contract." I made a quick, mental calculation. "We've only been here three."

"Yeah, I know, but who cares? I reckon we should just forget about that and leave. What's he gonna do?"

I didn't know what the landlord would do. He hadn't made us produce guarantors for the rent when we'd taken the tenancy, but he did have our parents' addresses.

"What about the deposit?" I said. We'd given the equivalent of a month's rent.

"Well, we'd lose that."

"Marcus, I don't want to lose that money … and anyway, I don't *want* to leave!"

He shrugged his shoulders. "Why not? What's here for you, man? Why did we even stay? Let's just fuck it off."

It was alright for him – he had Nina's to go to. But what about me? "Where do you expect me to go?"

"I dunno – home?"

"No fucking way!"

"Somewhere else then."

"Yeah, right," I said. "How can I even afford to move?"

He stared me straight in the eyes, "Well … you could always get a job."

I stared back. "What do you think I've been trying to do for the last couple of months?"

"I dunno what you've been doing," he said. "What *have* you been doing?"

"What?!"

"Well, have you actually *applied* for anything?"

"Of course I have!" I lied.

"Really? But you haven't even had any interviews, have you?"

"No, not yet. These things take time."

"Bullshit! *I* found something pretty quickly."

Yeah, and I know how much you love YOUR job!

Marcus sighed and sank back into the armchair. "Look, you should just take anything you can get at the moment … for the money."

Who was he to tell me what I should do? What business was it of his?

"I'm not going to just take *anything*," I said defiantly. "And why should I? I've got a degree."

He laughed. "So what?! You and everyone else. What job d'you want anyway?"

Avoiding the question, I picked up my can and resumed drinking.

"What about teacher training?" he suggested. "Loads of others are doing that. Nina's thinking about it."

I wasn't going to do teacher training – I didn't like kids and I was certain I wouldn't like a roomful of them … and then there were the early mornings. Was the job even about *teaching* anymore? It seemed to be about tests, targets and a whole lot of stress.

"If people wanted to be teachers," I said, "why didn't they choose to do that in the first place? They're only doing it now because they've run out of options and imagination." I wanted to add that was a common theme with Nina, but resisted. I lowered my voice. "What about when it all goes to shit with Nina again?" I'd lost count of the number of times they'd split up … and got together … and split up … and got together. "Why don't you stay living here and see how it goes with her – give it a couple more months?"

"Nah, it'll be alright this time. Things will be different." He spoke quieter himself. "Look, I can't stand commuting anymore – three fucking hours … on a good day! I'm going, man. Sorry."

Sure he was, but it was clear there was nothing I could say. He'd made up his mind.

That week, I spoke to the landlord about the situation – not through any sense of right or loyalty, but because I didn't see another choice. I wanted to stay, and he didn't want the place empty, so we came to an agreement: I'd live in the flat at a slightly reduced rent covered by housing benefit, if I signed a new six month contract as a single tenant. I signed.

Marcus packed up and left at the weekend; he thought he was being generous by not asking me for his share of the deposit back. Part of me was glad he was going – he wasn't there anyway – and I wasted no time moving myself into the bigger bedroom.

* * *

Our graduation happened in October. Everyone came back for the ceremony – Marcus with Nina, and Holly was there.

Inside the cathedral, the monotonous hum of the speeches

echoed like a fly in a dustbin. Amongst a sea of mortarboards, I stared at the backs of people's heads. Holly's was three rows in front of me, just to the left. I focused on her straight brown hair beneath the cap, and visualised the curves of the body I knew were hidden under the shapeless gown. I decided to talk to her at some point during the day, but in the end, I didn't.

Afterwards, most of us went down to the pub by the river, and we drank, laughed and talked about old times. A few stayed into the late evening, but not Nincus, and not Holly.

Then everyone left and that part of my life was over.

I was on my own.

4

The first university students I saw in town after the summer break were sitting on the low wall that circled the fountain. There were six of them: four girls and two boys. A blonde girl wearing a long Indian skirt and red boots was trailing a hand in the water behind her, while a boy in pale jeans and a yellow sweatshirt sat next to her awkwardly, combing his fingers through his pop star hair. A couple of them were eating shop-bought sandwiches out of the plastic packaging, and a girl dressed entirely in black was smoking. They didn't look like they belonged together and were probably the first people they'd all met; they were a collection of 'types' who hadn't yet found their own groups.

Bunch of dicks.

They were who we'd been three years before, and I remembered how I'd felt at the beginning. Everyone was new to me, from all around the country with different accents and different words. They didn't know me and I didn't know them, and for a few days it was difficult to be myself – or to remember who 'myself' was – until I found the people who'd become my friends. Those people had moved on to jobs, or travelling, or unemployment elsewhere, and these new students had taken their place … had taken *our* place. It hadn't been our choice to leave university; the time we had was finite, and it had inevitably, and abruptly, come to an end.

The town was different too – the places I went to had changed. What would once have been the campus and the cafés and the pubs, became the park and the library and the Jobcentre. But it didn't occur to me to revisit the old hangouts; I lived in a parallel city where they didn't even exist.

I should have been looking for a job, but I wasn't. It would have been easier if I'd known what to look for, but I didn't.

Everything had always been simple for me. I'd been given the part-time jobs I'd applied for (cleaning in a supermarket, and a brief stint behind a bar), and passed my driving test on the first try. I hadn't struggled at school and achieved good grades with the minimum amount of effort. I was an all-rounder – as capable at sciences as I was at arts – above average, and in the top sets for the subjects streamed by ability. I knew I'd do my A-levels then go on to university; it was expected – by my parents, by my teachers, and by myself. But it didn't matter to me what I studied. It was just about being there for the three years.

I enjoyed English at school; I liked the teacher – all the boys did. She was engaging and enthusiastic, and when she bent over to read our work we could see down her top. So I chose English as my degree course, and assumed the next thing would become clear along the way.

But it hadn't.

So now what?

Get a job.

What job? Where?

A good job, I was sure. I would have a highly-valued, well-paid career.

There's so much choice of what people *can* do, but not always the opportunity to do it. To be really successful at things like sport and music, you have to start at a young age. But when you're young you don't know what you want. My parents should've insisted I continue my piano lessons. Maybe I'd be fluent in another language if they'd pushed me to do that, or I could be learning how to run my dad's business ... if he hadn't been a headteacher. If only I could invent something – a thing so simple it was crazy no one had had the idea before, so indispensable to people's lives that every home had one. Something that would make me a lot of money and give me recognition.

I had no practical skills or trade, only qualifications, and there was no clear profession that I wanted to pursue. I'd had the idea of becoming a writer and felt I knew enough to be successful at it, but after all the enforced writing during university, I'd lost interest and wasn't prepared to put in the time and effort. I wanted a book, as indeed I wanted my life, to appear fully formed in front of me: to be perfect and immediate.

And anyway, I didn't particularly have a story. In my first year, I'd begun working on a novel called *Abra-Cadaver*. It was about an illusionist framed for his glamorous assistant's murder, who evades the police and hunts down the real killer using a series of elaborate tricks. I hadn't made much progress with it; I knew nothing about magic. To be honest, I came up with the title first and the story came from there. I thought it was a genius title, before I found out it had already been used … at least twice. The more books that are written, the more difficult it is to have an original idea. I'm sure someone's even said *that* before.

To write about what you know is supposed to be the best way, but what did *I* know? Maybe I hadn't lived enough yet. But I was sure that if I *did* have a story, I could write a great novel – probably prize-winning. An idea would no doubt come to me one day and I'd look out for it.

I would only be a writer of books though, not newspapers. I couldn't see myself penning articles about vandalism, charity fundraisers, or the closing of community centres; I'm not a deadlines and headlines kind of a person. Although, 'Freelance Headline Writer' would be a perfect job for me if it existed. I'd find it easy to think up puns for stories about drunken soap stars, cheating footballers and political scandals … not that I'd ever work for their lying, tabloid rags though. They can all fuck off.

I know it's probably stupid, but I've always thought I should get a sense of something – a job or a place or a person – as if it were meant to be. It'll be familiar before it happens, like a feeling of déjà-vu. Perhaps that idea has influenced my choices more than I realise.

Without a job, the only difference between the weekdays and the weekends were the programmes on TV. Weekdays were best and sometimes I'd watch all day – chat shows, Australian soaps, children's cartoons, game shows, early-evening news, dramas and late-night comedy. I particularly enjoyed afternoon episodes of *Columbo*, *Quincy*, and *Murder, She Wrote*, but I could never bring myself to sit through *Jeremy Kyle.*

Certain programmes were the highlights of the week, the distractions I could rely on. Mealtimes were also important as there were at least three, and they happened daily. Straight after breakfast I looked forward to lunch, and after lunch, I thought on to what I'd have for dinner. But they weren't often the meals I wanted – it was the food I could afford.

I'd had to work out a detailed plan of my income and outgoings; even if you don't think you're spending much, it's surprising how quickly money runs out if you don't pay attention to it. Every pound counted, if not every penny. The rent was covered, but there was still gas, electricity, water, food and other things to pay for. Not able to afford to keep my phone contract, I got a cheap pay-as-you-go handset.

I lived mostly in overdraft – often close to the limit – and there was no chance of credit beyond it. I allocated money on a weekly basis and tried not to spend more. A couple of times I did overspend, using money from the following week, but I was essentially stealing from myself and making life more miserable down the line.

With the money allocated, I made sure there was an amount available to buy alcohol. Nearing the end of the week – or middle of the week, or Tuesday – when I'd drunk it all, I used some of the remaining food budget to buy more.

I *did* mean to do something about my situation, there was always some guilt about the time I was wasting, and even the benefits I was claiming. In the beginning I had no problem as I knew I'd spend a large portion of my life contributing back to the system with tax. But it had gone on too long. Most evenings before bed, I'd think about getting up early the next morning to try and sort it out. But when it came to it, the need to roll over and go back to sleep would win over, and it was usual for me to stay in bed until eleven or twelve.

As I sat in front of the TV, I'd be thinking that I must tidy up / go to the shops / clean the bathroom / look for a job, but I'd rarely do any of it. I seemed to always be on the verge of doing something useful without actually doing it. I could never do much after three in the afternoon anyway (and certainly nothing like a job application), so before the day was even half over, I'd write it off and begin to focus on the next one – how early I could get up, how much I could get done …

5

It was the beginning of December and had rained every day for almost two weeks. Not owning a coat, I'd hardly left the flat, but it looked likely to be a dry afternoon, so I decided to go to town and buy one. And I was pleased to have given myself a mission, to have something to do.

As I stepped out of the front door, I smiled. It was starting to turn colder, but not too bad yet. It was the right time to get a coat, a good plan, and I'd been clever to think of it.

Standing for a moment on the metal platform at the top of the staircase, I peered down to the yard below. I had an impulse to vault over the rail and wondered what would happen if I did. Would I be able to land on my feet without breaking at least one of my legs? Probably not – it was a long way down to the concrete floor. I imagined myself lying there on the ground. Would I die or just be injured? If I called out, would anyone hear me? And if not, when would I be found?

I walked down the stairs.

In town it was busier than I'd ever seen it; I realised it was a Saturday.

A Saturday in DECEMBER – of course it's fucking busy!

Perhaps not such a good plan.

The shop windows were dressed for Christmas and there were dozens of market stalls set up in the square selling hot food, decorations and cheap gifts. Somehow resisting the smell of burgers and frying onions, I made my way past it all to the indoor shopping centre.

Inside, there were far too many people and there was not

enough room to move amongst them. Mothers wielded pushchairs laden with screaming children and carrier bags, and slow-moving husbands were reluctantly herded by their wives. I found myself stuck behind an enormous man whose skin could no longer contain his fat in a shape that resembled a body, and it hung below his T-shirt like a fleshy mini-skirt.

Get the fuck out of my way you fat bastard. How could you do that to yourself?

As I dodged past him, I realised my face showed my disgust and changed it to a neutral expression.

Wanting to be in the shopping centre for as little time as necessary, I went straight to one of the cheaper clothes stores and negotiated a path through the crowded women's department to the men's at the back. I found the coats, but even in there they were more than I was able to afford. With equal feelings of homicide and suicide, I made my way out to the ground floor atrium and headed in the direction of the escalators.

There was so much going on – the lights, the displays, and the echoing noise of the people walking and talking. Every unit was vying for attention and the whole place was making me dizzy. The background music started to come into the foreground – Slade, East 17, The Pogues and Kirsty MacColl; snippets of the same few songs as I passed each open doorway. They didn't seem to be playing at the right speed – sometimes slower, sometimes faster – and the voices sounded as if they were mocking me. My head felt like it was in the middle of my chest one moment, and floating away from my body the next. There was another shop I'd wanted to try, but it was up two floors and I couldn't do it: I needed to leave.

Near the exit I saw a Santa's grotto (playing 'I Wish It Could Be Christmas Everyday') with a long queue of impatient children and parents waiting their turn. A life-sized model of Rudolph stood by the entrance to the grotto, which got me thinking about the proper reindeer and what their names were. I remembered all but two.

What are those two?

I listed the six again over and over in my head, but still couldn't get the others.

What ARE they?!

Stop it, Lyle, it doesn't matter. Forget it. Forget it!

In one of the charity shops (where I should have gone in the first place), I found a grey, hooded jacket for six pounds. It was a bit big but would do, and the fresh air would get rid of the musty smell.

Back in the street, I passed a hairdresser's with a board outside advertising a special deal for men: a wash, cut and dry for a fiver. No appointment was necessary – just walk in. Five pounds seemed crazily cheap, and having been prepared to spend up to fifteen on a coat, I had at least that to spare. My hair had grown longer than I usually had it and was nearly down to my shoulders. I walked in.

Directed to a waiting area, I was told 'Laura' would be with me in a few minutes. I seated myself in a red leather chair and scanned the low table in front of me scattered with magazines. The title of one was partly obscured with only the upper half of a word visible:

REALITY

'REALITY' struck me as strange name for a women's magazine. But when I uncovered the whole title, I saw the word was actually 'BEAUTY'.

Pretentiously noting the profundity of my mistake, I nodded.

Yeah, half of reality IS beauty.

I continued to wait. It was noisy with hairdryers, talking and the radio. I started to think it had been a bad idea, and was contemplating getting up to leave when Laura came over. She was around thirty with short, bleach-blonde hair, and piercings along the edges of both ears. She took me over to the sinks. Tilting my head back, my neck rested in the indentation of the basin.

"Does that feel comfortable?"

"Yeah."

"Is the water too hot?"

"No."

Laura was wearing a tight, white shirt with the top three buttons undone. She had good-sized tits. I tried not to look at them but it was difficult not to – from the height we were both at, they were close to my face. I could see a lacy bra through the material of the shirt, and the shape of slightly raised nipples.

As she leaned over and wet my hair, one of her tits brushed my shoulder. She reached for the bottle of shampoo and did it again. As she massaged the shampoo into my scalp, she rested it on me for what felt like a full minute. Was she doing it deliberately?

The contact ended as she rinsed my hair clean. Her nipples were noticeably harder, the shape more distinct.

Did you like that, Laura?

They were right there. I wanted one in my mouth, and then the other. I was sure she wanted that too. Maybe at the end of this I'd ask if she'd like to go out for a drink sometime.

Laura guided me to a chair in front of a mirror, then left me alone for a moment to fetch her scissors.

I regarded my appearance; the bright lighting of the salon showed a different person to the one I'd only glance at in the bathroom as I brushed my teeth. My cheekbones were more prominent (they could almost be described as 'chiselled') and my eyes seemed bluer and larger, although slightly baggier underneath. I hadn't been shaving. My dad had a beard as did my uncles, and I remembered a time in my early childhood when I'd assumed that all men have beards. It felt right that *I* had one, and it suited me. I looked good – no wonder the hairdresser liked me. Smiling kindly at my reflection, the smile was momentarily reciprocated before it was replaced by a sneer. I slowly and subtly shook my head in disapproval.

In the mirror, I watched Laura return and stand behind me. She asked how I wanted the cut, and I was glad when she didn't talk more than that; since her tits had gone away from my face I'd lost interest. So I just stared at the objects on the small glass shelf in front of me: the bottles of hairspray, the tub of wax, and the black and white clippers that reminded me of a killer whale.

It didn't take long for her to finish. She'd done a good job, but wouldn't be getting a tip. I paid the five pounds to the girl at the counter by the door and stepped onto the street. My ears and neck were cold after the loss of their previous insulation, so I bought a black woolly hat for a pound at a market stall.

Back in Oldchurch, I stopped in at the Co-op to buy food with the eight pounds I had left. On the door, I saw a poster for the lottery. Believing it *could* be me, I went straight to the stand, picked my numbers and queued for the ticket.

They were selling scratchcards at the till with pictures of Santa's reindeer on. Their names were written underneath.

Dasher and Vixen – that's who you are!

Convinced it was a sign, I bought one of those too.

The symbols hidden behind the silver revealed I'd won a pound. With that pound, I bought another card … and lost. Wanting to win again I returned to the counter and bought a different one, without a Christmas theme. Another loser. I should've persevered with the reindeer.

I'd spent half of my money and had four pounds left. I wanted to keep going with the scratchcards, but couldn't risk wasting more cash, so shopped for food instead. I chose a sliced loaf, a jar of beef sandwich spread, a Pot Noodle, bananas and a carton of milk. There was enough money to include a couple of cans of beer. I wanted to get more alcohol, but having hardly anything left in the kitchen cupboards, had to buy the food. But there was still the lottery ticket for that evening and a chance I'd win the jackpot.

Later, as I watched the draw, I thought about all the things I'd buy with the money: the big house by the sea, the cars and the holidays. When I had money everything would be different.

The numbers were chosen. Only one matched mine.

I'd been stupid to think I could've won ... but maybe it just wasn't my time. Maybe it isn't good to get something from nothing, so it had probably been for the best.

I ripped up the ticket and turned off the TV. Stepping into the corridor, I found the floorboard that sounded like a person whistling when you stood on it. I got it to make the noise a few times before heading into the kitchen. Opening the cupboard, I saw the food I'd bought and remembered the scratchcards. There were lots of things I could've got with those few pounds – I could've had more beer – and I wouldn't be wasting my money like that again. I closed the cupboard and went to my bedroom.

Not wanting silence, I put on a CD. I prefer them to downloads in the same way that I prefer real books to ebooks – to have a physical copy, to see the covers. The saying that you can't judge a book by its cover is so wrong as I've discovered many good albums and novels purely on the strength of their artwork.

Scanning my stack of CDs, I thought about which were my favourite three. I brought those to the top of the pile, before changing my mind and swapping them around. Turning my attention to books, I again tried to find the three favourites, but that was more difficult. I had to put *Catch 22* in there and *Steppenwolf*, but how could I decide between Orwell, Poe, Homer, Dostoyevsky and Kafka? And then there was the old

Illustrated Book of Fairy Tales that my sister used to read to me. I upped my selection to five, and then ten.

Next, I thought about what I'd choose if I could only keep ten things I owned. I didn't have a lot of stuff, and there wasn't much that I cared about or was irreplaceable. I decided my CDs, books and porn collection counted as one thing each, and along with those I chose my laptop, stereo, TV, and the vintage Smith & Corona typewriter my granddad had given me. Then I got bored and gave up.

Lying down with my head at the foot of the bed, I placed my feet on the wall above my pillow. Through the window from that position I could only see dark sky and clouds, their edges highlighted in silver by the moon. There was nothing to indicate where I was – I could've been anywhere – and I imagined I was in a house on the top of a hill.

One curtain was pulled back too far creating an imperfect frame, so I got up to make it symmetrical, being careful not to glimpse the real world outside. I lay back down and stared straight up. The holes at the top of the light shade made a pattern on the ceiling like stylised rays of the sun. I closed my eyes and I was lying on the hill in the summer; I could feel the warmth of the sun on my face and see its light through my eyelids. It was not winter. It was not night time. I was not indoors. Taking a deep breath, I held it and told myself it would be my last. And then, after the longest time, I took another.

As I pretended to be somewhere else, I thought about *that* place. There really was nothing left for me after university had ended, and it occurred to me for the first time that staying *had* been a mistake. It was like an epiphany. Why the hell hadn't I gone when Marcus had?

You should've gone.

You should go.

I'd have to stay until the tenancy ended in March – I wanted the deposit back – but then I could start again somewhere else. Everything would work out then; a change of environment was all I needed.

But *where* would I go? I knew that back home was the only option as I had no money to go elsewhere. Even though I'd discounted it before, the more I thought about it, the more it seemed like a good idea. It wouldn't be *so* bad living with my parents for a while – and it would only be until I could save enough money to move out again. I decided to talk to them about it when I went back for Christmas.

Knowing I wouldn't be staying much longer, I didn't have to find a job there anymore, or feel bad about not trying. I was back to the holiday feeling of the beginning of summer with no sense of guilt when I watched TV, or looked out of the window, or the other things I did when I did nothing.

I went into town despite having no reason to go. It was even busier, but I didn't mind so much. Passing the old boundary walls, the fountain in the square, and the cathedral, I saw it all as I had when I first arrived: it was a beautiful city. And I had a lot of good memories. Maybe I'd even be a little sad to leave.

I walked back through the park in the bright winter sun and smiled at a baby being pushed in a buggy by its young mum. I smiled at the mum.

An old man in passing said, "Lovely day."

I said, "Yeah, it is," and was glad to have exchanged words with a stranger.

I whistled a happy tune: 'You Are My Sunshine'. As I neared the edge of the park, I almost wanted to turn around and shout, "So long!" I laughed at myself for thinking it. I was sure I'd never said that in my life. But it seemed like the time for 'so long'.

6

Winter began properly with the New Year, and a few days after, as I travelled back to the flat by train, we passed through areas which had a thin covering of snow on the rooftops and verges.

I opened the envelope again and leafed through the notes: three hundred pounds. It was unusual for my parents to give me money, but then it wasn't usual for me to ask – a difficult conversation for everyone. And having said I needed two hundred to pay off my overdraft, I'd been surprised to receive extra. But I wouldn't be asking again; they'd made it clear there would be no more. I tucked the envelope into the front pocket of my rucksack and zipped it shut.

From my window seat in the half-empty carriage, I stared at the ghost of my reflection in the glass, then refocused beyond it to the landscape flashing by. Countryside changed to towns and back again until the high-rising blocks of flats indicated we'd reached the suburbs of London.

Graffiti covered any surface alongside the tracks: bridges, walls, across some windows. The majority of it wasn't artistic or even colourful, it was just repetitive marks – tags; ugly vandalism that said nothing other than someone had been there.

We passed rows of small, run-down terraced houses, their gardens that backed onto the railway line were littered with trampolines, washing lines, bikes, bins and dogs. I wondered about the people who lived there. What had brought them to places like these? But, not just *these* places and *these* people, why did so many live in bad areas on the outskirts of cities?

Was it circumstance rather than choice? There must be nicer towns elsewhere in the country that were cheaper, but was it even to do with money? Perhaps they'd grown up there and it hadn't occurred to them to go, because surely if it had, they'd find a way to make it happen.

The familiar landmarks of the Houses of Parliament and the London Eye came into view as we approached Waterloo where I'd catch my connecting train. Calculating there was enough time before we stopped, I took out my pencil.

The day before, I'd watched *Animalympics* – I loved that film, a cartoon from my childhood – and a song from it had been playing in my head throughout the journey. I folded down the tray table from the back of the seat in front of me, and on the plastic, wrote out some of the lines:

THERE COMES A TIME WHEN YOU MUST CHOOSE

ABOUT THE PATH YOU'RE GONNA TAKE

AND YOU MUST TAKE IT WIN OR LOSE

AND IF YOU LOSE IT'S YOUR MISTAKE

I returned the table to its upright position, grabbed my bag, and left the train.

I wouldn't be moving in with my parents and hadn't even told them I'd considered it. It was obvious on the first day that it wouldn't work. It was no longer my home – it was their home – and my bedroom was the newly-redecorated spare room, my things boxed and stored in the attic.

I was bored back in Shitetown-upon-Fuckall. Even though at the flat I was used to not doing much, at my parents' house I was doing it with an audience of judgement and disapproval. As a headteacher, and as a father, Dad was all about 'Fulfilling Your Potential'. He asked a lot of questions and my answers weren't good enough.

I looked forward to leaving, but stayed a fortnight; it was good to benefit from their heating and eat their food. Our lives intersected most days for the evening meal, but for the rest of those long two weeks, I avoided my parents by watching my films and taking walks along the river, sometimes with Isaac.

Isaac was doing teacher-training in Exeter but was back for a few days visiting his family. I went round to his house and *his* room was still the same. As we slumped on beanbags and played video games, his mum brought us up sandwiches and drinks like we were kids again. Before he left, Isaac sorted me out with a couple of memory sticks containing porn – I could always count on him for that.

Christmas Day was enforced boredom. I can only be thankful that once the magic of Christmas has dissolved and we progress into adulthood, there is alcohol.

My sister and her husband came over for Boxing Day. We sat around the table eating leftover cold meats, freshly-baked cranberry bread and an array of salads off Mum's best china laid out on a white tablecloth.

Elspeth was fulfilling *her* potential and always had. She'd got her PhD and was now a research scientist working on … something, somewhere. She'd secured the job before she'd even completed her doctorate.

Dad asked her questions using an entirely different tone to the one he had for me. They talked about the paper she'd had published and the house she and Alex were renovating. She showed us photos of it on her brand new iPhone.

Smug bitch.

Putting her phone down, Elspeth seemed to pointedly ask, "What are *you* up to, Lyle?"

Everyone's attention shifted. "Uh … me? I'm still trying to find a job."

"So you're signing on then?"

Before I could answer, Dad cut in. "Yes he is, and has been

for the last six months."

"Alright," I said defensively. "Not everyone gets a job straight away."

I reached for the shop-bought piccalilli which had been presented in a crystal-cut glass bowl; even the day before the cranberry sauce had remained in its jar, and we'd eaten from the usual plates. I knew Mum would hate it if any of the yellow stuff were dropped on the spotless tablecloth. I thought about doing it 'accidentally', but spooned it carefully onto my turkey.

"What are you looking for?" Elspeth asked.

Dad answered for me again. "He doesn't seem to know."

I chewed a mouthful of bread.

Alex joined in. "Have you thought about teaching?"

"Great suggestion, Alex!" I said with sarcastic enthusiasm. "I'll get right on it. How can I ever thank you?"

"No need to be rude, Lyle," Mum warned.

"Yeah, but why does everyone keep saying I should teach?"

"There's nothing wrong with teaching," Dad said.

"I know. It's just not for me."

"Well, it's about time you worked out what *is* for you!"

"Yes, it is," Mum agreed.

The decision that I would never live with them again had been underlined.

Elspeth and Alex didn't stay that night, preferring to drive the two hours back to their house. I had a feeling I'd have been made to give up the spare room if they had though. My sister didn't have a room there anymore either – it had been turned into a study – but it *had* remained her room for a few years after she'd left, only changing when she married Alex.

After a second train, I couldn't be bothered to walk, so waited for a bus to Oldchurch. The glass in the shelter had been smashed and the shattered fragments along the bottom edge of the window were like a mountain range. I touched the peaks to see if they were sharp. They weren't.

On the bus, I sat at the back. On the grey plastic of the seat in front of me, someone's shoes had created dusty marks that resembled Godzilla fighting a duck.

At a stop along the way, a woman and her two children got on. The kids ran straight to the back, seating themselves on the opposite side to me, and their mum sat in front of them. I listened to the conversation between the girl (who I guessed was around eight) and her younger brother. She asked him, "What's your favourite stripe combination?"

I couldn't help smiling; I thought it was a strange and brilliantly-posed question. The boy gave it some serious consideration and finally settled on black and red because it was like Dennis the Menace. She said hers was black and yellow like a bee. I didn't tell them, but I decided mine was black and white. There wasn't a specific reason.

As we approached my stop, I pressed the button to inform the driver.

Bye Bee and Dennis. It was nice listening to you.

I stepped through the gate in the wall and locked it behind me. Someone in the flat across the yard had just had a shit – I heard the toilet flush and looked up to see the bathroom window being opened; it seemed an appropriate welcome back. A small scene of bottles and tubes was revealed on the windowsill, usually just silhouetted against the frosted glass. The people who lived there used the same toothpaste I did.

As I let myself in the front door, it felt equally as good and bad there was no one else there. I went straight to the living room to work through the porn Isaac had given me.

He was a connoisseur of porn of many types from all eras, and amongst the collection was a file entitled 'Retro' from the 1970s. In one scene, two guys and a girl were fucking on a large leather sofa, but I barely noticed what they were doing as I was more interested in the wallpaper behind them; although green instead of brown, it was exactly the same pattern of trees and hills as in my living room. Throughout, I was frequently distracted by the décor; there were some amazing lamps and chairs.

When I took a break to use the bathroom, I found an icicle had formed from the dripping tap in the sink, extending halfway down to the plughole. I snapped it off and threw it down the hallway as if it were a javelin, and it broke up as it hit the wall, the pieces falling onto the lino outside my bedroom.

Hours later when I went to bed, I noted the ice hadn't completely melted.

7

The cold helped destroy any motivation and positivity I might have had.

I hadn't anticipated how bad winter in the flat would be. The only heating was from two ancient gas fires – one in the living room and the other in my bedroom – which gave off warmth within a radius of around a metre, inexplicably failing to heat up the rest of the room. During the coldest times, I sat with the armchair close to the fireplace, my feet and legs burning and the rest of me not quite warm enough. I rarely used the fire in the bedroom as I was scared I'd succumb to carbon monoxide poisoning in my sleep.

The kitchen, bathroom and hallway were all unheated, and in them, throughout most of January and February, I could see the vapours of my breath. With the exception of sleeping, I spent as little time as possible outside of the living room: baths were infrequent, I pissed into a pint glass, and the food I cooked became things I could microwave, toast or add boiling water to.

Despite extra clothes and blankets at night, I'd wake lying on my back with my arms wrapped around my chest in order to conserve the heat around my body. It was so bitterly cold in the early mornings that it wouldn't have surprised me to see frost on the carpet.

Two months passed. I'd exhausted the new porn. I had a birthday. I frequently drank, and it was just as well I had no access to other drugs. Sometimes I guarded what little money I had, and other times I bought things I could've done without. I added more drawings to the scenes on the wallpaper: animals and birds, a house on a hill, and stars in the sky above the man in the boat. I longed for warmer weather and regretted the time I'd wasted the summer before – if I had it back, I'd do everything differently. I looked ahead and waited.

The list I'd made shortened. I stopped reading. I'd attempted several books but found nothing that either spoke to me or entertained and couldn't get beyond twenty pages. But there was always TV and porn, and there was sleeping and getting drunk.

I was finding it increasingly difficult to go outside. Initially I didn't want to because of the cold, but I slowly realised it was more than that; I had to psych myself up to buy food or collect my post, and would have avoided it altogether if I could. I hardly saw or talked to anyone. Days could go by and the only person I'd spoken to was on the checkout at the Co-op … and that was just "Hello", "Thanks", and "Bye". On several occasions, I found myself in the small room, leaning against the wall, listening to the girl on the other side.

I felt different every day: sometimes anxious, sometimes numb, full of self-pity, self-loathing, or hopelessness. But not just every day, I could feel different every *hour* if not more frequently. Many times I experienced a sudden rush of overwhelming despair. The smallest thing could set me off and it wasn't always obvious why: needing to wash my clothes, getting a paper cut, switching the TV onto skiing, seeing an advert for an electric toothbrush. Conversely, I'd get a wave of something like euphoria from hearing a piece of music or from a smell that reminded me of my childhood. But it was fleeting and would leave me feeling restless.

The times when I felt unexpectedly good (or maybe not even *good*, maybe just not *bad*), I couldn't seem to enjoy the break. Instead, I put thoughts into my head to bring myself down. I wasn't consciously thinking I didn't deserve to feel

OK, but looking back there could have been an element of that. And on some perverse level, I think I liked the self-sabotage.

I knew I wasn't in a good way, but through it all there was never a day when I didn't get dressed, and that gave me some small sense of keeping it together.

One day I was in the kitchen making toast and opened the cutlery drawer for something to spread Marmite with. The drawer stuck halfway as it often did, so I kicked it closed and tried again. It opened properly.

The only clean item was a steak knife, which would have to do as I couldn't be bothered to wash up anything more suitable. As I waited for the bread to brown, I stared at the raised, geometric pattern of the tiles, and absently tapped the knife on my hand. It was sharper than expected.

Looking down at it, I turned the point towards my palm and pushed it in. It wasn't enough to draw blood, but it hurt. I rolled up my sleeve to expose my arm and rested the blade there. I drew it back, then increased the pressure and sawed with the serrated edge. The skin broke, but it was only a scratch.

People do this – cut themselves. YOU could.

The toast popped up.

No.

I placed the knife on the worktop and pulled my sleeve down to cover the mark.

"What the fuck are you doing?!"

But I was asking a bigger question, not just about the knife.

What *was* I doing? I'd been looking ahead to the time when I had to make the change, but why wasn't *now* the time? The cold wasn't a problem anymore – it was the middle of March – and I was making toast and contemplating self-harm.

I laughed.

Funny you're doing this today of all days.

But why had I thought 'today of all days'? What was special about today? No, there was nothing. It was like all the others. I was rambling inside my own head.

Am I going crazy?

What do you mean GOING, Lyle?

"Maybe you already are."

And now you're talking to yourself again.

I laughed. And then I laughed *because* I was laughing.

I couldn't go on like this. I had to get out of it; I had to get a job. No one was knocking on my door to offer me opportunities – they didn't even know I was there. I had to do it for myself. And I'd always known that.

I could do it tomorrow! Tomorrow I'd get up early (this time, I really would). Tonight, I could write a list of all the things I needed to do, and tomorrow I'd make sure I'd do them before the end of the day. It would only take one day of discipline – I could manage that. One day of hard work and I'd be getting somewhere. I could turn it all around. I would make finding a job my job and there would be no excuses.

In my room, I set the alarm on the clock for ten in the morning.

Not early enough!

I changed it to nine.

It begins tomorrow.

8

Nine o'clock: shrill beeping.

It didn't feel like I'd been asleep for long, but I knew I'd had more than eight hours. I lay on my side focusing on the clock face, watching the second hand tick past the three and the four and the five and the six. I closed my eyes, still visualising the movement.

It was warm in bed and I was comfortable there.

Get up.

I opened my eyes to check the time again: two minutes past. I should get up ... but maybe I could do it when it got to five past. That was a rounder number on the clock and a few extra minutes in bed wouldn't make any difference.

Yeah, five past is better than two.

Or a bit longer even – give myself more time to come round. It wouldn't matter, in fact I was sure it would be beneficial. Just a little rest until, say, quarter past nine. I shut my eyes.

The next time I looked at the clock it was twenty to eleven.

Twenty to eleven! This was supposed to be The Day when everything changed. It had barely begun and I was already fucking it up. I quickly got up and dressed. I didn't have a bath (although I was sure I needed one), and skipped breakfast – I'd eat at lunchtime.

Referring to the list I'd made the night before, I identified the tasks that wouldn't require much time or effort, but could be crossed off to make me feel I was getting somewhere. One of them was 'Buy newspapers'.

Across the road in the newsagent's, I bought both national and local papers. Back in the living room, I put them in a pile on the floor along with the dozen or so others I had lying around the flat – several weeks' worth that I'd only glanced through, if I'd opened at all. I turned to the 'Situations Vacant' pages of each one.

The positions available in the nationals were for Executive Officers, Team Managers, Project Supervisors, Regional Directors or Branch Co-ordinators. They were looking for candidates with at least two years experience, excellent IT skills, and knowledge of Quark/Excel/HTML/XML/PHP and other things which could have been random strings of letters and numbers for all I knew. Many wanted a high flyer or a key player, someone who was enthusiastic, dynamic, self-motivated and worked well in a team. In return they offered an outstanding package, performance related salary, benefits and the chance to work in a challenging environment.

In contrast, the local papers were full of vacancies for care workers, kitchen assistants, waiters, cleaners and bar staff. They rarely stated any requirements and offered minimum wage.

There wasn't much of a middle ground between the two extremes, and few jobs that were close to being relevant to my qualifications, experience or interest. I tore those adverts out as I found them.

I read film reviews, an article on global warming and one on Tove Jansson, took a quiz to determine my personality type (INFP), and completed a form to win a holiday to South America. I stopped for lunch.

After eating, I checked back through the adverts I'd put to one side. There were eight in total and none in particular excited me. I rejected three.

My CV and template letter weren't good and needed to be improved if I was going to secure interviews. I had some notes written on sheets of paper, and sat on the floor trying to organise them into an order. But I couldn't focus. After a while I couldn't even sit; I had an intense feeling of butterflies in my stomach which I tried to relieve by pacing the flat. I fetched a glass of water from the kitchen.

Standing in the doorway of the living room, I sipped the water and looked at the scrappy notes on the floor. I stepped forward, turned the glass over, and dumped its contents. The liquid splashed violently onto the paper and ran off the edges, the ink diffusing and the words blurring into each other.

You fucking idiot.

Immediately regretting what I'd done, I gathered the wet pages, blotted them on the carpet and laid them in a line to dry.

There was nothing more I felt I could do. Enough had been achieved anyway and I swore I'd continue the next day.

It was twenty past two.

The agoraphobia I'd been feeling was decisively overridden by my need to get out. I put on my jacket and, taking a pocketful of cereal, went to the park.

The other people in the park all had dogs. A scruffy terrier yapped at a Dalmatian retrieving a ball, and I could hear a woodpecker in the distance. The sky was grey. It wasn't raining but there was a light mist and I could feel the moisture on my skin and when I breathed. Taking a deep breath, I thought how good it was to be out.

A squirrel ran by the base of a tree, its tail following the movement of its body like a wave. I brought out some of the cereal from my pocket, scattered it on the ground, and without hesitation, the squirrel came to eat it. Another soon appeared and stood nervously with its legs splayed, belly near to the ground and tail twitching. Squatting down, I held out my hand and offered the food.

"Come here buddy, I won't bite you."

Keeping still, I attempted to gain his trust and he tentatively came closer. I smiled. It was nice to interact with nature. Why didn't I do this more often?

The squirrel was in front of me. He stretched forward to take the food … and his teeth sank into the fleshy pad of my fingertip. I shouted out at the shock of the pain. He let go and ran off. In anger, I threw the rest of the cereal after him.

My finger was bleeding and perceptibly throbbing. Wrapping a tissue around it, I left the park hoping I wouldn't contract rabies.

Fuck nature.

I headed through the industrial estate and into the retail park. When it started to rain, I took shelter in B&Q, wandering around the bathrooms and kitchens, deciding which ones I'd choose if I had a house. The square floor tiles were big enough for me to fit an entire foot inside, and I stepped into the middle of each tile, carefully avoiding the cracks.

When I'd exhausted that, I moved to the adjacent pet superstore and looked at the reptiles, fish and rodents in their glass cages. I squeaked some dog toys.

It was still raining when I got outside – a fine rain like pinpricks on my face. I walked into it, along the roads skirting the park, surprised at how quickly it was getting me wet – the front of me at least. The people passing in their cars would probably be feeling sorry for me, but they had no need; I felt sorry for *them*, confined in their capsules. When had they last walked in the rain? When had I?

By the time I passed through the gates to the churchyard, my jeans and jacket were soaked and my hair plastered about my face. I sucked the strands near my mouth and, although it had been a while since I'd last washed my hair, faintly tasted shampoo.

I stopped to read an inscription on the shared plot of a woman buried in 1935, her husband in '57, and his second wife in '63. It was a strange ménage-a-trois in death, a bizarre scenario, and I wondered if the first wife would've approved of the arrangement.

I made my way to Sylvia Avery's grave, and quietly saying hello, ran my hand along the curve of the top of her headstone. Daffodils grew by the wall. I picked them and decorated the ground over her. Not wanting to leave Robert Hix out, I placed a flower on his grave too.

Back on the path, a puddle had formed in a shape resembling the Isle of Wight. A boy of around thirteen sheltered from the rain in the porch outside the main doors of the church. On seeing me, he appeared alarmed, but he covered quickly and called out, "Got a fag, mate?"

"No, sorry. I don't smoke."

And I *was* sorry. I'd have liked to have helped him.

I went to the Co-op. I only had a few pounds to buy food, but I approached the counter and asked for scratchcards – two of them.

With the first I won nothing, but with the second …

Twenty pounds!

It was the most I'd ever won on a single card. I didn't quite believe it was real until the cashier verified it and handed me the money. But I stopped myself using it to buy more cards – having an unexpected twenty pounds was luck enough, and I wouldn't push it.

I picked up a basket and put in a joint of beef, a bag of potatoes, parsnips, carrots and broccoli. Adding it up in my head, I had plenty for gravy, horseradish sauce and frozen Yorkshire puddings too – I was going to do it right. I hadn't had a roast dinner since Christmas (or any large meals at all), and I was getting enough food to make a roast last over three or even four days.

As I walked towards the checkout, I thought again. Could I really be bothered to prepare and cook it all? It was going to be a lot of effort. And I'd have to do all the washing-up – before *and* after. Retracing my steps, I started to put everything back, but then abandoned the basket on the floor for someone else to deal with.

I bought microwave ready meals, a bottle of gin and two bottles of tonic.

After eating an unfulfilling spaghetti bolognese out of its plastic tray, I filled a pint glass with near equal amounts of spirit and mixer. It tasted bad, so I drank half of it quickly and topped it up with tonic. After that had gone I poured another with a better ratio. Sizing up the gin, I wondered if I'd be able to drink the whole bottle in one night. I decided to see.

Putting music on in my bedroom, I turned it up loud. It was something I hadn't listened to in a while, and I sang along. Halfway through, I was reminded of another song I hadn't heard in ages, so put that on instead.

Raising my glass, I silently toasted the music, and the room and myself.

Yeah, this is fucking awesome, Lyle!

Thinking of more songs, I played those, but soon ran out of ideas. So I closed my eyes and chose a disc and a track number at random.

It was 'Pyramid Song' by Radiohead – a beautiful song, and at first I was happy to hear it. But everything I'd put on up to then had been upbeat; this was a complete shift in mood.

Sitting on the bed, I listened. The video played out in my head: a solitary man wearing an oxygen tank dives down into a flooded world. He swims through an underwater town, past houses, street lights, cars and skeletons. Reaching his own house, he goes in, sits in his armchair, and removes his oxygen …

This wasn't the music I wanted. I turned it off.

In the living room, the TV was on. I changed channels but couldn't find anything to watch amongst the football, politics, cookery, and shit films.

I glanced around the room at the brown wallpaper and the green carpet and the pieces of paper, dry on the floor. Next to my half-empty glass on the table was the 'to do' list. I hadn't crossed much off – not what I'd intended at all. There I was, at the end of a day when I should've done much more, drinking on my own.

You're fucking pathetic, Lyle.

Drinking alone because there's no one to drink with.

Because everyone has their own life.

Marcus has got a job ... and he's got Nina.

And you've got nothing and no one.

Who *was* I anyway? Did I know anymore? Did I even have a personality? I supposed I must have – I took a quiz and got a result – but did I actually *like* things? I couldn't remember. I definitely *dis*liked a lot. What did people think of me? Was it in a particular way? Did they think of me at all? If I died, would anyone even care? Would they notice?

The self-pity flowed easily and so did the tears. The capacity I had surprised me. Maybe it was because I hadn't cried in a while so my stores were full. But were tears stored or were they created as you went? Would I keep producing them as they were needed or would I run dry?

A heavy drop fell on to my top and shattered into smaller, perfect spheres. None were bigger than 2mm in diameter and they remained on the fleece material for a long time without sinking in, sparkling in the light like miniature crystal balls.

It felt good to cry – like it had been necessary. Wiping my face dry, I laughed about it.

I said out loud, "Lyle, don't take life so seriously!" and filled my glass all the way to the top. The evening turned around and became enjoyable again. The things on TV didn't seem so bad after all.

Before long, I reached the bottom of the glass. There was gin still in the bottle but I couldn't drink more.

Can't even finish what you've started with THAT.

Adverts were on. I tried to remember what programme I'd been watching, but had no idea. I felt dizzy and a bit sick, and the pattern on the wallpaper didn't help. The room seemed smaller.

I stood up.

I sat down.

I stood up again.

I needed fresh air.

For the second time that day, I had to get out.

9

The rain had stopped. Opening the gate, I paused as I considered where to go. It was closing time at The White Horse and people were leaving. Three girls exited the pub through the double doors and stood talking and laughing. Their laughter was overly loud and jarring. They may as well have been shouting, "Hey everyone, pay attention to us!"

They were younger than me – maybe not even twenty, maybe not even eighteen – and by the clothes they wore, I could tell they were locals, not students. The one I noticed in particular was wearing a short, red jacket, blue-patterned trousers and white high heels. The trousers showed off the curve of her arse which was almost cartoon-like in contrast to her slim waist. Her friends hugged her before leaving together arm in arm, and the girl in the red jacket turned to go up Market Street on her own. Watching her go, I closed the gate and took the same direction.

The sound of the girl's heels on the pavement echoed in the quiet night. I walked not far behind, focusing (as much as my eyes were able to) on her arse – the lift and drop, the sway from side to side, and the slight wobble with each step.

Her thin, cotton trousers were elasticated at the ankle, and loose fitting, except around her arse. No sign of an underwear line – maybe she wasn't wearing any.

It was exactly how I would've sculpted the perfect arse. But perhaps I couldn't have – the proportion was so right, it was possibly even more right than I'd imagine. Had I ever seen one as perfect? I didn't think so.

Fuck, it's SO good!

I wanted to be up against it. I wanted to take her into the churchyard, pull down her trousers and bend her over the tomb. It had been a long time since I'd last fucked anyone, and I was getting hard thinking about it. There were so many things I would do to her, and I imagined a few as I followed behind that lift and that drop.

It occurred to me that in my scenarios, the girl hadn't consented. Had I been thinking about forcing her, of attacking her? Could I actually do that?

No.

It was just a fantasy. I was sure it was something I'd never do … to her, or anyone else. But it was a fantasy that was turning me on. To appease my slight shame and guilt, I decided to see her home safely.

I walked quicker than she did and was only a few paces behind when she reached the end of the street. Traffic made her stop. Although I hadn't meant to catch up, I couldn't avoid it, and drew up next to her by the kerb. She looked around, startled, and I could tell she hadn't been aware of me. To not appear threatening, I thought the best thing to do was talk.

"Hi."

She reluctantly said, "Hello," and faced forwards again.

Seeing the front of her, her tits were pretty good too – quite big, and the tight top she wore showed them off. As we waited for a car and taxi to pass, she glanced at me again and I brought my gaze up to her face. I grinned. She pulled her jacket tightly around her.

The road became clear and she began to cross. I caught up again before she reached the other side.

"Do you want me to walk you home?" I said. "It's not safe on your own at this time of night." Impressed by my effort not to slur the words, I doubted she'd know I'd been drinking.

"Thanks, I'll be fine."

"I don't mind."

"I'll be fine," she repeated.

I stayed with her though and we continued for a few steps in silence. Then I found myself saying, "Do you know you've got a great arse?"

"Fuck off."

"What? I'm just trying to give you a compliment."

She ignored me.

I leaned back to have another look, "I'd say it's definitely one of the best I've ever seen. It may even be *the* best."

She kept walking, maybe a bit quicker.

"What? What's wrong with saying that?"

No response.

"Sorry, I don't mean to annoy you. I just want to walk you home. Do you live near here?"

"I'm not telling you where I live, and I said I'm fine."

"Yeah, but there are plenty of dodgy people around."

She looked me in the eye and raised an eyebrow.

"Not me!" I laughed, "I'm not dodgy – not at all. My name's Lyle, what's yours?"

"I'm not telling you my name."

"OK, you don't have to … but let me walk you home."

"Can you go away now."

"Hey, don't be like that. I just want to make sure you get home safely … and if you want to invite me in for a coffee, that's OK too." I smiled. She wasn't smiling.

"I'm only joking," I said. "Well, I'm not actually – I *would* like to come in for a coffee. But I don't really like coffee …"

She said, "I just want to walk on my own now. Please."

Her "Please" affected me for a moment. Even though her voice was quieter when she said it, it had emphasis. Was I scaring her?

"OK, if you're sure," I said. "Are you sure?"

"Yes, I'm sure."

"Alright. Can I get a hug goodbye then?" I really wanted a hug, to feel her body up against mine, her tits against my chest. I wanted to reach round and grab her arse.

"No, I'm not hugging you."

"Just a quick hug?"

"No!"

"Right, no hugs … so … how about a fuck?" In my defence, I was drunk, horny and desperate.

She increased her pace, trying to pull away from me. I slowed to let her.

"OK, OK. Sorry, I'll go."

"Good," she said without turning back.

Taking another long look, I called after her, "I'll be thinking of your arse later."

"Fuck you!"

She reached the corner, then was gone. I didn't follow to see where she went – I thought about it, but didn't do it.

I headed to the park for a piss.

It was a cloudless night and the thin, crescent moon smiled like the fading Cheshire Cat. Tilting my head towards the sky, I found the North Star using the pointers from the Plough. I felt dizzy, so steadied myself by lying on the dewy grass. Searching for constellations I knew, I found Leo, Cassiopeia's 'W', and Perseus. I tried to see the cluster Pleaides – the Seven Sisters – but it seemed to vanish if I looked directly at it, only appearing clearly when I averted my eyes a little.

With the vast sky above me, I had the usual sense of complete insignificance. With billions of people in this world and an unknown number of other worlds out there, I was just one tiny, pointless thing in all of it.

But my thoughts switched. Maybe I wasn't pointless. Maybe I was *important*. Maybe life was the most important thing of all and I was lucky to have it. Out of all the atoms in the universe, all the sperm and eggs from my parents and from the many people who had been my ancestors, *I* was here. What job I had didn't matter, nor how I lived my life …

… or was how I lived my life *all* that mattered? And who did it matter to – just me? Was it enough that it *just* mattered to me? Or did I need the Universe to care?

But was *anything* important or was it our own perception that made it that way? And how can we tell the difference between what's real and what's perception – like the advertising that alters the way we view a product? We're all conditioned to think and feel in particular ways. But can we ever know what we *actually* think? Can we work it out for ourselves, strip it down without the opinions of parents, friends and society getting in the way and clouding our judgement? Is it possible not to be influenced?

We have to question everything, but what if the answers we're given are lies? There's so much information and much of it is contradictory. So what *should* we think? There's not necessarily a black or white, a right or wrong, so we have to open our minds and see things from all sides …

… or should we pick a side?

Is reality really real anyway? Maybe we all live in a video game or The Matrix.

Glimpsing a shooting star overhead, I wanted to make a wish. But what for? To have three wishes isn't too bad, but just one is difficult. What's the single most important thing? World peace? Health? Money? Love?

I wish everything will be alright. That covered it.

I sat up. My back was damp. I scrambled to my knees, then stood. I had an impulse to run across the grass and sprinted as fast as I could, my arms and blood pumping until I could no longer continue. I hadn't got far.

I wanted to cartwheel. Could I even cartwheel? I tried, but collapsed to the ground onto my shoulder.

I meandered back to the flat.

In the light, amongst walls, I realised I was more drunk than I'd thought. I downed some water and switched on the TV. But I wasn't watching the screen as much as I was giving my eyes something to focus on. But I was tired and it was difficult to keep them open. When they closed, my head spun violently making me nauseous, and I had to snap them open again to stabilise my head and stomach. I tried to remember what those spinny things were called that NASA use to train astronauts.

I hoped to get away with not being sick, but it was inevitable. When I couldn't fight it off, I rushed to the bathroom to vomit in the toilet. Kneeling on the floor, seeing the stains in the toilet bowl made me even more ill, beyond the point in which I had anything left inside.

Running the cold water from the sink, I cupped my hands and drank. I splashed some onto my face. The water was flowing from the tap too fast making me feel anxious. When I turned it off, the slow drip had the same effect, so I had to get it to a steady stream that didn't bother me. Watching the water swirl around the plughole, I concentrated on breathing deeply.

My head felt heavy, so I rested it on the taps. I must have been leaning a bit too hard as my head slipped in between them and wedged there, my forehead resting on the sink. I tried to carefully free myself but in the end had to give my head a good wrench to get it dislodged.

After about an hour (or it could've easily been two), I felt well enough to leave the bathroom. I went to my room and lay down on my bed where I either passed out or fell asleep – at that point I'm not sure a distinction could've been made between the two.

10

Standing in the bathroom, I had my doubts. But everything seemed OK; there was the sink, the bath and the toilet – all as it should be.

It's fine, go.

So I started going.

It was an effort at first and it hurt a bit, but once it came, the piss kept on coming. There was a lot of it and it sprayed out in all directions, like putting a finger over the end of a high-pressure hose pipe. I had no control, but even if I did, there was nothing to aim for – the hole in the toilet that had been there a few moments before had disappeared, leaving a flat wooden surface like the seat of a chair.

I knew it wasn't right.

I woke to a disturbing warmth spreading out from my groin, creeping up my back and down my legs: I was wetting the bed.

"For fuck's sake!"

Pushing the covers away, I got out. The piss trickled down from my soaked pants, onto my feet and into the carpet. I stripped the sheets to try to save the mattress and went to the bathroom to clean myself, dropping the ball of wet bedding in the hallway as I went.

It was not yet eight o'clock and, once I'd had a wash, I wanted to return to bed and get more sleep. But the mattress was too wet. I blotted it dry with a towel as best I could, and as I did, became aware of how unwell I was feeling; it wasn't a good morning to be up so abruptly. The fire was on in the bedroom and I couldn't recall putting it on. I thought it more likely that my pounding headache was due to hangover rather than toxic fumes from the fire, but nevertheless turned it off, opened a window and relocated to the living room.

I switched on the TV and lay on the sofa. Feeling sick, I made it worse by imagining bacon and eggs – sloppy yolks oozing over white undercooked fat. I always torture myself. It's like when I'm scared and my brain can't help thinking about horror films I've seen or stories I've heard; I conjure up ghosts and psychopaths with their faces at the window, their fingers tapping on the glass.

Why had I drunk so much? Of course this was going to be the result.

You did this to yourself.

I remembered a few things from the night before as I touched the twin bruises on the sides of my head. And there was a girl! What was her name? No, she hadn't told me. I'd said some stupid things. At the time I was convinced I was being playful, but I suspected I made an idiot of myself, or worse, I may have frightened her. I put my head in my hands, then went to the bathroom to vomit.

I did nothing but sit on the sofa, watch TV and drink water for the whole of the morning. I would've spent the rest of the day trying to recover in that way, but in the afternoon, I had to go to the Jobcentre to sign on.

I opened the gate at the exact moment the girl passed by. As we made brief eye contact, I didn't recognise her, but by the look of something close to alarm on her face, she recognised me. She had light brown hair tied loosely in a high ponytail, dark eye make-up, and pink lipstick. If it wasn't for the same red jacket she was wearing, and if I hadn't turned my head and seen the back of her, I wouldn't have known; I didn't remember her face at all.

I was sure I'd never seen her before last night, and here she was again, just when I didn't need it. But perhaps there was a reason, perhaps I'd been given the opportunity to apologise. Watching her enter the café, I followed.

Expecting to see her in the queue, I was surprised when she wasn't there. I glanced at the tables, but she wasn't there either. As I wondered where she'd gone, the girl came out from the kitchen and stood behind the counter: she worked in the café.

I couldn't just go up and talk to her – there were three or four people wanting to be served – so I joined the queue and waited for my turn to come. When it did, the girl did her best to look nonchalant as she asked if she could help.

"Hi," I said, keeping my voice low. "Uh … I just wanted to say that I was sorry about last night."

She stared at me with her eyes wide.

"I'd had quite a bit to drink."

"Yeah." She laughed nervously, but without any hint of friendliness.

"I hope I didn't scare you. I didn't mean to."

Rising up on her tiptoes, she peered over my shoulder at the customers behind.

"Well, anyway – I'm sorry."

She said, "OK." But it sounded like an acknowledgement rather than an acceptance of my apology.

"Right …" I said.

I wasn't satisfied with the way the conversation had gone, but instead of repeating myself, and to make it all seem normal, I did the only thing I could and ordered some food. I scanned the baguette menu above her head: ham, cheese, ham and cheese, egg salad, chicken salad, chicken tikka, halloumi … too much choice and I wasn't capable of making a decision.

I couldn't stomach a sandwich anyway, so contemplated the cakes in the glass case between us. They didn't appeal either, but I had to choose something; she was waiting, and we both wanted me to hurry up and leave.

"Can I have a gingerbread man, please?" As soon as I'd said it, I regretted it; it sounded so childish.

With the tongs, she picked one with red and yellow Smarties for buttons. "This one?"

"Any." I would've preferred orange Smarties – they were the best – but I wasn't going to say that.

She put it in a paper bag. "That's a pound, please."

I found the correct money in my jeans pocket and gave it to her. She handed me the bag, put the coin in the till, and transferred her attention to the next person in line.

I left the café.

Walking through the park, I recalled the cartwheel and rubbed my sore shoulder. A squirrel was by the side of the path. I couldn't be sure if it was the biter, but it looked like him. I transferred the gingerbread from my hand to my pocket, hissed at the squirrel and muttered, "You're not getting any you tufty little prick."

Keeping my head down as I reached town, I went straight to the Jobcentre. The outside of the building was grey and austere, and the inside claustrophobic with low ceilings and harsh, fluorescent lighting. Nobody ever looked like they wanted to be there, and that included the staff.

I sat with everyone else who was waiting to be called, surrounded by propaganda posters of happy people in jobs. We were a mix of different ages, but I did note that men under thirty were well represented. Before I'd joined them on the dole, I thought they'd be scroungers or the unemployable. But the vast majority didn't look that much different from me; I had the same clothes, the same unshaven face and the same solemn expression as half the men in there.

There were a couple of the unemployable there too, and one of them slouched near me. He was a man of indeterminate age (he could have been anywhere between early thirties or late forties) with a weaselly face, greasy hair and dirty jeans.

His fingernails were nicotine stained and as long as a woman's. I could smell him – cigarettes and unwashed clothes – and it made me feel sick again. Breathing just through my mouth, I leaned as far back from him as I could without making it look as though I was. I couldn't guess what sort of a job he'd be going for but hoped it wasn't in catering.

Across from me was a man dressed in a navy-blue suit and red tie, a briefcase by his feet. He was noticeably smarter than anyone else there and seemed out of place. Maybe he was new to this and thought you had to be presentable for them to give you the money – but they'd give it to you anyway. He saw me looking and smiled. I shifted my gaze to the grey carpet tiles.

They expect you to be on time for your appointment, but *they* rarely are, and forty minutes late, it became my turn. I sat down in front of the desk of a lady I'd never seen before. She was overweight, and had thick make-up and big bouffant hair. The smell of her strong perfume made me feel as sick as the stale smoke had. She told me her name was Janice.

I handed over my papers.

"Mr ... McNorton. How are you today?"

"Fine." I sometimes worry that I'll suddenly develop Tourette's and involuntarily say inappropriate things to embarrass myself. It was the perfect time, and the voice inside my head was shouting: "You're not fine, you're hungover ... and you wet the bed last night." I moved my hand to cover my mouth.

She read my job search diary.

"It looks as though you've been busy."

It certainly *looked* as though I had – I'd filled it in an hour before and made most of it up.

"Yeah," I said.

I opened my mouth to speak, but shut it again.

Just answer the questions you're asked, Lyle. Do what you need to do, and go.

"You're looking for clerical work," she stated as she read my information.

I wasn't, but when I'd first come in to apply for the benefit they'd had to put something down for their records. That was what we'd agreed on.

"Yeah," I said.

"And you've been unemployed for some months now – nine?"

"Yeah."

"Hmm, we need to broaden your horizons and consider other things. You should start coming in once a week, and we need to think about a back-to-work plan, maybe get you doing some voluntary work."

What the hell was this? I knew they were clamping down, trying to improve their statistics, but I hadn't expected it for me.

She typed something into her computer and swivelled the monitor around so we could both see.

"First, let's see if anything new has come up shall we?"

She went through the list of available clerical jobs, taking her time to read them out to me even though I could read them well enough myself. I could've done them all easily, but I was over-qualified; I had a degree – how many other people in that fucking place could say the same? Let them take these jobs.

I could sense the impatience in the room from the people waiting, and tapped my foot. Why was she bothering to go through all this? Why didn't she just let me sign on and go? Everyone's time was being wasted.

Where was Robin? I liked it when I got to see him, but he hadn't been around lately. He didn't put pressure on like this. He was as keen for me to go as I was.

"Does Robin still work here?" I asked.

"Robin? Oh, he's taking some time off."

Time off probably meant stress. I could easily believe that.

He always seemed a little hunched and edgy. Janice didn't hunch. She was robust. She was in control. I noticed the wedding ring constricting her fat finger and wondered if her husband was happy about that.

She said, "There's a temporary contract at the council offices – in the parking department. You'd be dealing with permits and tickets."

Office work. Parking tickets. Not anything I wanted to do.

"They want someone with Maths and English GCSEs," she continued.

Yeah, Janice, you can see I have those, but I also have eight other GCSEs, four A-Levels and a degree … and I wet the bed.

My hand covered my mouth again.

"What do you think? Shall I see if I can get you an interview?" She was already reaching for the phone.

As I left the Jobcentre, I saw the weaselly man smoking a cigarette outside the doors. I expected he'd finished one just before he went in and lit one up the moment he came out.

You loser addict – spending your dole money on that.

God, how I hated him … and everyone else. I hated the students in the street, I hated myself, but most of all, I hated Janice; in my vulnerable, hungover state, she'd almost pushed me into an interview.

But I'd managed to stop her. I made up a quick story about an interview I already had, and told her I'd be sending speculative letters to several companies that week (not necessarily a lie – it was something I *could* do). She was on my case, though – I knew she wasn't going to let me continue the way I had been – and I would have to go in the following week to discuss it further.

Walking through the pedestrian precinct, I squeezed my left hand with my right in reassurance. I pretended to myself that I was invisible and could almost believe it. Feeling detached from the world around me, I was just a part of my own. No one else was real in my world. They didn't exist. There was only me.

A man, around my age, was busking with a Spanish guitar underneath the clock tower. Unwilling to part with any money, I passed by as if I hadn't noticed. But the music was beautiful. I stopped around the corner to be out of sight but so I could still hear him play. Leaning against the wall, I stayed there for some time.

In my pocket, apart from pennies, the only money I had was a two pound coin. Doubling back, I dropped it into his open guitar case.

11

I found myself getting on with things and somehow it just happened. Before had been a false start, but now I was doing it. And *doing* it was not as difficult as I'd thought, or as time-consuming as *avoiding* it had been. One afternoon, I updated my CV, and the next day, I wrote the template letter.

I went to the library to search for jobs online. That was where most were advertised anyway; I'd been limiting my choices by just using newspapers. I made myself open to ones that I would've previously dismissed. It didn't matter if they were far away – I could commute or move – and if they didn't exactly match my qualifications or experience, it was worth seeing if they'd give me a chance. I even found one that I actually wanted – at a magazine publisher's in London. I sent out some applications by email and post.

I didn't have a letter box for my flat, so my post got delivered to the antiques shop. I usually went in there every couple of weeks to collect it, but after applying for a few jobs, went most days to check for replies. Sometimes the shop was closed and there'd be a handwritten sign on the door saying 'Open again at 2' or 'Back in 5 minutes'.

The antiques dealer owned the entire building, with the shop being on the ground and first floors, and my flat at the top. Keith was a stout man in his fifties with curly black hair who wore colourful waistcoats. From time to time he'd ask if everything was OK with the flat, but apart from that we hadn't said much to each other since Marcus had moved out. After I'd been in four days in a row, he started a conversation.

"Back again? Expecting something?"

"Yeah. I'm waiting to hear about some jobs."

"Oh? What for?"

"Uh, a few different things." I glanced at the two envelopes in my hand – they both looked like junk mail. "I've applied for so many, I've forgotten what they even are!"

"You've applied for a lot then?" he asked.

"Yeah, probably a couple of hundred since I graduated – I've lost count." It was twenty, if that.

"And still no luck?"

"No. Not even any interviews. Most places don't reply at all."

Keith shook his head and tutted, "That's terrible. I thought it was easy to get a job if you'd been to university."

"It should be."

"That's not right." He shook his head again. "After all that hard work."

Yeah, all that hard work!

I said, "I didn't expect to study for three years just to end up on the dole."

"No, of course you didn't."

"And I'll probably have to get something that I'm overqualified for just to earn a bit of money."

Keith thought it was an awful situation for me to be in. It was so sad when a young man of my obvious intelligence and will to work couldn't get anything. And what a poor reflection on our country where even a good education can't guarantee you a job.

I agreed. It was an injustice; I'd been let down. Beginning to believe the role I was playing, I actually felt quite angry.

I went to the library most days, scouring the internet for jobs, and *did* lose count of how many I applied for. As well as the advertised vacancies, I sent out my CV to anywhere I could think of that could be relevant to my degree.

Application deadlines came and went and I began to realise

that it wasn't that easy to get a job – even one I didn't want. Although I was losing hope of hearing from any prospective employers, I continued going down to the shop; I liked talking to Keith.

Keith took an interest in my life. He asked about my job search, my degree, and where I was from. We spoke about the weather, how difficult it was to keep up with technology, and that there was never anything decent to watch on TV. Keith complained about antiques shows – mostly the David Dickinson ones. He said they made people think they knew everything, and that their "crappy old tat" was worth a lot. It made them forget that a dealer has to make money too.

He hated one programme in particular and asked, "Do you remember *Lovejoy*?"

I hadn't watched it.

"That was so unrealistic," he said. "The antiques business isn't at all like *Lovejoy*. He was always ducking and diving, driving round in his bloody Morris Minor, knowing everything about rare items and making thousands on them."

But it still didn't mean anything to me.

One day, Keith was quite animated. "Lyle, I'm glad you've come in today. If you hadn't I'd have come up to see you."

I thought he was going to tell me some post was in, but it was something else.

"I've had an idea … I don't know why I didn't think of it before. I could do with someone to look after the shop for me on a casual basis. My wife used to do it but she's not been well …"

It was the first time he'd mentioned his wife; I didn't even know he had one. I made my face show concern and debated asking what was wrong, but then he continued.

"It'll be a couple of days a week … or just the odd morning or afternoon. What do you think?"

He was offering me a job.

I didn't want it, but what could I say?

I said, "I don't know anything about antiques."

"You don't need to. You'll just have to be here to keep the shop open."

"But I wouldn't want to let you down. I'm sure I'll get a job soon so you'd be better off finding someone else."

"That's not a problem," he said. "When that happens I'll sort it out, but it's going to be hard for me to employ someone anyway because I might only know the day before that I need them to work. You won't have to do much – just serve a few customers – and the rest of the time you'll be able to apply for jobs. I've thought about it and it's the perfect solution for all of us. I already know you, and you said you could do with the money …" He smiled at me expectantly.

The person he thought I was couldn't say no, so I smiled back, thanked him and agreed to work in the shop until I found something else.

12

Keith went through the things I needed to know. He showed me where he kept old newspapers, boxes and carrier bags for wrapping, how to process card payments on the hand-held machine, and fill in receipts in the duplicate book. Everything was priced, and I could knock off ten percent for trade buyers. I had to write the sales from the day on a notebook and keep it face down on the desk so entries were hidden from customers' view. I didn't have to be taught how to use the till; it was an antique itself and opened by pressing down any button without the amount being registered.

I met Keith's wife, Maggie, who wore patterned cardigans that clashed with his waistcoats. She'd been diagnosed with ME and was apparently exhausted a lot of the time. We got onto the subject of *Lovejoy*. Maggie liked *Lovejoy*, or more specifically, she liked Ian McShane who'd played him in the series. He reminded her of Keith.

Maggie did the accounts for the shop and found out that if I worked for at least sixteen hours a week, I could get extra money from Tax Credits. She helped me fill in the forms to claim it. I'd been expecting a more informal arrangement – cash in hand – but this way meant I had the satisfaction of going to the Jobcentre for the last time and informing Janice.

The shop opened at ten o'clock, and I only needed to get out of bed five minutes before to dress and brush my teeth.

It was bigger inside the shop than it seemed from the outside, as there was a long narrow passageway going quite far back. At the end of the passageway was Keith's workshop, and from there he had access to the yard.

The desk was positioned so that almost all areas of the downstairs could be seen. It was arranged to minimise shoplifting (only large items and furniture were upstairs), but people still managed to steal sometimes. Behind the desk was a door to a small back room, and beyond that, behind another door, was the toilet. I always had opportunities to nip to the loo, but learnt to close the shop if I needed a shit. Once, I got caught out – I heard the shop door open and had to finish before I was ready. It was Mrs Valensis who'd come in, and I wasn't sure if she'd known what I'd been doing because her face had an expression like she'd smelt something nasty anyway.

The back room was used for storage, but also had a kitchen area with a sink, fridge and kettle. There was an old armchair in the corner and this was the place where I ate my lunch. I didn't get an actual lunch hour, but as the shop was often quiet, I always found time to eat.

On the first day, Keith stuck around to supervise. Shortly after we opened, a woman with a strong Yorkshire accent came in and remarked, "It's just like an Aladdin's cave."

Keith told me I'd get to hear that a lot, and he was right. After the third time, I started to keep a tally chart on the inside cover of the notebook. The comment annoyed me not only for the frequency, but because they always preceded it with 'an' – surely it should just be 'Aladdin's cave'. I also hated it when people used the term olde worlde, or referred to things as old-fashioned.

The next customer was a man with Einsteinesque hair. He had an orange Sainsbury's bag with him. As he placed it on the desk, he eyed me with suspicion.

"Hello Eddie," Keith said pleasantly, "how are you today?"

Eddie didn't reply to the question. "Tenner."

"Well, let's see what you've got." Keith reached into the bag and brought out a selection of brass items – an ashtray in the shape of a fly, a coal shovel, a shell case and a door knob.

"Tenner," Eddie repeated.

"I'm happy with that," Keith said, and opened the till. He took out a ten pound note and handed it to him.

Eddie bowed slightly. "Fank you very much, sir." He bowed again as he left the shop.

"That was Eddie," Keith explained. "He brings me a bag of bits once a week. If he comes in and I'm not here, just give him what he asks for."

"Really? Are you sure that's OK?"

"Yeah. It's never more that twenty quid. He doesn't look it, but he's quite switched on. He knows the things I'll buy and what I'll pay for it."

A few other regular customers came in that first day – Mrs Valensis, the man who asks for thimbles, and the lady who only wears purple. There was a man with a big nose, dark-rimmed glasses and a bushy moustache who looked like he was wearing a Groucho Marx disguise. Keith said he came in a lot but never bought anything. I named him Ian Cognito.

I found out who my neighbour was; Keith pointed her out as she passed the window. Her name was Amy and she'd lived next door since she was a baby. Keith had seen her grow up over the years.

Also through the window, I saw Mr and Mrs Stephenson holding hands. And I saw the girl-with-the-arse.

We'd been out on the street at the same time on a few occasions since I'd tried to apologise, and I would've smiled. But although I was sure she'd seen me, she went past as if she hadn't. After that, I pretended I hadn't seen her either to make it easier.

The pound coin that was glued to the opposite pavement turned out to be a great source of entertainment. People often tried to pick it up, and they all looked mildly embarrassed when they couldn't. I wondered who'd stuck it there in the first place. Maybe someone from another shop in sight of it.

Keith usually came and went, moving furniture in and out of the shop, going to auctions, or doing restorations in the workshop or yard. Often I'd go to work and not see him at all. I had a key so I could open up in the mornings and close at the end of the day. I locked the takings in a safe in the back room and left a note on the desk with anything that needed his attention.

The job was easy. As he'd said, I just had to sit there and take people's money, or if there were no customers, I just had to sit there. I took a folder in with me which supposedly contained letters for job applications, but mostly had blank sheets of paper in it. Sometimes, if people tried to talk to me, I'd write on the paper so I'd look busy and they'd stop. I wrote: go away; shut up now; you're boring me; not interested; leave me alone. I just wanted to earn my money and go and have the easiest day I could doing that. There was a sign on the door of the shop which read 'Please Come in and Browse'. I would've liked to have taken it down and not given people the encouragement.

I was doing one or two full days along with two or three half days most weeks. Keith tried to give me enough work so it averaged out at least sixteen hours, and any extra that I worked, I was paid cash in hand at the end of the month. One of the first things I spent my wages on was internet access for my flat. Along with all the new porn, I downloaded some episodes of *Lovejoy*. I quite liked it.

Although pleased to benefit from my availability to work for him, Keith was increasingly frustrated on my behalf that I couldn't get another job. Every now and then I'd make up an interview I'd been to, or a rejection letter I'd received, but in fact I'd long given up looking or applying for anything at all.

When Holly came in, I'd been working in the shop for almost a year.

PART 2

HB

13

Holly looked good. She was wearing a short denim skirt, Converse and a grey jumper. Her hair was longer than I'd ever seen it, and she'd lost a bit of weight – enough to look better, but not too much to lose her shape.

"Lyle! What are you doing here?"

"Me?" I said, "Working. What are *you* doing here?!"

"Um, I've been to stay with Annabel for the weekend. The train was passing through so I thought I'd get off – see some of the old places."

"What, here? Oldchurch?"

"Yep. I used to go to the park all the time."

I hadn't known that.

"And I, um, saw that in the window." She pointed to the wooden house I'd placed there earlier.

"The music box? Do you want to look at it?" I started to move out from the desk.

"No, don't worry now." She waved her hand in dismissal. "I'd rather talk to you!"

"Actually, I'm just about to close. I live upstairs. Do you … do you want to come up for a cup of tea … or something?"

"I've got to catch a train …" She checked her watch. "But, I've got time."

I locked the shop door behind us and took Holly through the side gate. I let her go before me on the stairs; she had good legs.

Inside the flat, I asked her to wait in the hall so I could quickly sort the living room. But she didn't wait long, and came in before I'd made much progress.

"This is nice," she said with sarcasm.

The curtains were closed. There were chips in a wrapper on the sofa, plates on the coffee table, clothes on the floor. I could've filled half a bin bag with all the empty beer cans, bottles and discarded rubbish. I hadn't ever dusted and didn't own a vacuum. It probably smelt bad.

"Sorry about the mess," I said, "I haven't had a chance to tidy lately."

"I can see."

I let in the daylight and cleared a space for her on the brown, corduroy sofa. Taking the chips and as many plates and bowls as I could carry to the kitchen, I pushed clothes and other things out of sight with my foot as I went.

With the kettle on, I washed up two mugs and a spoon.

"Tea?" I called.

"Yes, please."

I knew how she took it.

As I brought in the drinks, Holly was surveying the room. "Nice décor. Great carpet." She turned her attention to me. "Not sure about the beard."

"Oh, really?" I self-consciously rubbed my overgrown bristles. "I like your hair long though."

"Thanks." She ran a hand over the back of her head.

Placing the mugs on the table, I sat next to her on the sofa. It was a two-seater and we were close, our knees just a few centimetres apart – my jeans, her bare skin.

I said, "It's strange you came into the shop."

"I know!" she agreed. "I can't believe you were there."

She crossed her legs and her skirt became even shorter. I glanced at her thighs, then down at my feet, then at the blank screen of the TV.

"Uh … whereabouts are you living now?"

"I'm at my mum and dad's."

"Yeah? How's that?"

"I can't stand it."

Recalling staying with my family at Christmas, I said, "I can imagine."

"I want to move out as soon as I can – I'm saving up. I've got a job as a receptionist, but it's only covering someone's maternity leave. I need to find something else."

"Yeah, I'm trying to find something else too – I'm just working downstairs for a favour really."

Holly uncrossed her legs and shifted in her seat. I stared at the loose threads hanging from the bottom of the curtains. We both picked up our tea.

"So," she said, "have you seen anyone else from uni lately?"

"No, not since graduation."

"Not even Marcus?"

"No. How about you?"

"Well, Annabel – obviously. And I'm in touch with a few others on Facebook."

"I'm not on it."

"Yes, I know you're not into that. You didn't hear about Marcus and Nina then?"

I shrugged my shoulders. "Did Nincus split up again?"

"No, Nina's pregnant."

It was the last thing I'd expected.

"Crazy isn't it?" she continued. "I think the baby's due in September or something."

"Yeah, crazy."

Good one, Marcus. You've fucked up your life.

After Holly had filled me in on what some of the others were doing (not that I was particularly interested), it was time for her to catch her train. I showed her to the door.

"Thanks for the tea," she said.

"No problem. Good to see you."

"You too."

"Uh … I hope you find somewhere else to live soon."

"Thanks, me too." She was standing by the door, touching the handle. She took a deep breath. "OK then. Take care."

"Yeah, you too."

Letting go of the handle, she leaned towards me for a hug goodbye.

We hugged.

Then we kissed.

Then we took off each other's clothes.

Then we went to my bedroom.

Then she missed her train.

In bed, Holly turned to face me. "I still hate you, you know."

"I hate you too," I said.

"Why didn't you talk to me at graduation?"

"I meant to, but you had your parents there and everything. Why didn't you talk to me?"

"Yep, same thing – Mum and Dad were there – and then we had to go and I didn't see you to say goodbye." She got out of bed and started to dress. "So … are you still a lazy, selfish prick, then?"

"Pretty much," I answered. "Still a self-righteous control freak?"

"Hey, I was never *that* bad." She half-smiled as she pulled on her skirt.

I didn't want her to go. "Isn't there a later train you can get?"

"Not really – it's half ten now."

We'd been in bed for over four hours.

I said, "Why don't you stay?"

"Because I've got to work in the morning."

I grabbed her wrist and pulled her towards me.

"Lyle, I've got to *go*. The last connection through London is quarter to one."

"Just stay. Call in sick."

Looking down at me, she removed her wrist from my grasp. "I can't – they're relying on me."

"Get an early train in the morning then. You'll still make it."

Chewing on her lip, she said, "I suppose I could ..." Finding a timetable in her bag, she checked it. "There's one at six fifteen."

"Yeah, get the six fifteen. We can have breakfast and I'll walk you to the station."

"Hmm ... OK. I'll stay."

She undressed and joined me back under the covers. We didn't sleep for a while.

In the morning, I was tired so we didn't have breakfast together, and Holly walked to the station on her own; there was no sense in me getting up when I didn't have to, and she said she hadn't expected I would anyway.

Before she went, Holly hesitated in the bedroom doorway. "What are you doing at the weekend?"

"Not a lot."

"Well ... I could come back on Friday night?"

"Yeah?" I said, "We could fuck the whole weekend."

She laughed, "If I've recovered from last night!" She glanced around the room, "You've got to clean your flat though ... and wash your sheets."

"Anything you want."

She moved back to the bed and kissed me. With my hand up her skirt, I stroked the curve at the top of her thigh.

"See you Friday," she said, and left.

That week, I shaved off my beard. I took my bedding and towels to the launderette, and cleaned the kitchen – the plates, the pans, the worktops and the floor. I bleached and scrubbed the toilet to get it back to the only brown it was meant to be, borrowed a vacuum cleaner from Keith, and wiped dust from every surface. It felt good to have a clean flat and I should've done it before.

Keith and I delivered Mrs Valensis's furniture; she lived in exactly the kind of house I'd expected – large, immaculate and filled with antiques. She directed us as we carried the heavy washstand in, speaking politely to Keith without even acknowledging my presence.

I worked in the shop on Friday and time dragged more than usual. Staring out of the window, I saw the Stephensons on their way from the café. The girl-with-the-arse passed them as she headed there.

Too bad arse-girl, I don't need you anymore.

I sold four items in a row for six pounds. They included a jug from a tea service which, the lady who bought it told me, was exactly the same as one she'd broken that morning.

Coincidences.

I thought about what had led Holly to the shop.

I thought about the little wooden house.

I don't like giving presents on birthdays and Christmas when I'm supposed to, and I don't give things unless I'm sure the person will like them. But I knew Holly liked the music box. The price on the ticket was eight pounds; I'd buy it for her if Keith let me have it for six.

When I gave Holly her gift, she said she loved it. She wound the key all the way and in her hands it was a different tune - happy, and not evocative of a horror film at all. She wished the chalet were real so she could live in it, in a forest or on a mountain, somewhere far away from cities and people. I liked that idea, and she invited me to live there with her too.

Holly stayed until Sunday night. I'd forgotten what life could be like and it came back to me over those few days. I felt I was living, not just existing; it was like the last two years hadn't happened. We only left the flat once – for extra stocks of food, alcohol and condoms – and the rest of the time we watched films, cooked dinner, drank and stayed in bed. We fucked in every room – in all the usual ways and some new – but mostly we talked.

I had things to say; I had opinions and knowledge that she respected and found interesting. I could be funny; she laughed at my jokes and understood my puns. I remembered *this* was me.

We talked about many things.

And we planned a holiday.

Twelve days later we were on a plane, flying to Rotterdam for the weekend. I hadn't told anyone where we were going and neither had Holly. It wasn't the best of destinations, but I'd heard somewhere that Rotterdam was the same as Amsterdam, with coffee shops and a Red Light District. And we weren't there to sight-see: we were there for the prostitutes.

14

The plane landed at nine o'clock on Friday night. We hired a taxi from the airport to our hotel, and the journey took us down a street lined with topless bars and strip clubs. I winked at Holly, reached over and gave one of her tits a playful squeeze. But she pushed my hand away, glancing at the rear view mirror, worried the taxi driver had seen.

Holly had found us a cheap, last-minute hotel online. It was a tower of fourteen floors, close to the city centre. Our room was on the first floor and had French doors leading onto a balcony overlooking a car park. There were twin beds in the room. We pushed them together.

We dumped our bags and went out to explore the city. The air was still and warm and we followed the sounds of music to a fairground nearby. Not wanting to be in amongst the lights and noise from the rides, and laughter and screams from the people, we stood and watched for a few moments through the fence. Holly put her hand in mine and, although it felt strange to have the contact, I didn't let it go.

Wandering aimlessly, we didn't stumble across the Red Light District. Not that it mattered – we weren't intending to go there on the first night anyway.

Back in the hotel room, I opened the door to the mini bar.

Holly said, "What are you doing."

"Getting a drink. Want one?"

"I don't think we should – have you seen the prices?" She read from the tariff. "Five euros fifty for one of those little bottles of beer … a Coke is six!"

"Yeah, but I want a drink." I unscrewed the lid of a

miniature gin bottle and popped a can of tonic. "Sure you don't want one?"

"No, I'll save my money."

But after I'd had the gin and started on the beer, she changed her mind and opened the vodka.

We soon finished all the alcohol and ate the two tiny tubes of Pringles (which Holly said were four euros each). We talked about what might happen the next day and it got us both so excited, I bent her over the mini bar and fucked her from behind. I fell asleep shortly after, drunk and happy.

We were woken at half past three by a long rumble of thunder. Holly opened the curtains. The weather had changed dramatically from how it had been a couple of hours before and the trees swayed wildly in the wind. We lay together, watching lightning split the sky every few minutes.

The storm came closer. At around four o'clock, a startlingly loud boom and simultaneous flash of light triggered the hotel alarms.

Holly was unsettled. "We should get up."

"Probably." I continued to lie there.

"Do you think we need to get out?"

"I don't know." I didn't want to move.

We listened for sounds of an evacuation, but it was impossible to hear anything through the shrieking of the alarms. Reluctantly, after much urging from Holly, I got out of bed and put on one of the hotel's white, towelling dressing gowns. Opening the door, I peered into the corridor. A hotel porter strolled down it towards me, not seeming to be in a hurry.

"Hey," I said when he'd reached me, "what's going on?"

He was Dutch, but like everyone else we'd met, he spoke in perfect English. "Nothing to worry about, we got hit by lightning. It's fine."

"Uh, OK … so, shall I go back to bed?"

"Of course."

I retreated into the room to do what he'd said. I was glad I didn't have to go outside, but if it came to it, the ground wasn't too far away from the balcony – I could jump.

Holly wasn't convinced. "He said you should go back to bed?"

"That's what he said."

"Really?! Maybe we should see what they say at the front desk?"

"Yeah, if you want." I lay down and pulled the covers up. "But I'm staying here."

"Come with me."

"No."

"Please!"

"No."

The alarm stopped and Holly did too.

"There you go," I said. "It's all OK now."

I rolled over, closed my eyes, and with the sounds of the storm moving away, drifted back to sleep.

In the morning, complimentary breakfasts were delivered to the room to make up for the disruption in the night. It was a nice gesture, but I'd have rather gone without it and been left alone to lie in.

Holly was eager to get up and go out into Rotterdam. I suggested she do that for a few hours on her own, but my idea was not received with enthusiasm. I tried to doze as Holly ate the food, showered and dressed. But she didn't do any of it quietly. I got up.

On our way out of the hotel foyer, Holly picked up a map of the city; neither of our phones had internet access, so we had to do it the old way. There were no clues as to where the Red Light District was – no sign saying 'Hookers Here', and no cartoon depictions of busty women in tarty clothing. Even though we wouldn't be going there until the evening, it made sense to find out where it was in advance.

I folded the map and put it in my pocket; my sense of direction is pretty good, and I was sure my instincts would lead us the right way. And before long I'd found the clubs and bars we'd seen from the taxi. The signs on the doors were in Dutch but it wasn't difficult to work out that they all opened at eight or nine o'clock on a Saturday night.

But the clubs weren't what we were seeking. Using the logic there'd be similar things nearby, we investigated around the area. But that one street was all we found.

We continued to search the city. We ate lunch on the roof terrace of a café, discovered amazing street art, and followed a sculpture trail where we saw a statue of Santa holding what looked like an enormous butt plug. We spent some time in a market and found a stall that sold porn DVDs for one euro each. I bought the five that looked the best (the least bad).

After hours of walking, we came to the river near the Erasmus bridge. We were tired and it was getting late in the day, so we stopped at one of the tables outside a bar. Holly sat down, while I brought out the map and approached the barman.

"Excuse me. Could you tell me where the Red Light District is please?"

"You want the … Red Light District?" He looked confused. Maybe it was lost in translation and he hadn't understood the terminology.

"Yeah … with the girls … in the windows?"

He laughed, "Oh, we don't have that in Rotterdam. You go to Amsterdam for that."

"Uh … but I thought … are you sure?"

"Yes, of course I am sure."

Disappointed, I thanked him. Then ordered cocktails.

I returned to our table to deliver the bad news and a large strawberry daiquiri.

Holly frowned at the drinks. "How much were *they*? We can't keep spending money – I can't believe we emptied the mini bar last night."

"It's OK," I said, "it's happy hour – two for the price of one."

As we drank, I told her we'd just wasted our day searching for something that didn't exist. And that we may have wasted the weekend.

"But you told me they had one in Rotterdam!" she accused. "Where did you hear that?"

I couldn't remember.

"That's typical. Why didn't you check it out properly before we came here?"

I didn't know.

"Why didn't we just go to Amsterdam in the first place?"

We should have done.

"You had to be different and go to Rotterdam – you always have to be different. What are we going to do now?"

I wasn't sure.

"You're an idiot!"

I had to agree.

After we'd finished our cocktails, we made our way back to the hotel. We'd decided to go to the clubs later; there was the possibility they'd offer extras, but if not, at least I'd get to see some tits which would be better than nothing.

On the way, we called into a shop. Holly noticed the same bottles of beer that we'd taken from the mini bar, but for a quarter of the price. They also had the small cans of Coke and tonic, so we got enough as replacements. We bought alcohol for ourselves for that evening too – a bottle of wine and more beers.

Drinking wine in the bath together as we got ready for the evening, Holly finally began to cheer up. Both slightly drunk when we left the hotel, it suddenly occurred to me to forget about Rotterdam and go to Amsterdam – at least we knew sex would definitely be on offer there.

Holly was unsure. As fantasy headed towards reality, she

was nervous about the whole idea.

I said, "We can always change our minds when we get there and not go through with it." But I didn't really mean it. I didn't want to travel home without doing what we came for. And I was sure she could be persuaded – especially if she kept drinking.

So Holly agreed to go, and we didn't have to wait long till we caught a double-decker train from the station. Sitting on the top deck of an unfamiliarly clean train, I took in the flat landscape as the sun set and remembered the word 'polder' from my Geography GCSE.

We arrived in Amsterdam a little over an hour later.

15

Out of the station, unsure in which direction to head, we consulted the map conveniently displayed on a board in the street. As with the map of Rotterdam, it didn't indicate where we needed to go; we both knew it was by a canal, but it seems there are lots of canals in Amsterdam.

So we started walking, watchful for bikes and trams. We went down a number of streets – some busy with people and some quiet, some leading to canals and others to squares – but none took us where we wanted to go. We followed anyone we thought might be going there (i.e. groups of men) but that strategy didn't work out.

We didn't mind wandering at first; Amsterdam was a much nicer city than Rotterdam. Many old buildings were tall and thin and no two seemed the same. They were packed tightly together like men standing shoulder to shoulder, propping each other up. But after an hour or so, Holly had had enough.

It was clear we needed to ask for directions, but she wasn't keen; she worried people would know what we were there to do. But how could they? We might just be going for a look – like others did. But even if they *did* know, so what? Was it *that* bad what two consenting single adults and a paid professional get up to? Why should we feel ashamed and immoral? It should be fun, not sordid.

I took us into a coffee shop for a smoke and to ask the way. Choosing weed described as 'medium' on the menu, I rolled it into a joint to share. It might have been medium for Holland, but it was stronger than the stuff I used to get.

After a couple of tokes, and knowing the right direction,

Holly relaxed. She agreed to forget about the earlier setbacks and start enjoying our adventure.

She held my hand.

We were back near the station, going down a street we'd passed before. Crossing a wide bridge, we paused for a moment to look down at the pleasure-cruise boats moored on the water. A drunk old man wearing a green, woolly hat lurched up next to me. He spoke to us with a strong Dutch accent. Maybe it was a guess, or maybe he could tell that's what we were, but he spoke in English.

"Hello to you. Nice evening."

I agreed it was, and asked him if we were still going the right way.

"Ah, you are window watching," he said. "You are close. It is near to the Oude Kerk – old church."

"Oldchurch?!"

"Yes. You will find it there." As we left him he said with a chuckle, "Enjoy."

I'm sure we will.

We located the church and, attracted by a glow of red, took the bridge to the other side of the canal. Making our way through a narrow alleyway, we caught our first glimpses of women in windows. It was something of a shock – they were just there! – but we didn't stop or even hesitate, and passed by as if it were a normal sight. When we came out at the other end of the alley, we finally found what we'd been searching for.

This was the Red Light District I'd expected. On either side of a canal were sex-shops, bars, clubs advertising live shows, and all the women in the windows. The whole place was bright with fluorescent red and ultraviolet strip lights, the vibrant colours reflecting off the water. There were so many people moving along the pavements that it was difficult to find the space to join them. Although they were mostly men, I was surprised to see there were also a lot of women.

The hooker-windows here were either just lower than street level, or up a few steps on the first floor. Women in underwear sat on tall stools, or stood posing to attract potential customers. In some windows there was one girl, in others, two or three. Some showed empty rooms with unoccupied stools, and others had closed curtains.

I watched a man descend to a lower window. The girl there came to the door to talk to him. They exchanged words and he went into the room. The curtain was drawn.

The weed had worn off and we both felt quite sober. I didn't want alcohol in case it affected my performance, but Holly needed some Dutch courage – so to speak. We went to the nearest bar.

I ordered drinks – gin for Holly, juice for me. She noticed Pringles on the shelf behind the barman that were the same sized tubes as in the hotel room. I added two to the order and Holly put them in her bag, pleased to have saved us a few more euros on the mini bar bill.

I asked how she was feeling.

She screwed up her face. "I don't know."

"Nervous?"

"Yes … but it's weird – them on display like that. It's like they're merchandise."

"It is what it is." I spoke matter-of-factly. "In this context, they kind of *are* merchandise."

"But they're not," she said. "They're just people doing a job. And I'm not sure I like the way they're being looked at by everyone."

"It's what they're here for. And what *we're* here for, don't forget."

What I assumed was a stag party entered the bar. They were dressed as superheroes and were very obviously British, making a loud, collective "waaaaaay" sound: the call of the football fan.

Holly said, "I feel like everyone's looking at *me* the same way too."

"I doubt it," I said. But when I glanced over at the stag party, noticed two of them (Wolverine and Batman) staring at her.

She leaned in towards me conspiratorially. "Hmm, I reckon they are … because that's pretty much what *I'm* doing. I'm checking out all the girls – the ones in the windows *and* the ones walking around like me."

"Really?" I said. "Welcome to my world."

She rolled her eyes.

"Do you still want to do it though?" I asked.

"Yes. I feel a bit weird about it, but excited too." She downed the remainder of her drink. "Right, let's get on with it then."

We started looking for our girl.

Almost immediately, I pointed to one, "What about her?"

Holly didn't like my choice. "I don't want one with fake boobs."

I agreed – nor did I. And they probably were too big to be true.

"How about that one?" I said.

"No, I don't like her hair."

The next had "too much make-up" and the fourth had "trashy tattoos", so I left it to Holly to pick someone; I wasn't as fussy as her.

Seated in a lower window, an attractive brunette wearing glasses caught Holly's eye. It was a good choice. I approached the door and beckoned the girl over.

"Hi, you want some fun?" she said with an eastern European accent.

"Yeah, I'd like some fun. And my … girlfriend would like to watch us. Is that possible?"

Bemused, she shook her head.

"She doesn't want to join in, just watch."

"Sorry honey, not for me." She closed the door and resumed her position on the stool. She waved and blew us a kiss as we continued window-shopping.

There were five or six more that I would've picked before Holly decided on someone. This girl had strawberry-blonde hair and was pretty in a natural way; she looked like a normal girl and not at all like a prostitute – as much as that was possible, displayed behind glass in Amsterdam's Red Light District in her underwear. She was in one of the upper windows.

As I climbed the steps on the outside of the building, I rose out of the crowd, exposing myself to be a customer and not just a browser. The girl greeted me at the door with a friendly smile. I asked if it would be alright to bring my 'girlfriend'.

"Of course," she said, still smiling, "but it will cost extra."

She thought for a moment and settled on a hundred euros. I wasn't sure if it would be disrespectful to negotiate, but it didn't feel right, and besides it was around the figure Holly and I had estimated. I didn't argue.

Turning around, I signalled to Holly who was trying to look as inconspicuous and nonchalant as possible. She hurriedly joined me on the steps and we went through the door.

16

I entered the room but backed out as I realised the people on the street could see me; some looked up as they filed past. The girl pulled the curtain closed and ushered us in.

The room was lit in ultraviolet which made her white underwear and our eyes and teeth glow. It was small and sparse with a narrow bed along one wall (more like a mattress on a shelf than a bed), the stool she sat on, and a sink with a large mirror above. On a table in the corner were folded towels, a box of tissues and a bowl of condoms. Under the table was a half-full bin of used tissues and condom wrappers.

I told the girl our names. She said hers was Marina. I asked where she was from: Italy. I asked her age: Twenty three – the same as us.

"This is the first time we've done anything like this," I said. "We're from England." The comment was unrelated – just small talk – but it sounded like some kind of explanation.

"I know." Her English was good. "So you are here together? I also like to do this with my boyfriend."

"Oh, you have a boyfriend?" I asked, surprised. "And he doesn't mind you … doing this?"

"No, of course not."

What kind of a man would be happy to go out with a prostitute? Not that I think there's anything wrong with prostitution in principle, it's just not an occupation I'd choose for my girlfriend. But each to their own. Who was I to judge?

Holly was glaring at me; I could tell she wanted me to stop talking and start doing something. I stopped talking.

I moved towards Marina, but she held up her hand and said,

"Money first." I hadn't known the correct etiquette of paying upfront, assuming it was like a taxi where you pay after the ride. And were you supposed to tip? I should have researched it, but doubted the guide books would have covered that.

With the financial transaction complete, Marina reached down to undo my jeans. I had to stop her as I was suddenly aware I needed a piss. She directed me out of the room and down the stairs to the toilet.

In the toilet, it was good to have a bit of time to myself; I worried that my dick hadn't been inspired much by the scenario so far and hoped it would soon. Graffiti covered the walls there, and after I'd zipped up my jeans, I got the pencil out of my pocket and wrote amongst it:

LM & HB woz ere

Back on the stairs, I passed another of the girls dressed in just her underwear. I said, "Hi," as if she were an acquaintance in the street. She smiled politely.

On my return to the room, Holly was sitting on the bed looking awkward (but trying not to), and Marina stood next to the stool; she was completely naked. This was unexpected, mildly exciting, but also disappointing – I would've liked to have helped with the removal of her clothing. I got the impression she was trying to hurry things along.

I stood for a moment, unsure what to do next.

"Would you like to take off your clothes?" Marina suggested.

"OK." Slipping off my shoes, I pulled my shirt over my head.

"What do you want to do?" she asked, as I stepped out of my jeans and pants. I realised my socks were still on and quickly removed those too.

"Could you … uh … suck me?" I ventured.

She was obliging, but not without a condom. I wasn't hard enough for it to be put on, so Holly helpfully intervened to make it happen. After that, I had no worries.

Marina rolled the condom on and took over. I remembered the joint I'd kept from earlier and got Holly to retrieve it from my jeans for me. "Alright if I smoke this?"

Marina couldn't speak, but nodded her head to let me know it was fine. Holly found my lighter and lit the end; it glowed green in the ultraviolet.

Inhaling deeply, watching the prostitute on her knees in front of me, my mind inconveniently thought of Louisa – because of the smoking, nothing else. I pushed my old-lady friend from my mind.

"That's enough," Holly said. "You can fuck her now." She took the joint from me and smoked it herself.

I helped Marina up and laid her down on the mattress. Getting on top, I stared straight into Holly's eyes as I went inside. She smiled. I got into a rhythm and Marina gave every indication she was enjoying herself; it seemed genuine and not faked. After a couple of minutes, Holly said, "Can you change positions?"

Marina went on all fours on the bed with me behind. She made even more noise that way. Reaching around, I put both my hands on her tits, but Holly came over and took them off. I thought she had a problem with the way I was touching Marina, but she put her own hands there instead and began kissing me enthusiastically.

It didn't take long.

In a daze, I went over to the table and cleaned myself with the tissues.

"Thank you," I said to Marina.

"Thank *you*," she said. I knew she'd liked it.

After I'd dressed, Marina kissed us goodbye on both cheeks and hastened us out of the door. We descended the steps and were suddenly thrust back into the crowd flowing along the side of the canal.

It was like nothing had just happened.

17

We ducked down the first alley leading away from the area, and headed towards the station. It had gone one o'clock but the streets were as busy with people as they'd been before.

"So …" I said.

"So …" Holly echoed. We both laughed.

"How was that for you?"

"Um … good. How about you?"

"Yeah, it was good. A bit crazy … I didn't think you were going to join in?"

"I didn't much." She grinned.

"You were touching her!"

"It must've been the weed. I just thought I'd see what someone else's boobs felt like – while I had the opportunity."

"And what did you think?"

"They were alright. Quite nice. Different to how I thought they'd feel – seeing as I've got my own. I didn't want to go anywhere near her other bits though."

"Ha! Fair enough."

We agreed we were glad to have done it. I'd had better sex before – this hadn't been anything special – but as an experience, it was amazing. It was something we 'shouldn't' be doing. It wasn't 'normal'. It had been a buzz.

But it was over and it was late.

We waited on the platform for the next train to Rotterdam to arrive. When it did, it was a single-decker with full carriages, so we had to sit on two fold-down seats by the doors. Holly leaned on me, resting her head on my shoulder, and I stared through the window mostly at blackness, replaying the evening in my head. Halfway through the journey, as we reached Leiden station, the train came to an abrupt stop. It made us jolt forward and I just about managed to root my feet to the floor to stop us both from falling.

A woman wearing a smart suit and carrying a briefcase got up from her seat nearby and moved to the doors. She pressed the button to open them, but nothing happened. She pressed it repeatedly, but the doors remained closed. She looked at me, confused. I shrugged.

Soon, an announcement in Dutch was made through the loudspeaker system, followed by what sounded like all the passengers groaning as one. People began standing up and getting their coats and bags. Not understanding what was happening I asked the smart woman.

She said, "Someone has gone in front of the train. We need to get off and wait for another one."

So we joined the crowd, making their way through to the first carriage, exiting through the only open doors.

Passing the front of the train, several people turned. One man was even bending down to see under it and a guard was attempting to stop him and move him along.

Holly whispered, "Don't look back." I hadn't intended to.

As we walked down the platform to the concourse, three fireman ran past us towards the train. When we got there, all seats had been taken so we found a step.

Holly spoke. "Do you think he's dead?"

"I imagine so."

She stared down at the floor. "Horrible way to kill yourself."

"It's fucking selfish," I said. "If you're going to take yourself out, you should do it so you don't bother other people."

She faced me. "Don't be mean. You're always going to 'bother other people' – your family and friends."

"He might not have had family or friends."

"No, everyone's got someone – haven't they? I wonder why

he did it."

I sighed. "I really don't know."

She thought about it for a moment. "I just don't get why anyone does that. There's always another choice."

"Is there?" I challenged. "Maybe death was the *best* choice."

She shook her head. "I don't believe that. Things can get better."

"Yeah, but sometimes it can feel … … anyway, I don't suppose we'll ever know so don't think about it. All we know is that he's pissed off a train full of people and ruined the night of those firemen who have to scrape him up."

"Don't you feel sad about it though?" she said.

"Not really, I didn't know him … or her – why are you assuming it's a man?"

"Well, it seems more like something a man would do."

"What, more likely a *man* would commit suicide?"

"Maybe. Not necessarily. Just more likely a man would jump in front of a train. Women would take pills or something."

She was making a whole lot of assumptions and it was starting to annoy me.

"Is that right?" I said. "And you've got the statistics to back that up?"

"Well, obviously not. How would *you* do it then? *I'd* probably take pills."

I didn't want to think about it. "Can we talk about something else?"

She looked at me apologetically. "Sure."

But we didn't talk. I was too occupied with my own thoughts and Holly seemed like she was too.

We were waiting a long time. I was tired and it was cold on the step. "Open those Pringles," I said.

"No. They'll save us five euros on our bill."

"Are you serious?"

"Yes. You're not hungry – you're just bored. You can go without them."

"Don't tell me what I am!" I snapped. "And I know we don't have much money, but do you have to constantly mention it?"

"Well, we've got even less because we've had to pay for the train to Amsterdam ... which we wouldn't have had to if we'd stayed there in the first place."

"Oh, you're bringing that up again – fucking great."

She looked away towards the platforms and said in a quieter voice, "And we wouldn't be sitting here now."

"You're making *this* my fault too?"

She didn't answer.

We sat in silence and when the train eventually came, the silence continued on board. By the time we'd got to Rotterdam station and back to our hotel it had gone five.

The concierge stopped us as we tried to pass him.

"Hi, Miss Boskin? Mr McNorton?"

"Yeah?" I said.

"I am sorry, but we need to put you in a different hotel."

"What? Why?"

"The lightning last night. It damaged the electrics."

The lights were on in the foyer – the electrics looked fine.

"That's OK," I said. "We just want to sleep. We don't need anything else." I turned in the direction of our room.

"But for safety, you cannot stay here tonight."

I turned back. "It's not safe?"

"Yes, it is safe ... but the fire alarms are not working, so you need to go. We have made the arrangements. We will take you there."

"You've got to be joking," I said. "Why are you telling us this now? We've been stuck in Leiden station for hours, and we're exhausted. Please, we just want to sleep."

"I apologise. We have been moving guests all evening – you are the last to return."

I didn't need this ... but perhaps I'd be able to turn it to our advantage. "So, do we get compensation?"

"Compensation?"

"Yeah – a refund for tonight?"

"No, we cannot do that. I am sorry."

I wasn't about to give up; I needed a small victory. "How about you don't charge us for what we've had from the mini bar then?"

"Mini bar? Yes, of course, we will not charge for it."

I glanced at Holly thinking that would please her, but she just looked tired and past caring.

When we packed our bags, to mine I added in the drinks we'd replaced.

Holly said, "What are you taking those for?"

"They're free."

"Are you going to drink them now?!" she accused.

"No, I just want to sleep."

"But you won't be able to take them on the plane."

"I'll have them for breakfast then," I said. "Along with the Pringles we could've already eaten."

The porter from the night before walked us around the corner to our new hotel.

When I got into bed, I immediately fell asleep.

The next day we had to be up at ten in order to make our flight. I drank one of the beers even though I didn't want it.

On the plane we barely talked. Holly managed to sleep a bit, but I stayed awake.

We took the Tube into London. When Holly got off to join the Victoria Line to King's Cross. I said I'd call her later. I continued on to Leicester Square and then to Charing Cross to catch my train.

I didn't call Holly later.

18

On Monday morning I wanted to stay in bed but had already agreed to work for Keith; I didn't want to let him down, and I could also do with the money after the weekend. This time though I wasn't going to be working in the shop: Keith needed my help for a house clearance in a village nearby.

He picked me up outside the gate in his van, warning me it wouldn't be pleasant. "Wait until you see it, Lyle. It's revolting. The lady who lived there couldn't look after herself."

He pulled up at a house in the middle of a terrace in a quiet street, and the outside gave no clue as to what we'd find inside. Through the front door into a small hallway, the stench hit me. It reminded me of the guinea pigs I'd had as a child, the smell of their cage a mixture of sawdust, piss, animals and food. In front of us were the stairs. Tall towers of newspapers and magazines were stacked along one side leaving a narrow and barely passable route up.

In the living room, every surface of every piece of furniture was thick with dust – the kind you only get when it's built up over many years, if not decades. The carpet was almost black, the pattern hardly visible through the ingrained filth, and all around the edge of the room were more piles of newspapers and books. Next to the fireplace there must have been at least thirty supermarket carrier bags full of ashes and cinders.

"Didn't anyone care, or *know*, how she was living?" I asked.

"She didn't have close family – no husband or kids. Her niece is dealing with it now."

I looked from the papers, to the bags, to the papers again. "Sad to get old by yourself and not be able to cope."

"No, she was only about sixty. Nothing to do with age."

We went from room to room to see what we had to contend with. The kitchen had buckets on the floor of what can only be described as slop. Trays of grease were piled on the oven hob, and every worktop was covered with used plates and bowls. Empty cat food tins littered the floor in the corner, and I was grateful the weather wasn't that warm yet – the smell would have been much worse in the summer. Opening the cupboards, I found them full of food packets – empty and in neat stacks.

I walked through to the bathroom. The once white bath was grey, and in the dirt were scratch marks that looked as if they'd been made by a cat. Around the plughole were three separate piles of shit, presumably from the same animal.

My phone rang; it was Holly.

"Hi, how are you?" she asked.

"Tired."

"Yes, me too." She paused. "You didn't call yesterday."

"No, I just went to sleep."

"Thought so … but I wasn't sure if you were still annoyed about the Pringles." She laughed. "Sorry about that … and thanks for getting the mini bar bill cancelled."

Finally some gratitude. "That's OK."

I moved back to the kitchen and opened a drawer in the dresser – more empty packaging.

"How are you feeling after the weekend, though," she said, "apart from tired?"

"Fine. You?"

"I'm alright … well, I do feel a bit strange about it. I mean it *was* a weird thing to do."

"Was it? It's only weird if you make it weird."

"Yes, you're right. It was fun."

"Yeah, it was."

Despite the environment I was in, I started to get a little excited at the memory of being in that room with both girls.

Keith had gone upstairs. He called to me, "Lyle, you've got to come and see this!"

I said to Holly, "Listen, I've got to go – I'm working. You'd hate this house we're in. It's more of a mess than my flat."

"Wow, that bad?!"

"Yeah. Anyway, I'll call you later – definitely. I want to talk to you about something."

"OK, speak later then. Glad you're alright."

I ended the call, and carefully made my way up the stairs.

At the top, Keith said, "In here." He was in the lady's bedroom.

I stepped into the room and recoiled – it reeked of stale piss. There was no carpet and the only furniture was a double bed, wardrobe and a dressing table.

Keith drew my attention to the ladder that was leaning against a wall behind the door. There were dozens of used incontinence pads draped over the rungs as if drying out.

"Oh, that's nice."

Keith went over to the dressing table, crouched and rummaged through the drawers. More packaging – cosmetics, perfumes and jewellery – but none of the contents.

He stood up. "I hoped there'd be some treasure in here. Oh well. The bed will be worth a few hundred quid once it's cleaned up. We'll have to dump the mattress."

I gestured to it. "Is that where she died?"

"God no! She didn't die here … can you imagine? She wouldn't have been found for years!"

"I thought … oh, that's OK then."

Keith picked up a roll of black bags. He tore one off and gave it to me, "Right, I think we'll have to do a tip run first. Let's get as much of this rubbish in the van as we can."

We both put gloves on. Starting with the stairs, we filled around twenty sacks from there alone. The newspapers were quick to bag up, but we went slower and more carefully through other bits. We had a pile for charity, a pile to be dumped, and a pile for the shop. I had to ask Keith a few times if an item I'd come across was keepable or chuckable. Sometimes I was surprised by the things he wanted to keep.

I said, "I hope they're paying you well for this."

Pausing from the work, he grinned at me, "They're not paying me anything. I'm paying them – four hundred quid."

"Seriously?!"

"Yes. I keep what I find, and they get the house cleared."

"Oh." I looked around the room, not sure he'd got a good deal. "Is there enough here to make this worth it?"

"Hope so." He went to the mantelpiece and picked up one of a pair of dirty grey candlesticks. He showed me the base. He'd taught me the difference between Britannia metal (marked EPBM), silver plate (EPNS), and solid silver. These were hallmarked with a lion, anchor and the letter f: silver.

"There are a few bits like this and some decent pieces of furniture. I should do alright out of it. And you never know, we might even find some treasure."

"So, basically you want a 'Lovejoy moment'?" I said.

Keith laughed. "I suppose I do."

He *did* do alright out of it. We worked all day Monday, then Tuesday and Wednesday; Maggie had just about felt well enough to sit in the shop and keep it open, but had struggled by the third day. I found I actually enjoyed the hard work and the sense of achievement when it was over. And despite not being a young man, Keith was fitter and stronger than me.

Most of it was clearing rubbish, but we had three van-loads for the shop too. As well as the good furniture, we filled several boxes with small items that he could sell – things like cut glass tumblers, jug and basin sets, brass oil lamps, old kitchen utensils and plant pots. I was pleased to see the lady had a thimble collection in a wooden display shelf hanging on the wall; next time the thimble man came in and asked his question I'd be able to say yes. There were more silver items

– a small tray and a single candlestick – and I found hallmarked sugar tongs and pickle forks amongst the cutlery in the drawer. A lot of the knick-knacks though – the figurines and vases – were heading to charity.

As we sorted through, I held up a small but heavy, red glass vase. "What about this? Shop or charity?"

Keith appraised it. "It's probably worth a few quid, so stick it in the shop pile. But I wouldn't care if it went to charity – I'm not keen on all that sixties glass."

"Really?" I said. "I quite like it."

"Well, if you like it, you can keep it if you want."

"Are you sure? Thanks!" Turning it over in my hands, I noticed something stuck to the bottom. "There a sticker on it – Whitefriars."

"Whitefriars?!" Keith laughed. "Oh well. I've given it to you now … and you've worked hard."

I'd never heard of it. "Is that good then?"

"It can be. Check them out in the Miller's."

When we came to clear out the furniture from the lady's bedroom, a flat box slid off the top of the wardrobe. In it were some documents and a few black and white photographs in an envelope. Most of them were of a child on a beach, and on the back was written: Ramona, Torquay.

I showed Keith. "Is this her? Was she called Ramona?"

"Yes, that's her name. We'll pass those back to the family."

I scanned the photos. The child looked happy. How did she get from being that girl on the beach to the woman who'd lived in this state? When and why did she lose herself?

Picking the happiest photo, I wrote on the back:

RAMONA, SORRY YOU GOT LOST

I posted it through a gap in the floorboards.

19

Everyone has sexual fantasies and it's a shame if you don't explore them, satisfy that part of your personality. At the beginning of your sexual life you're just happy to be fucking and might not particularly care how you're doing it, or even who you're doing it with. But you'll soon try different things and maybe discover what *really* does it for you. There's nothing wrong with that – as long as you're not hurting people (against their will). And we hadn't hurt anyone; Marina was completely into it, I was sure.

I wanted to do it again and looked into going back to Amsterdam. But with flights, accommodation and girls, we wouldn't be able to afford it anytime soon. Saving up would take a couple of months at least and I couldn't wait that long. We'd have to find something closer to home.

It had been my first time with a prostitute so I didn't know the best way to go about it. Could we pick someone up on a street corner? No, I didn't want to do that, and besides, neither of us had a car. A strip club? But did they even offer sex? Probably some did but I had no idea which ones and I was pretty sure they wouldn't advertise it. I knew 'massage parlours' existed but didn't know where, and then there were the cards that you'd see in phone boxes …

What, if anything, was legal here anyway? I went online and typed 'prostitution UK'. According to the Wikipedia page, street prostitution, brothel-keeping and pimping were, as I'd thought, illegal, but working on your own as an escort was not. I typed 'escorts UK'.

It came up with escort agencies – lots of them – and many

were London-based. Their websites displayed profiles of the girls, with professional glamour shots of them in various poses and states of undress. They gave their names, ages, vital-statistics, locations and nationalities (hardly any were English), and were priced by the hour or overnight, for incalls (at their place) or outcalls.

Several agencies went further and listed the services a girl would provide; I noted that quite a few were prepared to see couples. Some of the services were acronyms and I had to Google them to find out what they were: GFE was girlfriend experience, PSE meant porn star experience, and OWO was oral without a condom. It took a while to realise that when it said A and O-Levels, it was code – for anal and oral – and not their qualifications. I'd wondered why it hadn't mentioned GCSEs.

This was a far better way to do it than Amsterdam even; we could trawl these sites and easily hand-pick a girl to match our specifications. When I spoke to Holly on the phone, I told her about the agencies. She agreed to it.

I said, "Let's book something for this weekend."

"*This* weekend?! I can't do that – I haven't got much money left after *last* weekend. Let's do it in a few weeks' time."

"No, I want to do it sooner than that … what about the weekend after – could you do it then?"

She thought about it. "Um, I don't know. I'll probably only have fifty pounds or so."

The escorts I'd seen charged between one and two hundred for an hour. I was getting paid the following week and had worked more than normal that month so I'd have extra money. I said I'd make up what Holly couldn't afford.

"Are you sure?"

"Yeah, it's fine. I just think we should try and do this as much as we can."

"I bet you do!" she laughed.

"So … what's happening *this* weekend then?" I asked. "Are

you coming down?"

"I'd love to, but like I said, I haven't got any money."

"Well, how much is the train?"

"About thirty pounds."

That wasn't too bad. "I'll pay for it," I said.

"Really? Pay for that as well?"

"Yeah, that's fair anyway – you've been down a couple of times. It's not like I'm ever going to come and stay at your parents' for a weekend."

"No, that wouldn't work," she agreed. "OK, I suppose that would be fair."

"Besides, thirty quid isn't much to pay for sex all weekend. That makes you quite a cheap whore."

"Huh! Thanks very much!" she said in mock indignation.

For the rest of that week Keith was working on the furniture in the yard. He got me cleaning the china and glass in the sink in the back room, or polishing the oil lamps and silver at the desk. I also brought my laptop into the shop, managing to connect it to the internet using the Wi-Fi from my flat.

I had two tabs open – one for eBay and one for escort agencies – although it was difficult to stay on the escort tab as customers kept coming in. On eBay, I was looking at Whitefriars vases, and some had bids of hundreds of pounds. I found one identical to the vase I'd got from Ramona's. It was up for twenty three pounds so far with two days left to go on the auction.

Keith needed me to work on Saturday and I spent the morning anticipating Holly's arrival and researching on the laptop. Louisa came in, coughing as she slowly made her way over. Steadying herself with her stick, she stood next to me, staring at the screen. I hoped she wasn't looking too closely.

"Whitefriars?" she said.

"Yeah," I answered, surprised, "do you know it?"

"Oh yes, I've got a couple of pieces. I've quite a collection of glass – Murano, Orrefors, Mdina, Kosta ..." I didn't recognise the names.

Louisa moved over to the chair and carefully lowered herself onto it. "So, where were we?"

She continued her James Bond stories from the time before – the stunts, the explosions, and the name-dropping. I asked if she'd been on the set of *Moonraker*. "Did you see the hovercraft-gondola in Venice – that's one of my favourite bits."

"No, that was after our time. Was that Sean or Roger?"

"Roger Moore." I said. "Late seventies or early eighties I think."

"Ah yes, well my Jack died in seventy-seven."

The conversation stalled. I didn't know what to say. Should I ask how? Should I change the subject?

She spoke again. "I never remarried you know."

"Didn't you?"

"No, Jack was the love of my life."

Holly turned up before lunch and I showed her some escort profiles. I showed her the vase on eBay.

"I think I'll put mine on there and see what I get for it," I said. "I've probably got other stuff I could sell too – raise extra cash."

"Good idea. Have you got an account? I have."

"Not yet, I thought I'd set one up today but it looks like there's a lot to it."

She shook her head and frowned. "It's really not difficult, you just have to follow the instructions step by step."

I wasn't good at following instructions. "You've done it before, can *you* sort it out?"

"For fuck's sake," she sighed. "Yes, I can sort it out. Switch places."

She sat in front of the laptop and began the process.

"You need a username and password."

"OK. Username: Lyle451. Password: hookerfund?"

"Perfect! I'll set up a PayPal account for you too. Have you got your bank details?"

I passed her my debit card.

Keith came out from his workshop carrying a table he'd restored. He saw Holly at the desk.

"Ah, I've got a new employee!"

She looked up. "Sorry, I'm just setting up an eBay account for Lyle … but nearly done."

"No hurry, stay where you are. I need to borrow Lyle anyway."

I helped Keith carry the table upstairs. As we shifted some of the furniture to make a space for it he said, "So *that's* what it is then."

"What *what* is?"

"Why you seem a lot happier lately."

"Yeah," I said, "*that's* what it is."

That weekend, Holly and I put a few of my items on eBay – Ramona's vase, a couple of DVD boxsets, PlayStation games and Star Wars Lego. We got a chance to look at the escort sites together properly and she liked that bit; for her, there was as much excitement in the planning, just like there was in the remembering afterwards.

We found a good site which comprehensively detailed services provided. We clicked on each profile and made a shortlist of the girls we liked who'd see couples. I made sure they also offered PSE and OWO. We chose 'Harmony'.

As I picked up my phone to call the agency and book, Holly said, "Will we have to give our real names?"

"I don't know. Does it matter?"

"I'd prefer it if we didn't."

"OK." I put the phone back on the table. "We could have pseudonyms. How about Fred and Wilma? Or Fred and Ginger … or Fred and Rose?"

"No. What is it with you and Fred?"

I shrugged. "It was the first name that came to me. What about Bonnie and Clyde then?"

"You can stop suggesting murderers too! And we don't have to be a double act so don't say Laurel and Hardy."

"You come up with something then."

"OK, I will." She looked around the room as though in search of inspiration and finally said, "How about we just choose some common names."

"Alright then … Tom?"

"Fine. And I'll be−"

"Jerry?"

"Stop it! Um, Emma?"

"Yeah, that'll do."

I rang the agency and spoke to a woman who sounded very much like Jobcentre Janice; maybe it was the same person and she was bringing down the unemployment statistics by encouraging women into prostitution. She told me Harmony wasn't available, but 'Kristal' would be. She'd been on our shortlist, and I clicked back to her profile. Kristal was twenty, from Slovakia and had long dark hair and 34D breasts (natural). She did all the good acronyms, took incalls in Bayswater, and would charge a hundred and fifty pounds to see us both. Holly nodded her agreement, and Tom and Emma made a booking for six o'clock the following Saturday.

20

Holly's train arrived in London first and she met me at Waterloo in the early afternoon.

With hours until our appointment, she suggested we visit the Tate Modern to view the free exhibitions. So we made our way to the river by the London Eye and headed along the Thames Path, past the skateboarders underneath the Southbank Centre. It was the beginning of May but as sunny and warm as summer.

In the museum, we spent much of the time with the Surrealists on 'Level 2', appreciating the paintings of Miró and Magritte, Dali and de Chirico amongst others. I kept a close watch on my phone, checking I still had signal; I was expecting a text from the agency with the address of where we were to meet Kristal.

Most of the artworks at the Tate were amazing, but some were pretentious crap. We enjoyed deciding whether they were "art or arse" and drew the same conclusions; it was difficult to believe some artists had been serious and weren't knowingly taking the piss.

I liked to read the titles which in many cases were as creative as the paintings or sculptures themselves. A good title enhanced the work as a whole: *Reborn Sounds of Childhood Dreams*, *Wedge of Chastity*, *The Reckless Sleeper*, *The Melancholy of Departure*, *Men Shall Know Nothing of This*, *Tiny Deaths*. It was a wasted opportunity to have an unimaginatively-named or even untitled work (one of Miró's was simply called *Painting*), and I wanted to cross out the bad names on the plaques and write better ones.

A picture I liked in particular (although not the name) was *Portrait* by Sir Roland Penrose. He'd used words to poetically compare parts of a man's body with things that were nothing like them:

His hand an encyclopedia
His lungs a street lamp
His teeth a church
His ear a bus

Holly approached, intrigued by what had caught my attention for so long.

"What's this about then?"

"I'm not sure," I said. "I can't work out if it's meaningless or metaphor … although is any of this supposed to have meaning? Is it the point that it doesn't?"

"Well, it's a lot about free-association and the unconscious mind," she explained. Her degree was in art history so she knew all about this stuff. "Surrealism was partly influenced by Sigmund Freud and his dream analysis."

"Didn't he think everything was to do with sex?"

"Pretty much," she laughed. "Surrealists often juxtapose seemingly random, unrelated objects. But the artist might deliberately or even *subconsciously* use those ideas because they have meaning to them."

I considered the painting again. "If it's meaningless, I still like it. But I hope the artist had reasons for choosing the words he did."

"Hmm, I'm not sure anything can be entirely random," she mused. "Anyway, we all interpret art differently and not necessarily how it was originally intended. But it's natural to look for meaning. I'm sure if you look hard enough you can find it in anything."

On 'Level 3' you had to pay to see the exhibitions, so we bypassed it and moved up to 'Level 4' to the 'Structure and

Clarity' collection.

Viewing the geometric paintings by Mondrian and Delaunay, and sculptures by Hepworth and Choucair, I felt the need to sit down.

After a few minutes, Holly joined me. I asked her, "Do you ever feel overwhelmed by ... by everything there is to know?"

"Um, what do you mean?"

"Well, there are things I wish I knew more about – like art ... and history and science – but there's so much of it, that I don't know where to start. It kind of makes me want to sit and do nothing. Do you know what I mean?"

"Sort of," she said. "But sitting and doing nothing doesn't get you very far. It's best not to think about everything at once – of course that'll be overwhelming. If you want to learn about it, just do it one book at a time."

In the gift shop near the exit, Holly encouraged me to buy several postcards. She said I should stick them on my walls because living without art around isn't good for the soul.

After leaving the gallery, we crossed the Millennium Bridge to St Paul's Cathedral on the opposite side of the river. Sitting on the steps leading up to the main entrance, I took the pencil out of my pocket and began to write on the white marble there.

"What are you doing?"

"Writing."

"You can't do that." Holly glanced around to see if anyone was watching.

"It's OK," I said. "It's only pencil. It's not permanent."

She leaned over to read what I'd written:

MY HEAD A CATHEDRAL

MY EYES A CLOCK

"Like that painting?" she said. "Why are you writing that?"

"Why? Uh … because I like writing on things. I like to think people will discover it at some point."

"You do this a lot then?"

"Yeah, sometimes."

"What do you write?"

"Stuff."

"Like what?"

"Just stuff. Whatever I feel like."

I added another line:

My BONES PENCIL LEAD

"What I meant was," she said, "why are you writing *those* things? What do they mean?"

"Nothing," I shrugged. "They're just things I saw around us."

"Ah, but *are* they though? How do you know you didn't *subconsciously* choose those things as metaphors?" She looked at the words again. "'My head a cathedral' could be all the empty space you have in there … or maybe you love yourself so much that you think you deserve to be worshipped?"

"Interesting theory – thanks for that!" But I didn't mind her teasing me.

She continued. "'My eyes a clock' is because you see time passing – you're aware of your own mortality. And 'My bones pencil lead' is because writing is so much a part of you that it's in your bones."

I was temporarily taken aback by her interpretations, then laughed them off saying, "Nah, like Freud reckons, it's probably to do with sex."

A single bell from St Paul's began to strike four as my phone played the four notes informing me I'd received a text.

21

We got to Bayswater Tube station much too early, so we walked to Kensington Gardens to see the Elfin Oak. Peering through the bars of the protective cage around the tree stump carved with tiny figures, Holly said, "Do you think we should have some kind of a plan?"

"A plan? What for?"

"What we're going to do with this girl."

"Oh … yeah, if you want." I hadn't thought too much about the specifics. But this wasn't the place to discuss it – too many children around.

Settling ourselves on an empty bench nearby, I continued the conversation. "Do you want to get involved this time?"

"I don't know. Maybe."

I sat forward. "What, do you think you'd join in *properly*?"

"Well, not *properly*."

"OK, but why don't you just let her do stuff to you?" I would've liked to have seen that.

"No, I'm not sure I'd feel comfortable."

I sat back. "See what you feel like when you're there then."

"Hmm." She watched a pigeon peck the ground nearby. "So, what do you want to do? Any positions you want to try?"

"Uh, not especially. A blow job is always good though – you know me."

"Yes, I know you." She smiled wryly.

I thought of how it had been in Amsterdam and said, "You seemed to have more of an idea last time – what do *you* want me to do?"

She chewed on her bottom lip. "Well, I'd rather you didn't

kiss her or do anything *for* her–"

"No, I don't want to do that anyway."

"I quite liked it when you were behind ... and maybe ... if you go on top ... you could pin her arms down to the bed?"

I blinked slowly. "You want me to pin her arms down? What, like I'm kind of *forcing* her?"

"Kind of ... but you're not, obviously. Is that OK? Would that make you feel weird?"

"No, it'll be alright. I can do that." I didn't feel like admitting it to Holly at the time, but I was into the idea of holding the escort down.

I checked the time: twenty to six. "We'd better go," I said. "I need to get money out first."

At the cashpoint, I fished around my pockets for my card. But the only cards I had were my Co-op loyalty, my driving licence, and return train ticket. I tried to remember where I'd had it last; I'd drawn some money out the day before ... but then what had happened to it?

I turned to Holly. "I can't find my card."

"Are you serious?! Have you lost it?"

"I don't know. I'm hoping it's just back at the flat somewhere."

She tutted. "It probably is. You'd better not have done this deliberately so I'd have to pay."

"What?" I was stunned. "Do you think I'd do something like that?"

"No ... no I don't ... sorry. You're disorganised and forgetful, not dishonest."

"Anyway you said you couldn't afford it."

"I can't." She breathed out heavily. "How much have you got on you?"

I brought out my notes and coins and counted them. "About thirty-three pounds."

"I've got forty ... look, I can probably draw more out but it'll put me into overdraft." She inserted her card in the machine.

"Let's see."

There was enough, and she withdrew all she could up to her limit – a hundred and ten – and gave it to me along with her forty.

"I'm so sorry, I'll pay you back," I said.

"Yes, you will."

We found the right street and the right number – twenty – and stood by the black door of a white-painted, Georgian terrace. A silver panel to the right of the door displayed buttons numbered one to ten. Ten flats in the building. Were any of the others used for this kind of thing? Did the neighbours know what happened in number nine? Glancing around to the street, I checked there was no one to see us, then pressed the button on the intercom that was shinier than the others – as if it had had more use.

A heavily-accented female voice answered, "Hello?"

"Hi. It's, uh, Tom … and Emma."

"Come up. Top floor. Use stairs, lift is broken." The door buzzed and we entered the building.

We didn't talk as we made our way up the stairs. Holly looked apprehensive and I forced a calm smile to reassure her. There were two flats on every floor so we had to climb up four flights. By the time we reached the top, my heart was pumping hard from the exertion and the adrenaline of excitement.

The door to number nine opened before I had a chance to knock, and we were greeted by our escort dressed in red, lacy lingerie and black stockings. She had long dark hair down to the base of her back and was attractive, although without the benefit of good lighting and Photoshop, a little different from her pictures. But I could tell it was the same girl and I wasn't disappointed – she *did* look to be a 34D.

"Hello, I am Kristal," she said. "Come in."

She took us straight into the bedroom. "Please, sit."

We sat on a double bed covered with a purple, satin sheet. There was a white wardrobe and matching bedside table, and on the table were a pack of wipes, a few condoms and some lube. The generic, canvas, flower pictures on the wall, and the lack of any other items in the room made it look more like a hotel bedroom than hers. Maybe it was her spare room. Or maybe she didn't live there at all.

Kristal held out her hand and with a smile said, "Please. The money."

I'd forgotten that bit. I gave her the cash and she left the room with it, returning moments later with a bottle of white wine and three glasses.

"Would you like wine?"

We both did. She poured, we drank.

"Shall we start?" she said.

"OK."

I stood up and went over to her. Sliding her straps off her shoulders, I got her tits out, then put her on her knees. She undid my belt, button and zip, and got to work on me; it was much better this time without a condom.

Holly moved so she could view from the side, but Kristal's long hair kept falling forward, getting in the way. I reached down, gathered it into a ponytail and held it in place with one hand. With that hand on the back of her head, I added pressure to make her go deeper and faster.

I finished and cleaned myself with the wipes she handed me. I sat back on the bed with my jeans and pants down by my ankles.

Now what? I was going to have to wait until I could go again. The three of us picked up our wine.

Kristal turned her attention to Holly. "Now I do you?"

Holly shook her head vigorously. "No, I'm just going to watch." She sounded embarrassed.

"If you're sure."

"Are you sure?" I prompted. "Why don't you … you know …

let her go down on you?"

Holly made a face to show she wasn't keen. "I'm OK, thanks."

We sat, mostly in awkward silence, drinking the wine. I thought about pulling my jeans back up (I should've done it before I'd sat down), but enough time had gone by that it would've seemed strange for me to get dressed at that point. And anyway, Kristal still had her tits out. My stomach made a noise like a cow mooing, which I thought was funny because I'd eaten beef spread sandwiches earlier.

When I was ready, Kristal and I took off *all* our clothes, and with a condom on, I went on top. As suggested, I held her arms down, my hands around her wrists either side of her head.

"Is this OK?" I asked Kristal.

"Yes, sure."

It was good that way, but I soon stopped. Holly looked at me quizzically. I stood Kristal up, bent her over the bed and continued from behind. With the escort's back to me I mouthed to Holly, "What's the time?" She came over and showed me her watch: twenty-five to seven. I nodded.

Changing positions again, I lay on my back and had Kristal ride me. She really got into it, and Holly moved around the bed, watching from all angles. I tried to last, but when I knew I couldn't go much longer, swapped places with Kristal and held her down again.

"Yes, that's it," Holly said, and ran her hand from my neck all the way down my spine. When she reached my arse, she pushed so I was in as deep as I could be. She kept pushing so she was the one controlling the movement. Everyone was enjoying that, and then it was over.

"Thank you," I said to Kristal.

"No, thank *you.*"

22

We were standing on the pavement outside the building.

"That was good," I said.

Holly agreed. "A bit too long though. I didn't think you were enjoying it at one point – you kept changing positions."

"I had to. If I came too quickly we'd have had loads of time left."

"Oh, that's what you were doing – getting your money's worth."

"Yeah, I definitely enjoyed it." It had been better than with Marina. "And I liked what you were doing at the end."

Holly laughed. "Me too. It kind of felt like I was you – like I was the man."

"Really? OK." If that was what did it for her. "You should do that next time."

"Next time? Are we doing it again, then?"

"Yeah, I thought we were. What do you reckon?"

"I suppose so ... but we'll only book half an hour."

We started walking towards the main road.

"She was nice," I decided. "And I bet she was grateful she got us."

"Grateful?!"

"Well, yeah. Why not?"

"Grateful we weren't beating her up or murdering her?"

"No! I mean she's probably had a lot worse. I'm not fat or old ... or ugly. Anyway, she enjoyed it."

"Did she?" Holly said sceptically. "It's all an act, though. They're just doing it for the money."

"But she genuinely seemed into it, don't you think? And why

would she need to pretend? I'm so good at what I do."

Holly scoffed, "You actually believe your dick is your gift to women don't you?"

"I'm only joking," I said.

"Nah, you're not really."

We reached the corner and Holly looked at her watch.

"It's only just gone seven," she said. "What are we going to do now?"

"Get some food and late trains back? I wish we could stay though – get a hotel for the night."

We had just over thirty pounds left between us, and Holly thought even a Travelodge would be at least sixty.

"Let's check." Taking us into the first hotel we came to, I asked how much a room for the night would be. It was a hundred and twenty. We left.

On our way back to the Tube station, we passed a casino.

"Hey, why don't we go in here?" I said. "We might win enough for a hotel … maybe even the money we just spent."

Holly was dubious. "Or we could lose everything."

"We haven't got that much to lose. Come on, it's worth the gamble."

"Is it?" she queried. "I'm hungry though. If we lose, make sure we've still got enough for food."

"Don't worry, I've a feeling we'll win."

After showing ID and filling in multiple forms to sign in, we ascended a wide, curving staircase with a polished brass handrail. Through the double doors at the top, we entered a large room with a bar area at one end and cashier's desk at the other. Along the walls were slot machines with their flirtatious, fluttering lights and seductive, Siren's jingles. In the middle of the room, two roulette and four card tables were spotlighted by the low-hanging lamps.

"I don't know how to play anything," Holly said.

"Stick with roulette, I'll show you what to do."

We took empty seats at a table alongside an elderly Chinese lady wearing red tartan slippers, and a man in a zip-up tracksuit top; the casino obviously didn't have a dress code. I laid down thirty pounds for the surprisingly unglamorous female croupier to change to chips. She slid a small stack towards me and said, "Place your bets please."

I put a couple of two pound chips on 'Black' and another two on 'Even'. The tracksuit man stared at me and, seemingly in response, moved some of his to 'Red' and others to 'Odd'. The Chinese lady took no notice of us and put her bets down; her hands moved quickly over the table dropping chips in precise places on corners or single numbers.

"No more bets."

The wheel span and the small white ball was added in the reverse direction. It came to a stop on number eleven. The croupier took my chips from 'Even' and matched the ones I'd put on 'Black'; I'd neither gained nor lost money.

"What do you want to bet on?" I asked Holly.

She looked at the table in confusion. "What's does '2nd 12' mean?"

"That's any of the numbers from thirteen to twenty four. And if you win, you get three times your stake back."

"Right, I'll do that."

"How many chips do you want on it?"

"Just one … but please stop saying 'stake' and 'chips' – it's making me hungrier."

I smiled. "Anything else you want? Red or black, odd or even? You get double back if you win on those."

"Black."

I put another down. The man stared again and put his on '1st 12' and 'Red'.

You got a fucking problem, mate?

"No more bets."

When the wheel stopped, the ball settled on number seventeen – a black in the second twelve.

Holly was excited she'd won, and I was equally as glad the man had lost. I pointedly looked him in the eye as his chips were removed. He left and joined a Blackjack table.

Yeah, fuck off!

We lost on a few spins but won on more, and soon we were up by twelve pounds.

Holly said, "Can we go and get food now?"

"No, not yet – we're on a roll. What about the hotel?"

"That's not really going to happen, is it? Let's quit while we're ahead."

"No, we can win more."

Folding her arms, she sat back, leaving me to make the decisions on my own. On the next few spins, I lost more than I won and soon we were down to the last ten pounds.

Holly was nervous we'd end up with nothing. "Come on, let's leave it now."

But I didn't want to leave when we were down. "No, I'll get it back. Just watch."

I bet on black: it was red.

I bet on odd: it was even.

Holly glared at me and said, "Yes, I'm watching ..."

There were six pounds left – three chips. I was going to gamble them all on one spin. But where should I put them? What spoke to me? What had significance? I remembered the number of the building we'd just been to was twenty, and it had a black door. Twenty on the wheel was also black. That *had* to be lucky for us. I put one chip on '20', one on 'Black' and one on 'Even'; I knew I was going to win with all three. Then I'd stop and we'd get something to eat.

"No more bets."

The wheel span.

The ball came to rest on number nine: red.

Nine had been the number of the flat! And the escort had been wearing red. Why hadn't I chosen those instead?

"That's it then," Holly said rising from the table.

131

I stood too, and we walked towards the double doors.

"It's a shame we can't get more money out," I said. "Our luck's bound to change."

She shook her head. "You should've stopped when I told you to."

"Yeah, thanks for that – easy to know in hindsight! But you wouldn't be saying that if I'd won and got us a hotel."

"Well, you didn't … I need the loo."

The toilets were just beyond the doors. She went into the 'Ladies' and I followed her into an opulent bathroom decorated with black patterned wallpaper and gold-coloured tiles. I locked the door behind us.

"Why are *you* in here?" she said.

"I don't know … I was thinking maybe we could fuck in here?"

"Maybe we can't – I'm not really in the mood."

"I'm sure I could get you in the mood."

"I'm sure you can't. I don't want to do anything until you've had a shower anyway."

"I could have a wash in the sink?"

"Forget about it." She pulled up her skirt. "Turn around, I'm having a wee."

I faced the door. The initials C and R had been etched into the black paintwork.

With my pencil, I wrote on the wall by the door frame. The marks were subtle but readable on the dark paper.:

QUIT WHILE YOU'RE AHEAD

"Writing again?"

"Yeah."

The toilet flushed and she came over to read the words. "Ha! Good advice!"

Outside the casino, I asked Holly what she wanted to do next.

"I'm kind of tired, I think I'll just get back."

"Really? Don't go yet."

"Why?" she said. "What are we going to do?"

"We could just have a wander around London?"

"We've walked loads today already and my feet hurt ... but most of all I'm *hungry*," she emphasised.

"There's still a bit of money." I had coins in my pocket. "You could get crisps or chocolate or something."

"No, I want real food."

She was determined to go home, so I accompanied her to King's Cross. A train was in already, and she ran to the platform to ensure she caught it, barely having time to say goodbye.

I made my way to Waterloo and got the next train back too.

When I got in, I found my cash card on my bedroom floor.

23

The Whitefriars vase and the other items all sold making me just under a hundred pounds. Watching the eBay auctions throughout the week, I was frustrated by how slowly the money was creeping up. I thought I was going to be left disappointed by the prices they'd reach, but most bids happened in the remaining few seconds, and they were enough.

This was a great way to generate extra cash and I searched the flat for more things to sell. I found books and a few items of clothing, including a smart pair of shoes I had no intention of wearing again. I considered selling the old typewriter and even got as far as taking photos of it. But I couldn't do it. My granddad had proudly passed it on to me when he found out I'd be studying English. His father had used the typewriter for his vanity-published poems, and my granddad himself had had ambitions of becoming a writer before the responsibility of providing for his family got in the way. He died during my second year of university so he didn't get to see me graduate. Not to say that I was glad – I missed him – but I was relieved that the burden of his expectations had gone. The typewriter though, which grimaced with a mouth full of black lettered teeth, frequently reminded me of what I was failing to achieve.

I went online to find cheaper escorts, discovering some who worked on their own and not through agencies. I clicked on the links and none were particularly appealing, but they were half the price of Kristal. I typed in a new search: 'independent escorts'. Within a couple of minutes, I'd found a site advertising tens of thousands of independents from all around the country.

You could enter preferences for proximity, age, ethnicity, dress and bust size. Filtering girls between eighteen and twenty-five within thirty miles, I got a couple of hundred results. Viewing a few of the profiles, prices were around fifty to eighty pounds for a half hour; we could see two or three girls for what we'd paid before.

Holly couldn't come down at the weekend – she had a cousin's wedding to go to. When I spoke to her on the phone she said, "You can come too ... if you want."

"Nah, I'll give that a miss. I'd avoid my *own* family weddings, someone else's would be hell."

She went quiet.

"So, anyway," I said, "check out that site I mentioned and let me know what you think."

"I will do. We're definitely not booking anyone for a few weeks though. We've got to stop spending so much."

"Yeah, probably ... or earn more."

I worked in the shop three days that week, with my laptop on the desk and the two tabs open. But I managed to find time out from the internet to look out the windows.

Mr and Mrs Stephenson were still holding hands, him in his hat and her in her coat despite the good weather. I saw Amy from next door walk past a couple of times with a skinny boy around her age. They looked sweet together, although I thought it more likely he was a friend rather than her boyfriend.

I packed the items I'd sold through eBay and labelled the parcels. I asked Keith if I could use a cardboard box and some bubble wrap that he had in the back room.

"Fine. What do you need it for?"

"I ... uh ... sold that vase." I immediately wished I'd lied. "I hope you don't mind."

But he didn't seem bothered. "That red one? It's alright, you can do what you want with it. What did you get?"

"Uh … about thirty quid."

"That's not bad. And that was eBay?"

"Yeah."

He nodded for a while. "So, can you sell *anything* on there?"

"Pretty much – clothes, toys, new or second-hand, antiques … whatever you want."

"I fancy giving it a try," he said. "But I wouldn't know where to start."

"It's fairly easy. But if you want, I can do it for you."

He nodded again. "There's a thought. I might take you up on that."

"I honestly don't mind. I've run out of my own stuff to sell now – until I find some more."

"Have you tried the car boot sale?" he volunteered. "I go sometimes. You can pick up all kinds of bargains there. That's where Eddie gets his bits from."

"Boot sale? Where's that?"

"In the park on Sunday mornings. Starts at seven."

Being up at seven o'clock on a Sunday morning was difficult, but I did it. As I trawled the fifty or so sellers' pitches, I saw Eddie there with his orange Sainsbury's bag. When he spotted me, he clutched it tightly to his chest as if he feared I'd take it from him.

In the end, I came away with four carrier bags full of an assortment of items I hoped to make money on, and a few CDs with covers I liked. I was anticipating a 'Lovejoy moment', to unearth something rare and valuable, but it didn't happen.

I took all my purchases into the shop with me on Monday, and spent the morning researching them in the Miller's guides and listing them on eBay. There was a glass bird that I'd bought for a pound which, on closer inspection, was marked on the base with 'Wedgwood'; I hadn't even known they made glass. I'd hesitated over a stack of seventeen old postcards with illustrations of kids by Mabel Lucy Atwell. I was vaguely aware of the name, and it was only a couple of quid for the lot, so I bought them. I listed them individually, each with a starting price of fifty pence. If they all sold at that, I'd make a good profit, but I'd only have to sell four to get my money back, and they'd be cheap to post too.

With the auctions started, I switched back to the escort website. Several girls looked good and I clicked on their profiles. I made a list of potential candidates and texted Holly their names.

Speaking to Holly on the phone that evening, I asked her what she thought of my choices.

"Well, I quite liked 'Sexy Sasha' and 'Candygirl69' ... although her write-up was a bit much."

I knew what Holly meant – Candy had been extremely detailed in describing what she'd do.

"And you can forget about 'Barely Legal Lolita'!"

"Ha! Yeah, I wasn't sure about her myself. Any others you liked?"

"Not really. A lot of them don't even have pictures of their faces."

"I know. I suppose they want to stay anonymous."

"Fair enough, but I wouldn't book someone without knowing what they looked like first."

I wasn't that fussed but said, "OK, we'll only consider the ones who show their faces then."

Along with the photos on each escort's profile, there was something called a 'Private Gallery' where you could pay, usually a pound or two, to see extra pictures. These were more explicit, or were face shots. Some even had short movie clips that you could watch at a price.

On the private galleries, I paid ten pounds in total to check out the girls I was interested in; I had to stop myself spending more. Some were worth the cash and stayed on the list, others weren't and got struck off. They were all normal girls though – none of them looked like models – and the photos were obviously taken in their own bedrooms or living rooms.

It seemed to be a good way for them to make extra money without doing much, and I wondered if they got more from the galleries than the escorting. Perhaps they didn't even need to meet men at all.

That was when I got the idea to set Holly up with a profile.

24

Holly came to stay on Friday night and complained my flat was a mess again.

"It's not that bad," I said.

"No, it's not *that* bad," she conceded. "But how difficult is it to give everything a place and put it there? If you don't keep on top of it, it will easily get worse."

She did think the Tate Modern postcards I'd finally Blu-Tacked to the walls looked good though.

We went into the bedroom.

"You haven't even made your bed!"

"So what? That'll take seconds."

"Exactly," she said. "You knew I was coming to stay, why couldn't you have put in a bit of effort?"

She pulled the duvet up and straightened it before emptying the contents of her bag onto the bed.

"I hope this is alright."

Surveying the selection of outfits and underwear she'd brought for our photo shoot, I said, "I'm sure it is." I couldn't wait to start.

She changed into the first item in front of me – a white, lacy bra which gave her an enhanced cleavage. It was getting me excited.

"Make sure you don't get my face in the frame," she said.

"I know. I won't."

"And I don't want you to show anything too graphic."

"OK."

I began taking the photos. She was shy in front of the camera.

"Just relax."

"I'm trying to."

I gave her direction. "Put your arms above your head ... ... stick your tits out ... ... push them together ... ... bend over ... ... arch your back a bit ... ... no, the other way."

"This actually hurts," she protested.

"Don't worry about it."

"You're not getting my face are you?"

"No, I already said."

"Can I see?" She came over to check out the shots. "Wow, I look great!"

"Yes, you do." I kissed her.

She changed again and she was a schoolgirl in a short pleated skirt, white shirt, tie, and long socks. She had no underwear on.

Unbuttoning her shirt part of the way, she said, "How about like this?" Standing in the doorway, she hitched her skirt up on one side.

"Yeah, that's good ... really good ... we might need to take a break."

"No! You can wait until we've finished."

Holly was getting into posing and enjoyed teasing me. She dressed like a maid. She dressed like a secretary. She dressed in nothing. We found props around the flat to make her look like a dominatrix. She put on an old Superman T-shirt I had and became a sexy superhero.

We ran out of ideas, but we had plenty of photos. And I didn't want to wait any longer.

"Can you put that schoolgirl outfit on again?" I requested.

The next day, I uploaded the photos to my laptop and we went through them.

"I can't believe how good they make me look," Holly said.

"They don't *make* you look good, you *do* look good."

We chose the best ones – some for the profile that anyone

could see, and several topless and naked ones for the private gallery.

We had to register a username and email address with the escort website, so set up a fake email account without using either of our real details. It was easy to do.

Holly said, "What shall I call myself?"

I reviewed the names others had used – there was a lot of alliteration.

"What about Horny Holly or Super Slut?" I wasn't serious. "Holly Golightly?"

"No."

"Holly Goodhead?"

"Who?"

"She's a Bond girl – from *Moonraker*."

"God, no – I hate Bond."

"You *hate* Bond?!"

"Yes … anyway, I'm not using my real name," she insisted. "Let's come back to that … where shall I say I'm from?"

"How about London?"

"No, I know a lot of people in London,"

"So what?"

"They might see my profile."

I laughed. "What are the chances that someone you know sees your profile, and even if they did, they wouldn't recognise you." With her face out of shot, there was nothing to give Holly away as being the girl in the photos; she didn't have identifying tattoos and her hair wasn't any different from lots of women.

"I'd just feel better if I was from a place where I don't know anyone. Maybe somewhere up north."

A town in the north popped into my head. "Yeah, what about Blackpool? If you were from there you could be Blackpool Pleasure Bitch!"

"Funny," she said, and laughed.

We both paused for a while, thinking about other places

around the country. But she got there first.

"What if I was from Plymouth? Then I could be Plymouth Ho!" She was pleased with herself, and rightly so.

"I think you're being overly paranoid," I maintained. "Be from London – more people will look at your profile then."

"Yes, you're probably right."

"We should decide on what you're called though. How about something like Trixie ... or Mitzi?"

Holly shook her head. "They sound more like poodles than escorts ... actually there's that thing ... what is it? ... where you take your first pet followed by your mother's maiden name to get your porn name."

"That could work. What's yours?"

"Well, we had a Siamese cat called Suki. And Mum's name was Cox."

"Suki Cox? Seriously?!"

"Yep."

"We have to use that!" We couldn't have made up a better one if we'd tried.

We added the photos, then had to choose from a list of what services she'd provide.

"I don't even know what half these things are," she said. "What's bukkake? And what's hardsports? I think I'll only tick the things I've heard of."

"Just say you do everything."

"Adult baby-minding and enemas are options! I'll tick the baby-minding but not the enemas."

She continued scrolling down the list.

"Filming – we've never thought of that. Next time we book we should see if we can film it."

That sounded like a good idea to me.

"There's pregnant and lactating on here too!" she said.

"Something for everyone."

"And unprotected sex. That's nasty – I'm not putting that."

"Just tick the box."

"I'm not–"

"Just tick the box!"

Between us, we wrote a description of Holly/Suki. It was a great piece of writing, and I felt we captured the right tone with touches of classy, sexy and dirty. It was the sort of thing *I* would like to read about an escort, and I got turned on doing it.

The last thing was selecting the rates for a half hour, hour, and overnight.

"Make me fairly high class," Holly said, "but don't price me out of the market."

Then we made the profile live, able to be seen by anyone who found it.

25

There'd been a table for sale in the shop since before I'd started working there; it was nothing special, just a narrow pine table meant for a hallway. One day it was bought by a couple who were in the process of moving house. They didn't want to take it for another few weeks, but paid for it, and I marked it with a red 'SOLD' sticker.

In the time between it being bought and picked up, I could've sold that table maybe three other times. People said, "Oh, that would've been perfect," or "*I'd* have had that, what a shame," and although I pointed out a similar one still for sale, they were only interested in the table that had sold.

It wasn't the first time that happened, and it occurred to me that the 'SOLD' stickers generated interest. If a person saw somebody else wanted an item, they wanted it too – its appeal had been validated. I mentioned it to Keith and he'd been noticing the same thing for years.

And it wasn't just stickers. Often it happened that something would be bought soon after it had been touched or commented on by another customer. It was as if people were subconsciously tuning into some kind of vibe that had been left. I attempted experiments and *willed* things to sell, but found it only worked if I genuinely liked it myself.

But by far the best way to sell an item was to put it in one of the 'selling spots'. There were two that I became aware of – the one in the window by the door, and the other in front of the desk. Things would be snapped up from there and I frequently replenished the empty spaces.

On eBay, the Wedgwood bird sold for sixteen pounds and

the postcards went for two or three pounds each. But a few of my boot sale purchases didn't get any bids at all, and I brought one of them – a turquoise vase – into the shop with me.

Louisa had said she collected glass, so I thought I'd offer it to her. But when she came in that morning, she told me she had far too many already and could do with selling hers rather than buying more. So, aware that Keith would be out for the whole day and would never know, I decided to write a price ticket and attempt to sell it in the shop. I put the vase in the spot in front of the desk.

It was a quietish day: Mrs Valensis ignored me, the 'Aladdin's cave' tally increased by one, and a French lady confused me by asking for a "sheep's cloak" before I realised she was actually saying "ship's clock".

Ian Cognito came in. He picked up my vase and turned it over to look at the base. He ran his finger around the rim, then handed me his first ever purchase. Even up close, it really did look like he had a false nose and moustache.

I got some newspaper and started wrapping the vase.

"I'd be interested if you get more like this," he said.

"Yeah? Well we might." I wrote down his phone number.

The next time I worked in the shop, I took a couple more of my unsold items – an Art Deco fingerplate and a plastic ice bucket in the shape of a pineapple. Positioning them in front of the desk, I waited for the customers. The fingerplate went, but despite drawing a lot of attention, the ice bucket didn't. Maybe I was asking too much for it.

Keith was supposed to be out all day again but turned up around three o'clock. I hoped he wouldn't see the pineapple, but he couldn't miss it.

"What's this?"

"Ah ... I bought it at the boot sale. It didn't sell online so I thought I'd bring it in here ... just for today." Standing up from the chair, I reached forward. "Sorry, I'll put it away."

"No, leave it. What have you got on it?" He looked at the price. "You'll be lucky, but worth a try."

"Yeah, I thought I was pushing it ... I only bought it for one pound fifty!"

"Did you? You got on alright at the boot sale then?"

I told him what I'd bought and the profits I'd made. I mentioned the turquoise vase too, just not that I'd sold it in the shop.

"Sounds like you've done well, keep at it." He made a move towards his workshop, but stopped and came back. "Actually, do you think you *could* sell some things for me on eBay? I can give you a cut of what they go for."

"Of course," I said. "But you don't need to give me anything."

"No, you should get something out of it." He glanced at the pineapple again. "I tell you what, you sell for me for, say, twenty percent, and if you sell some of your bits in the shop, I'll take twenty percent on those. Deal?"

It was a deal.

* * *

Suki Cox's profile exceeded a couple of thousand hits in a fortnight, and her first booking had been made within three hours of it going live. She got lots more bookings and Holly felt bad about cancelling them all. Some men would just re-book and then she'd feel compelled to message them to explain why they couldn't meet. But it wasn't with the truth – she made up a variety of excuses. Most gave up eventually but some got quite nasty about it, accusing her of wasting their time and not being real; this had happened to them before – it seemed we weren't the only ones to set up a fake profile.

If she'd have met up with all the men that had wanted to in those first two weeks, she'd have been paid just over two grand. We kept a record.

"I can't believe how much I'd have made," Holly said. She was sitting on the sofa with the laptop on the coffee table in front of her. "I wish I could earn that kind of money for real."

"But you actually *could* have done." I pointed out.

"Ha, I suppose so! I couldn't do it though."

"Couldn't you?"

"No! Sleeping with twenty guys? Maybe if it was fewer men and more money," she joked. "And if they weren't old, or fat, or ugly. And they were clean!"

"Yeah, I reckon everyone has a price."

"That's probably true."

"Go on then," I said. "What would your price be?"

"Just to do it one time?" She leaned back into the sofa and considered it. "Around ten grand … or five. Definitely not less than three … no, it would be five. Five grand – as long as no one ever knew. What's your price then – a pound?" She laughed.

"It's different for men," I said. "I probably *would* fuck anyone for a pound. Well maybe not anyone – I've got limits."

"Really? Do you? Maybe we should set *you* up with a profile!"

"I doubt anyone would pay to see *my* photos."

"I mean maybe you should become an escort."

"Oh. Do you think so?"

"I was only kidding!"

She leaned forward again and looked at the screen.

"Any more viewings?" I asked. I was talking about the private gallery.

"We're up to thirty-four pounds."

A few people had paid to see the private photos, but we weren't making money as quickly as we'd hoped. Holly found it exciting that men were looking at naked pictures of her though, and she'd been asked for more photos and even a video. Nobody had requested a face shot.

"What about new messages?"

"Um, there's a seventy-seven year old asking if he's too old for me," she said. "I'll just send a quick reply: 'Fuck off, you dirty old bastard!'" But I looked over and read what she typed and it was: Sorry, I hope you won't take offence but I think you probably are.

"What else is there?"

"Another one about feet." There were plenty of foot-fetishists. "And someone's asking if I've got a friend ... oh, it's for a stag party – they want to give the groom a threesome. Why do people even get married if they're just going to fuck around?" Shaking her head, she clicked on the next one. "Lyle, check this out – this guy wants to know if I'd consider 'mild torture'."

"Mild torture?! What does he mean by that?"

"He doesn't go into specifics."

"Makes a change."

Holly had had lots of messages, which she mostly ignored. Some were just compliments about her photos, but she'd also had many 'special requests'. There was a man who wanted to drink her urine, and another who wanted a thong sent to him after she'd had a 'day at work' (she *did* send one – for twenty pounds). They wanted her to do full-weight face sitting, wank them off with her feet, fuck through a hole cut in the crotch of a pair of tights, and pretend to be unconscious. We joked that nobody seemed to want 'normal' sex, but I suppose if you're paying a stranger there's no judgement; a lot of men probably hid from wives or girlfriends the things they wanted to do.

"Oh, that guy Woody's replied," she said. "Listen to this: 'Your smoking hot.'" She stopped reading to point out 'you're' was spelt wrongly – we both hated it when people did that. "'I'll save up my cum for you and unload it in your mouth. I want to see it run down your chin.' That's nasty. Why do men think we want to hear that? They watch too much porn."

"Yeah," I laughed uneasily. "I didn't think you minded doing that though?"

"Well, I don't mind with you so much, but quite frankly the less the better. The thought of some stranger's spunk in my mouth makes me want to throw up. Oh God, it really does!" She put her hand dramatically to her mouth. "I can't be bothered to respond. I don't think I'll message other people again – I'll just stick with Gregory."

"But *he* writes stuff like that to you though?" I said.

"Not quite like that. There's a difference between *good*-dirty and *gross*-dirty."

Gregory had been the first to message and was very flattering. He said she stood out amongst all the other escorts, not only by her photos which were 'sexy and artistic', but by the way she'd written about herself in an 'eloquent and arousing way'. I liked Gregory – a man who appreciated aesthetics and good prose. He lived in Edinburgh – too far away to make a booking – but he promised to schedule an appointment next time he was in London on business.

Holly had replied and they were regularly corresponding.

"It's not bothering you is it – me writing to him?" she asked. "If you feel jealous at all, I'll stop."

"Nothing to be jealous about." What Gregory wrote turned Holly on and I got the benefit from it. "He's probably fat and old and ugly anyway."

"Ha! Probably."

I said, "You don't get jealous of the escorts, do you?"

"No. You know that."

I knew that. I was just checking.

"Thirty-four pounds," she muttered to herself. "We need to start making more money – I'm out of a job in three weeks."

"Shit, is it that soon?"

"Yep, the woman I'm covering for is coming back."

"What are you going to do?"

"I was hoping the photos would pay and I wouldn't have to do much!" She laughed. "I don't know. I might look into teacher training. I could do with a new direction – I don't like office work."

"Did you just say you could do with a nude erection?"

She narrowed her eyes. "You know exactly what I was saying. Is there any time you don't have sex on the brain?"

"I don't think so. The trouble is, you're smoking hot." I winked.

"I hope you added the apostrophe."

"Of course! So ... do you need a nude erection?"

She closed the lid of the laptop. "You know what, I think I might."

26

When Holly's job ended, she didn't leave on Sunday night because there was nowhere she had to be on the Monday. But I did – I had to work in the shop. I left her in bed.

When I returned after work, the flat was tidy and clean. Everything had been returned to its place: my clothes were off the bedroom floor, rubbish was in the bin, and plates were washed up. The carpet in the living room had not only been picked free of debris, but the thick furry pile looked as though it had been brushed.

Holly was in the kitchen stirring a pot of bolognese simmering on the hob. She was wearing nothing but an apron which barely covered her tits and didn't remotely cover her arse. The 1970s décor seemed to complement what I'd come back to; all I needed was for her to bring me slippers and a pipe and I could read my newspaper.

Standing in the doorway, I said, "You've been busy today."

"I have. Do you like it?"

"Yeah, it looks great." I went over, kissed her and put my hands on her arse.

"I've sorted out your cupboards too, so it makes more sense." She moved away to show me. "Pans are here and food is in here now – at eye level so you can see what you've got. And in here …" she opened the cupboard next to the sink, "… there's a bag for all your recycling – cardboard, paper, glass and plastic."

"OK–"

"And this – I fixed it." The cutlery drawer ran smoothly, and she repeatedly opened and closed it to demonstrate.

"Nice one." I began to unbutton my jeans. "I think I might have another job for you."

Understanding what I meant, she said, "Is that a pencil in your pocket or are you just pleased to see me?"

Holly stayed for the whole of that week. She didn't cook every night, but the flat remained tidy.

Her profile on the escort website approached five thousand hits and the bookings and requests kept coming. A male escort on the site volunteered to make a video with her, and one guy offered to be her chauffeur to and from appointments, asking for nothing in return. She politely declined both.

We took more photos and posted them up in the hope of enticing more viewers; Holly sent some privately to Gregory for free. We'd reached fifty two pounds from the gallery – not a fortune, but we could put it towards paying for another escort. 'Sexy Sasha' was sixty pounds for half an hour and lived just three stops away on the train. We booked her for Thursday night.

Arriving at a modern house in a quiet residential close, Sasha answered the door in her dressing gown. When we were indoors and out of sight from the neighbours, she removed it to reveal bright pink underwear and thigh-length white PVC boots – clothes only strippers and hookers wear.

Sasha kept her boots on as I fucked her on the bed, while her pet poodle yapped constantly at the closed door. Holly filmed us on my phone and when we watched the footage back, the picture shook each time Sasha shouted, "Trixie, be quiet!" Holly had been trying hard not to laugh out loud.

There was a bit where I had Sasha on all fours. I gently pushed her head down onto the pillow, and with one hand, gripped both her wrists behind her back. Holly liked that; she watched it over again and got off on it.

On Sunday we went to the boot sale together. I found a set

of Hornsea storage jars, a collection of round glass paperweights, a 1950s magazine rack, and a coffee pot by Meakin. We saw Eddie there, presumably buying more things to sell to Keith. I said, "Hello, Eddie." But he just shuffled past hugging his purchases.

Holly enjoyed the boot sale and I liked having her there. She was keen to see the kind of things I was buying, and suggested a few items to me on the way round. She went off on her own for a while, coming back with a book on Surrealist painting. Presenting it to me she said, "For you to learn more about art ... one book at a time."

She'd also found a piece of green fabric that she thought was the same colour as the living room carpet, and she intended to make cushion covers from it. When we got in, she took out the fabric and held it against the floor.

"Yep, the same – I knew it. It'll look so much better in here with cushions."

I said I agreed, but didn't care one way or the other.

Glancing at the walls, she said, "It would be good if this place had a coat of paint too."

"Not over *this* wallpaper," I protested. There was no way I'd get rid of it.

"Maybe not in here. I like it – it's kitsch ... but what about the bedroom and hallway?"

I wouldn't miss the wallpaper in my room, and in the hallway it was ripped and dirty.

"You should ask Keith if he'll let you redecorate," she said. "And see if he'll replace the lino too – that's had it."

That afternoon, as Holly sewed the cushions and we watched the Formula 1 Grand Prix together, there was a moment when I realised how comfortable I felt in her company. Maybe I was even happy ...

And then it became too much. Holly was there all the time: when I went to bed and when I woke up, when I went to work and when I got in. I didn't know when she intended to go back home.

One day, after I'd got in at five, she was sitting on the living room floor going through the local papers' job pages.

"What are you doing?" I asked, even though I could see.

"Looking for a job."

"Here?"

"Wherever."

I sat on the sofa and took off my shoes. "What happened to the teaching idea?"

"I'm not sure I want to do that anymore."

"Oh, OK. What do you want to do then?"

"I don't know," she shrugged. "I've seen a couple of potential things for you, though. You should apply for this …" She held up a page for me to see. I didn't read it.

I said, "Why are you looking at jobs for me?"

"I'm not … but you said you wanted to find something else."

"Well, yeah. But I'm not looking."

"Why not?"

"Because I don't want to yet."

"Why not?" she repeated.

"Because I don't. Anyway don't worry about what I'm doing, concentrate on your own life."

She closed the newspaper. "OK, OK, sorry. I won't help then!"

In the evening we watched TV. I was drinking a beer and Holly was on her third can of Pimms and lemonade. With the remote, she put the guide up on the screen and scrolled through.

"There's nothing on," she said. "Let's go out."

I was fine sitting there with my beer. "No, I want to stay in."

"But we stay in all the time. I want to do something … why don't we ever go out for dinner?"

"Because you haven't got any money and I hate eating out."

"You hate a lot of things," she said under her breath. "Come on, let's go out. We don't have to spend anything, we could just go for a walk or something."

"I can't be bothered." I took the remote from her and started flicking through the channels. Finding an old episode of *Red Dwarf*, I left it on that.

"You're so fucking lazy!" she said, suddenly vehement.

"No I'm not, I just don't want to go out."

She turned her whole body and faced me. "Yes you are. You're one of the laziest people I know."

"I'm *not* lazy." I spoke calmly, but she was starting to piss me off.

"Do you honestly believe that?!" she scoffed. "I hope you get some good photos of the pyramids on your trip down de*Nile.*"

"Oh, that's a good one. You're funny." I wasn't laughing.

"Like with your degree – you could've done so much better if you'd actually tried."

How the hell had we got onto *this* subject?

"What the fuck are you talking about?" I moved my gaze from the TV to her.

"And then you wouldn't be working in a shop," she continued. "You're wasting your talent, you know."

"What's wrong with working in the shop? I'm doing the eBay stuff now, and I've got a space to sell in there …"

"Well, it's not a *bad* job, but why aren't you writing anymore?" she said. "You should be. Some of it was so good … like that story about the man who married his cat."

It was a short story I'd written in my second year, and it had received the most positive feedback from my tutor. It was the one I was proudest of.

"I'll get back to it at some point."

"Huh – some point! But why aren't you doing it now … instead of writing on walls?" Her tone had a touch of contempt. "That's just your half-arsed effort at writing."

"Half-arsed effort?"

"Yep. You're too lazy to write anything properly, so you do that. Why *do* you anyway? It's like you want people to see you – see how clever you are ... actually, I'm surprised you're not on Facebook or Twitter. Ha! Twitter's the perfect format for you: a hundred and forty characters, and validation for your ego."

I'd had enough of being attacked. "You're being a bitch now."

"Am I?" She sounded like that couldn't possibly be true. "I'm just saying that you're excusing yourself from getting on and writing something meaningful."

"You don't know anything about–"

"And that's what you do," she interrupted. "You never just get on with things. You put obstacles in your way like you don't even want the best for yourself. You make bad choices all the time."

"*I* make bad choices?" I said. "What about *yours*?"

"We're not talking about me, we're talking about you."

"Yeah? Why are we? At least *I've* got a job and somewhere to live," I shot back. "What are *your* plans? What are *you* going to do?"

"Great way to dodge a conversation – turn it round to me."

"But you're doing exactly that – dodging it by turning it back to *me*!"

This wasn't the way I wanted to spend the evening. I could see it wasn't going anywhere good so I stood up and said, "I think I *will* go out actually – on my own."

Walking around the park, I was angry at being forced out; I hated being judged, having someone comment on my life and choices. Instinctively I got out my pencil to write something, but remembered what Holly had said and put it away.

Half-arsed?!
It's none of your business whether I write or not.
And not doing something DOESN'T make me lazy.

I *would* get back into writing … in my own time; it couldn't be rushed, and it couldn't be forced. There was good writing in me, I was sure. I felt I had things to say, wisdom which I'd one day be able to tap into and put into words. I didn't know yet what that wisdom was, but it would come when I was ready. I wished I could go forward in time to confirm my abilities and achievements to myself. Then I'd return to the present with the impetus and confidence to get on and do it. Because I *knew* I could do it, I just couldn't seem to *do* it.

My feet were on autopilot and I barely noticed my surroundings or where I was heading. When they eventually brought me back to the flat, Holly was already in bed.

I went to sleep in the small room.

27

In the morning, as I surfaced into consciousness, I became aware of sounds from the other side of the wall: talking. Remembering where I was, I realised it was Amy. She was with someone.

Her voice was interspersed with the low pitch of a male. I lay there listening, but couldn't make out actual words. She laughed, then he laughed. Someone walked across the room and music went on – not too loud, but audible. The talking stopped. Then there was a creaking; it was rhythmic but not quite in time to the music. I didn't believe it was what I thought it was, until I heard the sex noises. It started with a few isolated high moans and low grunts, but soon resembled porn. Her bed banged against our connecting wall. Almost without thinking, my hand slid down my pants. But it didn't seem right, so I removed it.

I picked up my phone from the floor and checked the time: ten past nine. It was a Wednesday. Amy's parents would be at work and she should be at school.

I got up as quietly as I could and left them to it. I went to the kitchen to put the kettle on, but Holly was already on it.

"Hi." She brought two mugs out from their new place in the cupboard. "Cup of tea?"

"Yeah. Please."

As she poured the boiled water from the kettle, she said, "Sorry about last night. I didn't mean to say all that – I don't know why I did. I was just trying to be … encouraging."

"Is that what it was?"

She smiled apologetically.

I said, "Yeah, but the way you say stuff, like you know best – 'you should do this, you should do that' – I don't like it."

"I know." She strained the teabags. "I just get frustrated by what you–"

"I don't want to hear it." I cut in. "I can work things out for myself, you know."

She sighed heavily. "Yes, I know. And I'll try to watch how I speak to you. Pick me up on it if I start doing it again."

"OK, I will."

She stepped forward and hugged me. Putting my arms around her, I rested my chin on the top of her head. She spoke into my chest. "I'm having cereal, do you want some?"

"Yeah, I'll do it."

We let go.

I filled two bowls with Crunchy Nut Cornflakes and shared out the last of the milk. I threw the carton in the bin.

"No, that needs to go in the recycling," Holly retrieved it and rinsed it under the tap. "Why do you keep forgetting?"

"Uh ... you're doing it again," I said.

"No I'm not, this is completely different. It winds me up when you don't put things in the right bin."

"What does it matter? It's not a big deal."

"No it's not a big deal, so why can't you just do it?"

"Look, whatever. I've got to get ready for work." I picked up my bowl and left the room.

On my way to open the shop, I passed Amy on the street. I nearly said hello but remembered that although I knew who she was, she didn't know me. She was with the skinny boy I'd seen her with before, and neither of them looked the type to have had that kind of sex. But they say it's the quiet ones ...

I spent some time in the morning sorting out more of my items. Keith had given me the area near the bottom of the stairs to use, and the vases, pineapple, and ceramics made a colourful and eye-catching display.

Louisa noticed it when she came in.

"This is different," she wheezed.

"That's all mine. I'm selling now."

"Oh, are you? You like mid-century then?"

"Yeah, I do." Most of the things I'd put in the shop were from the '50s, '60s or '70s. It was what I was drawn to.

"That's my era," she said. "My house is full of it … maybe too full." She slowly made it to her chair. "Are you buying?"

"Uh, yeah."

"I've decided to move," she announced, as though the decision had been made then and there. "It's time I lived somewhere where they can keep an eye on me – I'm not as young and healthy as I used to be." She coughed up into her tissue and demonstrated the point. "I need to sell some things. Downsize – is that what they call it?"

"OK, well I'll talk to Keith and he can arrange a time to come round and–"

"No, no – I want you to do it."

The boot sale was one thing, but I wasn't sure I'd know what I was doing buying from her.

"Keith knows a lot more than I do," I said. "Wouldn't you prefer it if–"

"No, what I'd prefer is you."

I didn't have the chance to answer, because at that moment Holly came in. She stood in front of the desk.

"I'm off to the Co-op to get milk. Do you want anything?"

"No, thanks."

She moved her hair off her shoulders. "Um, I didn't mean to go on about the recycling before."

Not wanting a public conversation about it, I said quietly, "It's fine, don't worry."

I glanced at Louisa who was grinning broadly at us.

Holly turned in her direction. "Oh, sorry. I didn't see you there. Did I interrupt?"

"Not at all, I was about to go. The young man was just

saying he'd come round to look at the things I want to sell."

I smiled in surrender. "Alright then."

Louisa tried to stand up, and this time needed my help. I walked her to the door and held it open for her.

She said, "I'll sort it all out and be in touch."

As I returned to the desk Holly said, "What was that about?" She was sitting in Louisa's chair.

I thought you were going to the Co-op.

"Oh, she's got some retro stuff."

"Cool." Holly said, and gestured towards the stairs. "Anyone else in?"

"No, the shop's empty ... apart from Keith."

As if on cue, Keith appeared from his workshop carrying a rolled-up Persian rug. "Hello again," he said on his way past her and up the stairs.

She smiled at him, then spoke quietly to me. "Have you asked him about decorating?"

"Not yet."

"Are you going to?"

"Yeah, at some point."

Keith came back down the stairs. Holly said to him, "Lyle and I were wondering if it would be OK to do some painting in the flat – over the wallpaper in the hallway?" I couldn't believe she'd asked.

"Uh, yeah. I suppose you can."

She didn't stop there. "We'll do it ... but can you pay for the paint?"

Appalled, I said, "No, you don't have to do that!"

But he laughed it off, saying, "That's fine."

Holly kept going. "Also, there's a tap dripping in the bathroom."

"Right, I'll fix that later."

"Thanks," she said, and stood up. "OK, I'm off to the shops. See you in a bit."

She left and I said, "Sorry about that, you really don't have

161

to pay for the paint."

"No, I'm sorry. The flat's been in need of updating for years and I should've offered. So … is that girl of yours living with you now?"

"No," I said abruptly, "she's not living with me."

"Well, I don't mind if she is. It's not a problem."

After work, I returned to the smell of cooking.

Holly was in the kitchen adding onions to a pan. "I thought I'd do a curry tonight, that alright?"

"Yeah." I fancied pizza.

Opening the fridge, I saw she hadn't fully restocked it. And I was glad – it was a good reason to leave.

"I'll go get some beers."

Mr and Mrs Stephenson were in the Co-op. He carried the basket in one hand and held his wife's hand with the other. I passed close to them in the chilled aisle as they perused the meat. Mr Stephenson suggested they buy beef mince, but she said, "No." She picked up chicken breasts instead and put them in the basket.

I saw them a few more times as I wandered around; I wasn't in a hurry to get back. To all the things he suggested she impatiently said, "No." She was obviously the one who made the decisions while he complied. I started to feel irritated by them.

Just buy what you want. Don't let her dictate!

When I used to see the Stephensons, I thought they looked happy. But maybe they weren't – maybe they just put up with each other. What is there to talk about after decades of marriage anyway? All subjects will have been covered and what's left is memories. Conversations would be along the lines of, "Do you remember when …?"

Back at the flat with the beers, I went straight to the living room and opened one. Holly came to find me.

"Everything OK?" she asked.

"Not really."

"What's up?"

"What's up" I said, "is that I didn't like the way you confronted Keith earlier."

She folded her arms. "You think I *confronted* him?"

"What would you call it?"

"Helping," she asserted.

"That wasn't helping, it was embarrassing ... like I couldn't do it myself. And he's done so much for me already – giving me a job, dropping the rent when Marcus moved out ..."

"Yes, but this place needs sorting. Those gas fires look really old for a start – are you sure they're even safe?"

"Of course they're safe ... and I was going to talk to him in my own time."

"Yep, and I know how quick 'your own time' can be."

I flinched – she was getting nasty again.

"Why are you involving yourself anyway?" I said. "You don't live here – this is *my* flat."

"I'm just making it better."

"I liked it the way it was."

"What with rubbish everywhere? I tidied up for you, I fixed the drawer in the kitchen ... so what that I talked to him about the paint and the dripping tap? I'm just trying to help."

There was that word again, as if it excused her behaviour.

"I don't need your 'help'," I said.

"Well, you need *something*. You need to grow the fuck up – why are you still living like a teenager? I don't want to stay here when it's so messy."

"Don't stay here then. Who's asking you to?"

Glaring at me intensely, she said, "I'd better turn the rice off." She went to the kitchen.

I followed, but not to continue the argument.

She was by the oven with her back to me. I went over to her and put my arms around her waist. She leaned into me and we stood in silence.

Then, to change the subject, I said, "I can't wait till Friday." We had an afternoon appointment booked with 'Candygirl69'.

Holly shrugged me off and took the pan of rice to the sink to drain it. "I think we should cancel," she said. "I'd rather save up – go somewhere for a bit of a holiday at the same time like we did in Rotterdam." She plated the rice and then the curry. "We could visit art galleries and do other stuff. How about Prague? I've always wanted to go there, and it's supposed to have lots of sex clubs …"

"That could take months," I said. "I don't want to wait. It's OK, I know you're worried about money, so I'll pay on Friday."

"But you haven't got much either." She placed the empty pans in the sink.

"I'm doing alright, I've had bids on a few of the eBay–"

She suddenly raised her voice, "God, Lyle! All you think about is sex!"

I stared at her incredulously; I'd been trying to make it up to her.

"Are you fucking joking?!" My voice was equally as loud. "What do you think this is? *Sex* is what we're doing."

She couldn't have looked more shocked if I'd hit her.

"Fuck you!" She walked out of the room with tears in her eyes.

I thought she'd cry like all the times I'd seen before. She'd make me feel bad enough that I'd want to apologise, even though I didn't think I had anything to apologise for. She'd calm down, we'd have sex, and everything would be OK.

But she got her things and left.

And, as I stood next to the steaming plates of food abandoned on the kitchen worktop, I let her.

It was only later I realised she'd left the music box behind.

PART 3

THE WRITING ON THE WALL

28

In the churchyard, I sat in my usual place, and overhead, the full branches of the oak tree shielded me from the midday sun. Paper confetti in the shape of bells and hearts and petals had drifted against the side of the tomb.

Re-reading the inscriptions next to me, I thought about Robert Hix and his duel. What had been the reason for it? Had he been defending his honour? Was it rivalry over a woman? I had the idea it had something to do with Sylvia and that was why he'd been buried next to her. But I checked the dates and they'd lived at different times.

A fat rubber band lay on the ground beside my feet. I picked it up, looped it around the fingers and thumb of my left hand, and stretched it out. The sensation was familiar and it took me back to the Post Office car park behind our old house. When we were kids, Elspeth and I used to climb the wall to play there. We collected the bands discarded by the postmen and made them into balls. For a few weeks of one summer, finding rubber bands was my main focus, and it was my mission to make a bigger ball than Elspeth did. But she found more.

Most of my childhood memories seemed to be just me and Elspeth. Although Mum and Dad must've been there somewhere, I remembered only the two of us: flying kites, running around the ruins of Corfe Castle, rolling down the sand dunes …

Looking at my phone, there were no new messages.

I opened the texts Holly and I had exchanged the day before yesterday.

I'd sent the first: Sorry. X

It had taken a while for a reply: I'm sorry too, but I can't do this anymore

Me: Are you OK? X

Her: I will be

That seemed final, so I left it. What could I have said anyway? We'd had fun, but I didn't know what I expected from her ... or from us. In my mind we weren't actually *together*, and I wasn't sure I wanted to be. Because I knew how it would all go. I'd been there before.

I'd met Holly in the bar at university and we'd gone out for a while – towards the end of the second and into the third year of our degrees. It wasn't clear why she was with me as she seemed to find fault with most things I did. Except, that was, when we were in bed. And in the beginning she was happy to stay there with me as I missed morning lectures.

But soon she wouldn't miss lectures anymore. She went to them all and thought I should be doing the same. "It's our final year. You should take your degree seriously. You're going to regret missing this opportunity."

She said I spent too much time with my friends, drinking, and smoking weed. She wanted me to go out with her more, make an effort with *her* friends. But I didn't want to socialise and force small talk with their boyfriends who I had little in common with. Like Christophe who was with Holly's friend, Annabel. Christophe! He wasn't even French. He was a pretentious prick and I fucking hated him.

Holly expected me to "compromise", "be more considerate", and "work on our relationship". But they were just other ways of saying 'change'. And I shouldn't have to change for anyone. When she ended it, I wasn't too bothered – there were plenty more girls around, ones who didn't mind just having fun.

I looked at my phone again: half twelve. Time to go. The escort had already been booked so why shouldn't I keep the appointment and go on my own? I felt a sudden rush of nervous excitement – partly from the thought of sex, but also because I was going into the unknown and wasn't sure what I'd find.

Before I left, I checked Sylvia's gravestone to see if my name was still there. It was, but the words were faint. I went over them again, updating my age from 21 to 23. Underneath I added:

ADVENTURER

I pulled the rubber band back from my thumb and fired it over the wall.

Candy's profile said she was twenty-five but she looked more like thirty-five. She invited me into her house and we went straight up the stairs.

On the walls hung framed photographs of kids who must've been the reason she only took bookings in the daytimes. Unintentionally gurning for the camera were two boys with stuck-out ears, and a little girl with eyes that went in different directions. The pictures documented their years together from when the youngest was a baby; in the most recent, they were all in school uniform, and the eldest looked around twelve.

No way you're twenty-five.

In her bedroom, I was glad there was an alarm clock on the bedside table – it would be easy to check the time, to see how much was left. Another framed photo of the kids stood next to the clock.

I'm going to fuck your mum. I'm a motherfucker.

Candy wasn't the type I was usually attracted to with her straightened blonde hair and deep tan. I wouldn't have given her a second look in a pub or club and certainly wouldn't have gone home with her. Her tan continued under her bra but ended under her thong. She had a red rose tattooed on her shoulder and moles on her side in a V shape like the constellation of Taurus.

I briefly sucked her nipples and they tasted of tobacco as if someone – a smoker – had been there before me and she hadn't bothered to wash. As she squatted down to put a condom on with her mouth, her legs were apart and I could smell her.

She said, "Do you want me to talk dirty to you?"

Dirty body, dirty mind.

"Yeah, if you want."

It was clichéd porn-talk – laughable, and not much of a turn on. Holly would've definitely found it funny.

Candy said, "Give me some of your big throbbing cock."

I gave her some.

"Oooh yeeaah," she moaned. "My hot pussy is dripping wet for you."

Dripping?! Holly would've said that was in the realms of gross-dirty.

"Fuck me harder."

OK, I'll fuck you harder.

"Fuck me with your big hard cock."

Yeah I am, you slut. You fucking dirty bitch.

At the end, she looked proud, as if she'd just given me the best experience I'd ever had. But it's not a huge achievement to make a man come. And quite honestly I'd wanted to get it over with and get out of there ... even though it was before my time was up.

Back beside Sylvia's grave, I took out my phone, saw there were no new messages, and returned it to my pocket.

Bending down, I rubbed out 'adventurer', replacing it with:

IDIOT

29

The camouflage man had a new vehicle: a monster truck. It had bigger wheels for the bumpy terrain around the trees and handled the kerbs better. He drove it past a woman in a green dress who was trying to urge her dog towards the park. It was a fluffy, pedigree breed (Japanese, I think) with an upright tail that curled forwards. At its back end, the completely white fur had been clipped, displaying an obscenely large arsehole like a snowman's bellybutton. The dog was determined to take a crap in the middle of the pavement, and when he'd finished, despite the grooming, some of the fur around his arsehole wasn't so white. As the woman stooped to clear the shit from the ground with a plastic bag, she had a go at picking up the pound coin.

I saw Mr and Mrs Stephenson heading to the café. The hand-holding I once thought was endearing appeared fake and forced. And it was too hot for coats and hats.

It's July, you stupid people.

The door opened. Customers: a mum, dad, and two young sons. Even before they spoke, I could tell they were posh by their turned-up collars, deck shoes, and the dad's red trousers.

I hated it if kids came into the shop. They weren't interested in antiques and soon became bored and whiny. Their parents warned them not to touch anything, but they always did.

As soon as the family were through the door, the mum said, "Ambrose, remember not to touch."

Ambrose – ha!

The older boy prodded a Royal Doulton figurine of a lady

holding colourful balloons.

The mum's head shot around. "Gideon, you too."

Gideon! You poor little bastards.

Ambrose opened the lid of a black lacquer box.

"Boys! Are you listening to me at all?"

No.

The dad couldn't keep his hands to himself either and honked the rubber bulb of a taxi horn. He reminded me of someone – with his long, thin face, bald head, beard, and moustache. It bugged me and I kept furtively glancing his way to work it out. Was it an actor? Was it someone I knew? I thought it might even have been a cartoon character. As they were leaving the shop, I realised who it was: Richard from the game of *Guess Who* that Elspeth and I used to play.

I tried to recall all the characters on the board, spending the rest of the day writing them down in the notebook. There was Herman, Bernard, Frans, Max with a big nose, Eric who looked like Benny Hill. I thought about who had blue eyes, glasses, a hat or facial hair. I knew there were only five women and had already remembered Claire because she had glasses and a hat. Then there was Anita who I always fancied, and Maria was alright too …

The news was full of a school shooting that had happened in America. They showed yearbook-type photos of some of the victims – the seventeen teenage students and two middle-aged female teachers. They profiled the shooter. It was classic: a young, white, male loner.

What's the matter, didn't your mum give you enough attention?

I switched off the TV and wandered from room to room.

I went to the kitchen and got a beer from the fridge.

I drank as I leaned against the wall in the small room. Amy wasn't there.

I stood in the doorway of the living room; it *did* look better with cushions.

I went for a piss in the bathroom.

I got another beer from the kitchen.

Settling in my bedroom, I put on music. It was one of my boot sale CDs I'd bought for the cover art: a stylised man staring into the water below at his transforming reflection. The album was *Becoming a Jackal* by Villagers, and the chorus of the title track spoke about staring out of windows.

There are times when lyrics of songs resonate with you; it can be exactly the same with books. They seem to speak directly to you, almost as if the words were written *for* you, and can help crystallise your thoughts or just allow you to wallow. That evening, resonance was everywhere.

* * *

Some of the days I worked, some of the days I stayed in the flat. When I was working, I wanted to be in the flat. When I wasn't working, I didn't like being faced with a day of nothing in front of me, and looked forward to the distraction of the shop.

I couldn't stand the pointless conversations people were trying to have with me. Why did they bother saying something that I'd obviously agree with?

"Lovely weather."

Yeah, it is.

"Wasn't it dreadful about that school in America?"

Of course it was.

"It's awful how often those things happen over there. They shouldn't have access to guns."

Of course they shouldn't.

Two people referred to the shop as an Aladdin's cave and I really fucking hated it! I considered the words: Aladdin's cave – a lad in his cave. I remembered Bowie's album, *Aladdin Sane,* and wrote in the notebook:

ALADDIN VISIBLE

ALADDIN COMPLETE

ALADDIN DENIAL

In denial about denial, I rubbed out the last one.

Between customers, I went around the shop, choosing the three things I'd buy if money were no object. I settled on a teak sideboard, a copper Arts and Crafts mirror, and a bureau I'd use as a writing desk. Together, they were just over six hundred pounds.

Wondering how much it would cost to buy *everything* in the shop, I estimated twenty thousand. With a calculator, I added up the ticket prices and on the furniture alone reached over forty thousand pounds – I'd been way off. I couldn't be bothered to add the rest, but guessed the total would increase by at least another ten thousand.

Louisa came in and asked how it was going with the items I was selling. I told her it was good, but in reality it was slow. I hadn't sold anything through the shop for a while or listed on eBay; I'd stopped getting up for boot sales. Louisa hadn't got around to sorting out her stuff yet, but would do it soon. I assured her there was no hurry.

"Are you alright?" she inquired with concern. "You don't seem … yourself."

"Uh, I'm OK. Just a bad day I suppose."

"Oh, I'm sorry about that. I'm sure it will get better."

"Yeah," I said, unconvinced.

"That was a lovely girl I saw here before. Your girlfriend?"

"No, not my girlfriend."

"Oh." She patted my hand. "There will be other girls."

At that moment I glanced out of the window and watched the arse of the waitress from the café cross the road.

Yeah, other girls.

As I sat in my bedroom listening to music, so many lyrics made my thoughts turn to Holly.

I was startled by my phone ringing – it hardly ever rang – and the number on the display wasn't one I recognised. Ordinarily I'd have cancelled the call, thinking it was about PPI or something, but I knew it would be Holly; it had to be her – the timing was perfect.

"Hello?" I said.

"Lyle?" It was a man's voice.

"Uh … yeah?"

"It's Marcus."

"Marcus?" I was beginning to think the Universe doesn't like to be second-guessed. "Hey, how are you?" I probably sounded disappointed.

"You've changed your number. I had to ring your mum."

"Yeah, I've had a couple of different phones."

"And you didn't give me your new numbers?" he said. "I s'pose that's fair enough … look, I'm sorry about moving out. I felt like shit about it."

He seemed fine at the time. And I didn't change my phone for a couple of months after he left, but I don't remember him feeling bad enough to get in touch then.

"Don't worry," I said. "That was ages ago. I'm over it."

He laughed. "Glad to hear it. So, how are you, man? Still at the flat?"

"Yeah, I'm alright … still here."

"Living on your own?"

"Yeah, all alone."

"Good," he said. "Because I want to stay."

30

Nina had thrown Marcus out. He told me he'd considered leaving anyway, but this way he'd got the result he wanted without being the dick who'd left his six-and-a-half-months-pregnant girlfriend.

He brought a rucksack and a sleeping bag with him, and dumped them in the small room. When he came into the living room, I passed him a beer, but before he had the chance to open it, his phone rang. He went to the kitchen to talk; I could hear his side of the conversation.

"No, I'm at Lyle's," he said. "Yeah, same place … … Dunno … … Not sure … Maybe … … You *told* me to go! … … What d'you expect? … … … … Don't fucking start again … … I'll talk to you tomorrow … … … … No, I'll talk to you tomorrow … … Just leave it, I'll talk to you tomorrow!"

He returned, staring at his phone screen. Puffing out his cheeks as he exhaled, he dropped into the armchair.

"Nina?" I asked.

He nodded slowly.

"What's going on?"

"I dunno, she's fucking crazy. She's changed since she got pregnant – doesn't let me do anything."

"Changed?" I said. "She was always like that."

We both laughed.

"Yeah, maybe," he said. "She thinks I go out too much … just 'cos I didn't get in 'til four the other night. It's not like she's even had the fucking baby yet." He opened his beer. "Anyway, let's not talk about her … how are you? What's been going on?"

"Not a lot," I said. "I'm working in the antiques shop now."

"Yeah, your mum said you finally got a job." Raising his can, he tilted his head in congratulations. "Seeing anyone?"

"No."

"*Been* seeing anyone?"

I shook my head.

"Shit, man. No action at all?"

"Not lately."

I'm not sure why I didn't tell him about Holly or our adventures with the escorts. I suppose I didn't think it was anybody else's business, or perhaps I didn't feel as OK about it as I thought I did.

Marcus *did* talk to Nina the next day, but nothing was resolved. And I was glad, because I liked him being at the flat that weekend. We sat in the park with beers, went bowling, drank at the pub by the river, ate takeaways and watched films. We left our empties on the coffee table, the toilet seat up, and didn't bother washing-up. It was relaxed and it was easy. I told him he could stay for as long as he needed.

He commuted to London early on Monday and I worked in the shop. Afterwards, I waited for him to get back, and when he did, he'd brought some weed that he'd got off a guy at work. He rolled a joint while I went across the road to get us fish and chips. We ate, smoked, and spent the evening laughing and reminiscing.

"I missed this," he said.

"Yeah, me too."

The next morning I didn't feel too well and was glad to have a day off from the shop. I wasn't sure how Marcus had managed to get up for work, but then he still smoked a lot of the time; apart from that small amount in Amsterdam, *I* hadn't for a couple of years.

In the kitchen, I put the kettle on. There weren't any mugs clean; there wasn't much clean. Plates, bowls, cutlery and everything else filled the sink or cluttered the worktops. I picked out only what I needed and washed it.

I opened the fridge to get milk, but there wasn't any; the carton was on the side, the lid off. Picking it up, I could feel it was empty, but tipped it upside down over my tea anyway to get any remaining drops out. The cereal box was also out on the side, and Marcus had left the top and the inner packaging wide open. Closing it up, I put the box back in the cupboard where it was supposed to live.

Everything has a place.

The living room stank of stale smoke and greasy food. I created a small space on the coffee table for my mug, and moved Marcus's clothes from the sofa to accommodate myself. His breakfast bowl on the table in front of me contained soggy cornflakes floating in several centimetres of milk; he'd poured himself more than he needed and left me with nothing. I thought about spooning some of his milk into my tea, but didn't.

As I sat there trying to watch TV, my eyes kept going to the mess. Was this really the way we'd lived before?

I got a black bin liner from the kitchen and began throwing in the rubbish ... then I remembered, got a transparent recycling bag and put the bottles and cans in there. That afternoon, I did the washing-up. All of it.

Marcus didn't thank me when he got in – it wasn't even noted – and I resented clearing up someone else's mess when it was seemingly unappreciated. But he did have more weed, and I quickly got over it. We replayed the night before, even down to the fish and chips.

The next day was work for both of us. All day I felt bad – unhealthy, toxic. There had been too many days of excessive drinking, smoking and eating, and I made up my mind to have a proper dinner and not smoke. I planned to make food for Marcus too and waited for him to get back before I started. But at eight o'clock I was too hungry to wait anymore so cooked and ate without him. He got in two hours later.

"What time do you call this?" I said, half-serious.

"Yeah, alright Nina!" he half-joked back. "I didn't think it would be a problem."

"It's not a problem – you can do what you want. Just a bit of common courtesy would be good." I could almost hear Holly's voice speaking as I said it. It was a line she'd used before.

On Friday night, after a few beers in the flat, Marcus wanted us to go out to get drunk. Not scheduled to work on the Saturday, I agreed, and we went over to The White Horse.

It was hot and humid in the pub; going through the doors was like getting off a plane in a warmer country. There was live music – a band at the back of the room played covers of popular songs. They were rock versions of the originals and when we walked in they were halfway through 'Somebody That I Used To Know'. The band were actually quite good. If they were on *The X Factor*, they'd have been told they made the songs their own.

It was loud and I had to shout to be heard. "Do you want a drink?"

Marcus raised his eyebrows as if to say, "Of course."

It was packed in there. Around the bar, people at least three deep were waiting to be served. I managed to take advantage of a gap that opened in the wake of a large man who'd just got his drinks, but it was two more songs before I was served. I ordered us a couple of bottles each so we wouldn't have to go back so soon.

With no tables free, we had to stand. I leaned my shoulder against a pillar and surveyed the room. There were lots of girls – some with boyfriends, but a few groups were without men. The interior of the pub was decorated in dark red, and the wooden bar adorned with horseshoes and white horse figurines. On the walls were old black and white photographs of the pub, church, and local area. There was a picture of the antiques shop; it had once been an undertaker's.

Holding both of my bottles with my right hand, I tried to drink from one of them. Forgetting entirely the laws of physics and that both bottle tops had been removed by the barman, some of the beer from the spare drink flowed out over my nose and eyes. I wiped my face, hoping nobody had seen.

I saw her sitting at a table not far from us – the girl-with-the-arse – and she looked at me as I looked at her. She was with a friend who had dyed, paprika-red hair with a strip of dark roots along her parting. I casually faced back towards the band, but out of the corner of my eye could see I was being pointed out, and that the red-haired girl had turned in my direction.

"Do you want to go?" I said to Marcus.

"Go? We haven't been here long."

"Yeah, I know. I'm not sure I want to be out though."

"Just drink more!" he said.

So I drank more, and tried to ignore them. But I could feel their eyes on me and sense their whispering.

The band announced they were playing 'Billie Jean', which drew big applause from the crowd. But when it started it was almost unrecognisable after its makeover.

Someone brushed past my left arm: it was the girl-with-the-arse headed to the bar. I watched her as she passed and I wasn't the only one – every man in the vicinity had a look. She had on a pink miniskirt and a tight, black shirt. Her hair was in the high ponytail she always wore.

"Damn," Marcus said. "Check her out."

"Yeah, I've seen."

"Want another drink?" he asked, going without waiting for a reply.

He moved into the space next to the girl, and I saw him give a nod and a smile before bending to talk to her.

She laughed and went on her tip-toes. Cupping her hand around the side of her mouth, she spoke into his ear.

He was laughing.

What are you doing, Marcus?

I glanced over at her friend, perhaps in the hope of finding an ally who would stop them, but she was engrossed in her phone.

The band were finishing their final song as Marcus returned from the bar and handed me a bottle. I lodged it under my arm and clapped. Marcus put his fingers in his mouth and whistled loudly.

The girl-with-the-arse was with him. She smiled and said to me, "Try not to spill that one."

"You saw that?" My face reddened.

She gestured for her friend to come over, which she did, and it occurred to me then that, from where they'd been sitting, her route to the bar hadn't been direct. Had she detoured and brushed past me deliberately?

It was easier to talk without the music, but I leaned close to the girl-with-the-arse to keep what I said private.

"I don't know if you remember me … ?"

"I remember you." She placed her left hand on her hip and took a sip from the glass she held in the other.

I laughed nervously. "OK. I'm not sure if that's a good thing."

"You looked homeless then. You look better now."

"Oh, you didn't think I was actually homeless did you?!"

She laughed, "No, I didn't think you *actually* were."

You're sounding like an idiot, Lyle.

"I was just really drunk," I said. "You definitely got the wrong impression of me."

"Did I? You didn't want to fuck me, then?"

The boldness of her question nearly made me choke on my drink; it was such a change from the way she'd been before. I didn't know what I should say, but she was the one who brought it up so I figured I'd go with it.

"Yeah, of course I wanted to," I said, "but I probably

shouldn't have said it."

She smiled confidently and took another sip of drink.

Marcus was chatting to the red-haired girl; we seemed to have naturally paired up – me and her, him and her friend.

"I'm Lyle by the way."

"Carla," said the girl-with-the-arse.

"I'm Marcus."

"Danielle," said her friend.

A bell rang, and last orders called.

Marcus said, "We only live across the road. Do you both want to come over? Have a smoke?"

31

I tried to follow behind Carla on the stairs, but Danielle got in-between; she wasn't as good to look at from the back (or the front). Marcus reached the door first, unlocked it, and we all went inside.

Marcus sat on the sofa. Danielle chose the armchair, so Carla took the space next to Marcus. He threw me one of Holly's cushions so I'd be more comfortable on the floor, and with the tobacco and papers from the table, he began making a joint.

"Wow, this place is *old*," Carla said, scanning the room.

"Lyle likes it." Marcus smirked as he tore a roach from the Rizla packet.

"It's alright. I might redecorate soon, though."

"Good," she said, "this wallpaper's shit."

"It's kitsch," I defended.

"It's what?"

"Never mind."

Noticing the postcards on the wall, Carla pointed to one of them. "What's that? And why's it got an eye on it?"

"It's a metronome."

She looked none the wiser.

"It's by Man Ray," I said. He used to set a metronome ticking when he painted and had attached a photo of an eye to the swinging arm because 'a painter needs an audience'.

"Man Ray? Wasn't he in *Spongebob*?"

Marcus ran his tongue along the edge of the paper. He said, "Where do you both live?"

"Just up the road." Carla again. Danielle wasn't adding

anything to the conversation.

"On your own?"

"No – still at my mum's. But I'd love my own place."

"Yeah," he said. "It's good to have the freedom."

I didn't know if he saw himself as living there or if it was just pretence for the girls.

He lit the joint and passed it to Carla. Danielle was next. She looked dubious, but inhaled like a pro. It was my turn, then back to Marcus, and the joint went once more round the circle before I discarded the end in an empty beer can.

I was thirsty. "Anyone want a drink? Water, I mean … or tea – there's no alcohol. And I could do some toast?"

The consensus was water and toast.

I stood up. Marcus did too. "Don't worry, man, I've got it." I thought he was offering so I'd get some time with Carla. I thought he was doing me a favour. I took his place on the sofa.

He came straight back with the drinks, then went to do the toast.

"So …" I said to Carla. I hoped more words would form on their own, but before they had the chance, she asked, "Where's the loo?"

"Uh, across the hallway on the right."

She left, and I was alone in the room with Danielle.

"So …" I said again, making an effort with her. "What do you do? … Where do you work?"

"B&Q." She was staring straight ahead at the far wall, her eyes glazed.

"The one in the retail park? I've been there." We had common ground. "Which bit?"

"Paint. Mixing paint."

"Great, I'll come and see you when I redecorate then."

She nodded carefully.

"Uh, I don't know what colours to do yet, though."

"We-match-any-colour." She spoke as if she was in a rush to

get the words out.

"Yeah, I thought you could do that."

The End – there was nowhere else I could be bothered to go with the subject.

Danielle started breathing deeply.

"Are you OK?" I said. "Do you need your water?"

"Yeah."

I passed it to her.

"Do you want the TV on?"

"Yeah."

With the remote, I switched it on. It was a music channel – dance music that I didn't like – but it was probably as good as anything.

"This OK?"

"Yeah."

I didn't talk more because I knew she wasn't going to be capable of conversation; it was best that she just wait for the effects of the weed to pass.

Carla was taking a long time in the bathroom – I hoped she wasn't on a whitey too – and Marcus still hadn't come in with the toast. I went to see if he needed a hand.

The kitchen door was closed. I opened it, completely unprepared for what I saw.

Marcus was fucking Carla from behind.

I saw them side-on. His jeans, and her underwear, were by their ankles. Her skirt was up around her slim middle like a belt, exposing her hips and thighs and arse. As Marcus pounded against her, I was momentarily mesmerised by the quivering flesh of those parts.

She was bent over the worktop and had her shirt and bra pushed up, her tits splayed amongst the toast crumbs. From the way they were standing, and the proximity of the tub of butter, they may have been doing it *Last Tango in Paris* style.

Marcus's eyes widened as he saw me.

"Hi," he said, jovially.

Carla turned her head to see who he was talking to, and maintained eye contact with me as she was moved forwards and backwards (Marcus hadn't been put off his rhythm). It may have been an inadvertent twitch of her eye, but it looked like she winked.

"Shut the door on your way out, man," Marcus said. "Go and play with Danielle."

Backing out, I closed it, and stood there for a moment facing the white gloss paintwork; thick brush strokes were visible in the finish.

When I returned to the living room, Danielle must've been feeling better because she managed to move her head and ask, "Is he done yet?"

"What?!"

"Has he made the toast?"

"Oh ... nearly."

Minutes passed before Marcus and Carla came back in with the toast, acting like nothing had happened. Everyone picked up a piece, but I didn't want any.

We watched TV with the girls commenting on the music videos – they were some of their favourite songs. I wanted to talk to Marcus, but with no way to do it subtly, I just asked him to come to the kitchen with me. I closed all the doors behind us so we could talk without being heard.

"How the hell did that happen?" I said.

He shrugged and grinned, "I dunno, it just sorta did."

"But I ... she ..." What was I going to say – that she was mine?

He said, "Ask them if they wanna stay over."

"What? So you can fuck her again. No!"

"Why not? You can get with her mate."

"No thanks, I don't fancy her."

"So what? Just take one for the team."

"'Take one for the team'?!" I mocked. "Why are you talking like a cunt?"

"You know what I mean. You don't have to do anything – she can sleep on the sofa. Actually, that's better ... can I borrow your bed?"

"No, you can't borrow my bed!"

Doors opened and the girls appeared. Carla said with a hint of regret, "We'd better go. Danielle needs to get back."

Danielle was peering over at the place the other two had had sex – she'd obviously been briefed in our absence.

Marcus said, "Why don't you both stay?"

I glared at him, and Carla looked hopeful, but Danielle wanted to go.

"We'll walk you home," Marcus said.

We paired up again as we walked: me and Danielle in front, and Marcus and Carla behind.

We didn't have anything to say to each other and I was glad when we reached Danielle's place first and said goodbye.

The three of us remaining doubled back and headed up Market Street – the same route that I'd followed behind Carla the time before.

Halfway up the street Marcus said, "Lyle, why don't you go back and I'll see you in a bit?"

I agreed. I wasn't needed.

"Don't wait up," he called.

I waited up; he got in an hour or so later.

"What the hell are you doing?" I began. "What about Nina?" But I didn't care about Nina.

"What about her? She threw me out."

"Yeah, but don't you think you need to try and work it out with her? She's having your baby for fuck's sake!"

"I know that!"

"You've got to think about what she's going through – women get a bit crazy with hormones when they're pregnant don't they?" I was fighting Nina's corner because I wanted Marcus to get back with her. He'd pissed me off and I wanted him to leave. "To be honest, I don't think she's been *that* unreasonable not wanting you going out late. She's probably feeling scared – having a baby is a big deal you know."

"You don't have to tell *me* that," he said. "I'm shitting it."

"I know. I can see that," I feigned sympathy. "But it'll be worse for Nina. She's the one carrying it. She's going to give birth to it."

"Her," Marcus corrected.

"Her?"

"Yeah, it's a girl."

"You haven't mentioned that before."

"Haven't I?"

"No."

He rubbed his hand over his forehead. "It's all happening so fast – everything's gonna change."

"Well, yeah. You can't just carry on like you have. You've got other people to think about – Nina and your daughter."

Marcus looked shocked. "Fuck, man – daughter! I've never called her that."

Poking him with the stick of his impending fatherhood, I continued, "Yeah, she's your *daughter*. Do you really want her to grow up without you? Do you want to miss out?"

"No," he said. "I don't."

An apology was all that was needed for Nina to have him back – an admittance that he'd been wrong. They had a long talk on the phone on Saturday morning and he packed his stuff soon after.

"Thanks for letting me stay," he said before he went. "Although, I did pay half the deposit, so it's still kinda my place anyway." Picking up his rucksack, he swung it onto one shoulder. "You know, you should give Holly a call … I bumped into her a while ago and she asked after you."

"What?" I was thrown that he'd mentioned Holly. "When did you see her? Where?"

"A few months ago. Camden Market."

It was before she'd come into the shop.

"What did she say?"

"Not a lot, but she asked what you were doing."

"And what did *you* say?"

"That you were living over here."

"You told her where I lived?"

"Yeah."

I needed to clarify the details. "You mean you told her where the flat was? What did you say *exactly* … more or less."

"I said you lived above the antiques shop. What's wrong with that? I thought you still kinda liked her. Seriously, you should give her a call – she seemed really interested."

Holly had known where I lived. When she came into the shop she wasn't surprised to see me there. It hadn't been coincidence at all.

32

When I see coincidence, I look for meaning and often find it. It makes me wonder whether it's coincidence at all or something else – like a plan – and they're signs to the right track, private jokes from the Universe that I'm meant to get. Although I don't consciously believe in fate or providence, and know it's more likely a combination of cause and effect and random chance, part of me thinks that everything happens for a reason, and people get what they need, if not what they deserve.

I liked that it had been coincidence, that the Universe had put me and Holly in the same place at the same time. So did I feel duped, or was I pleased she'd made the effort to find me?

Wanting to ask her about it, I messaged: Hi, how are you? X

I waited for a reply.

The next day, as I sat in the living room with the TV off, I tried to phone her. It wasn't answered, and I didn't leave a message – she'd see the missed call was from me.

I waited.

Maybe Holly had changed her number and hadn't realised I'd got in touch? No, I remembered the answer message was a recording of her voice. She knew.

I sent another text: Please call me. X

Come on Holly, ring.

Staring at the wallpaper, I focused on one of the drawings I'd made – the man in the boat on the river. Something was different, so I went over to see. There was a second figure in the boat – a girl with long, straight hair – and the two people were holding hands; it was me and Holly, and she must've drawn it and left it for me to discover – she knew I'd like that. I was sure then that we'd be able to work things out. She'd get in touch and we'd talk it over and … … the train of thought derailed as I noticed what she'd added to the background of the scene: pyramids.

The arguments, the accusations of 'deNile', the reasons why she'd left and why I'd wanted her to leave all came back.

It didn't matter that she'd come to find me – we didn't work. Did we even have anything in common? I remembered she didn't like Bond. I shouldn't have tried to contact her, and it was obvious she wasn't going to answer me anyway. But even if she rang or texted back, I'd ignore her.

Leaving my phone on the sofa, I went down to the church. A hearse was parked outside the gates, a coffin manoeuvred from it by a group of solemn men dressed in black. Not wanting to intrude on their mourning or be witness to it, I changed direction towards the entrance to the park.

Once in the park, I skirted the outside of the churchyard wall looking for a place to climb over. Using a stone that bulged out from the wall as a foothold, I hauled myself up and noticed a solitary fragment of china set into the mortar near the top – a red rose on a white background.

Sitting on the tomb under the oak tree, I wondered who'd put the fragment there and why. Had they just found it on the ground, or had there been some forethought to placing it? It reminded me of the tattoo Candy had had on her shoulder. It seemed such a lazy cliché – a standard image. If people are going to graffiti their bodies, it should be with something beautiful, individual and meaningful.

It had been a pointless experience with Candy – a waste of time and a waste of money. The whole reason for visiting prostitutes was to do it with Holly, because I didn't see myself as someone who needed to pay for sex.

But having gone, I could've made more of the opportunity. There was no one else's needs to be taken into consideration, so I should've made it an experience for *me* and specified exactly what I wanted – like all those men who'd messaged Holly with their requests.

I knew what *I'd* ask for.

Perhaps I could book just one more …

Spending the evening on the laptop, I picked an escort – 'charliebabes' – based more on her proximity to me than anything else. Thinking it would be better to negotiate terms before the booking was made, I wrote out a message: Hi Charlie, I see from your profile that you do role-play. Would it be OK if you pretended you weren't into it, and I pretended to force you?

I re-read it several times. Writing 'pretended' twice was good – that made it clear – but did it all sound a bit *wrong* though? It was one thing having a fantasy, but writing it out was strange. I'd tried to word it carefully so I didn't come across like some kind of dodgy pervert, but it occurred to me that maybe I was.

Perhaps it was a bad idea … but lots of people did stuff like this – someone wanted Holly to pretend to be unconscious. And the point was: if I didn't ask, I wasn't going to get. I pressed 'send'.

Charlie didn't keep me waiting long for her simple reply: all good wiv me hun x

I was relieved she thought my request was OK, that *I* was OK. I composed another message: That's great. I want to make it clear that I don't want to hurt you in any way. I'm not going to be rough – just hold you down and that kind of thing.

Remembering something else, I tagged it onto the end: Also, can you make sure you have a shower before I arrive? (Sorry for asking, but I booked someone recently who wasn't very clean.) X

Her reply: no probs babe all good x

An appointment was made for the following evening at nine

o'clock. She messaged the address (on the other side of the city but within walking distance) and included her phone number so it would be easier for me to make contact.

I texted: Hi, it's Tom. (I still used that name.) This is my number. See you tomorrow at 9. Looking forward to it. X

She sent one straight back: c u 2moro x

Her text-speak, incorrect spelling, and complete lack of punctuation *did* bother me, but I reminded myself that I didn't need her to have those things.

The next day in the shop passed slowly and I was preoccupied with thoughts about how the evening would go. Would we talk about it first or just get straight into the role-play? I visualised different scenarios over and over, but they all began with me stripping her of her clothes. I had to put up the 'Back in 5 Minutes' sign to go into the back room.

After work, I had a bath and got ready in plenty of time before setting off. By half eight, I was already on her street.

The address was a modern three-storey block of flats, flanked by identical three-storey blocks of flats. Not wanting to be seen there so early, I passed the building without slowing or changing my pace, surreptitiously glancing at it without turning my head. Finding a kids' play park close by, I lurked on the roundabout in the dusk, impatiently keeping an eye on the time.

At five to, I was about to head off when I received a text: make it 9.15 soz busy 2nite x

If she was with another customer, she'd better have that shower.

But at ten past Charlie messaged again: where r u mate gotta go soon x

'Gotta go soon'? No, you'll stay for my half hour.

I made my way to the front of her building.

Me: I'm outside. X

Her: cum up x

She was on the first floor, wearing a black dress that I knew I'd soon be unzipping and taking off.

I'm going to fuck you so hard.

Following her through the door of a flat, she led me down a short corridor, past closed doors, and into a bedroom. I sat on the bed then shifted my body to remove the fee from my back pocket. Handing it to her, I realised I liked that aspect of it – the act of paying – and knowing the drill and not being asked. She counted the notes – eighty pounds – and made a fist around them.

"Back in a minute." She left the room and pulled the door to.

I heard her walk down the corridor. A door opened, then it closed. And then I heard nothing.

As I waited, I took in my surroundings. On the top of a chest of drawers was a trifold mirror, its reflections a triptych of the room – the wardrobe, me on the bed, and a blue teddy bear on a chair in the corner. It could be the ideal place to prop my phone to film us.

We hadn't discussed filming and I couldn't remember if it was on the list of things she'd do. Before it had been more for Holly's benefit, but I'd enjoyed watching it too, so I decided to ask Charlie about it when she got back.

She was taking a long time to return to the room: too long. I stood up, opened the door and stepped into the corridor.

"Hello?" I called.

No response.

"Hello?" I repeated louder.

I went back to the bed and texted: Where are you? X

Her immediate reply: gone mate lol x

33

She'd ripped me off, taken my money. I hadn't seen it coming yet somehow I wasn't surprised.

Me: So, what happens now? X

I think I added the 'X' to the end of my text to keep the situation light.

Charlie: im gone mate x

Me: Shame - I'm really horny. Why don't you come back? X

Still keeping it light.

Her: soz hun im gone x

Yeah, I get you've gone.

She sent another one: that aint even my flat lol x

I'm sure it was expected I'd leave at that point. I'd cut my losses and go, not reporting the theft to avoid embarrassing questions. That was probably what Charlie was counting on, and I imagined she'd done this to others.

My initial reaction *was* to get out, but it was swiftly overridden by wanting my money back. I assessed the situation to see how that could happen.

Firstly, whose flat was I in? Did Charlie expect me to believe she'd broken into somewhere just to steal from me? It was unlikely. It probably *was* her flat, but if not hers, then someone she knew – friend or family. And *I* hadn't broken in, nor was I doing anything illegal by hiring an escort. I had no wife or girlfriend to hide it from, so if the police became involved I didn't care.

What I needed to find out was whether I was alone in the flat. Out of the bedroom I cautiously opened the door opposite and discovered the kitchen. A knife block stood on the worktop. Thinking it was a good idea to arm myself, I took one out and slid it into my back pocket.

Looking out of the kitchen window onto an unlit area at the back of the building, I noted it as a possible escape route out of there. I took a moment to be impressed with how calmly I was handling the situation, and how acutely aware I was of everything that could happen; even though I'd made a plan of action, I was ready for surprises and modifications if required. Despite what the theme tune to *The Spy Who Loved Me* said, I doubted James Bond himself would do it better.

Stealthily moving through the flat, I found the bathroom, a second bedroom with boxes and piles of clothes on the bed, and finally the living room with a huge, flat screen TV dominating. No one else was there. At the front door, I attached the chain to make it difficult for anyone to get in.

Back in the living room, I noticed Charlie was in the framed photos hanging on the wall. In some she was standing next to a big man with no hair or neck

So, this IS your flat then? You're unbelievably stupid!

The window in that room was on the front of the building, and I carefully moved the curtain to peek outside. She, or *they*, were likely to be out there, keeping close watch, waiting to see me leave through the front door. Rows of cars were parked on both sides of the street, but I couldn't tell if anyone was in them.

I sent a text to her: I think you should come back and give me my money. X

Opening drawers, I saw stationery, bank statements, benefits notices, a torch, a hammer and other things.

Her: lol that aint happnin mate x

I knew it wasn't, so continued with my plan. I moved quickly back to the bedroom and opened more drawers: underwear, half a dozen sex toys, make-up, and jewellery (cheap crap). But no cash and nothing valuable. The only thing I'd seen that was worth anything was the TV – but there was no way I'd get it out of there.

Me: I'm just going to wait here until you do. X

I opened the wardrobe: women's clothes, shoes, handbags – nothing I wanted. A black rucksack was on a shelf at eye level. I took it down.

Fuck her then, if there was nothing of value to me, I'd take things of value to her just to piss her off! I began stuffing some of her clothes into the bag. The underwear, the sex toys, jewellery and make-up all went in. I grabbed the blue bear from the chair.

Her: my pimp is massiv stay there and ull c him soon x

In the living room I took paperwork that looked important, some DVDs, a phone charger, and all the remote controls. I took her photos from the wall.

I thought about smashing the TV with the hammer, but decided it would be too noisy. Finding a black marker pen, I wrote in big letters on the screen:

KARMA

I bet you won't even know what that means, dumb bitch.

By the time I'd returned to the kitchen, the rucksack was nearly full. I opened the cupboards, put in a jar of Nutella, and all the packets and tins that would fit. I didn't take anything from the fridge, but I poured her milk over the floor.

Me: OK, I'll be here waiting for him. You've left enough knives and hammers around to give me a fair chance.

No kiss at the end this time. I wanted them to see the game had changed and I had the upper hand.

Her: fuk u talkin bout knives u wanna c a gun!!!!!!

I was shocked – shocked she'd used a 'k' in the word

'knives'. And there was punctuation: exclamation marks – six of them. But she'd mentioned a gun, so it was probably time I got out of there.

Even one floor up, it was still high. After throwing the bag out of the kitchen window, I climbed out (wondering what the hell I was doing). I somehow managed to lower myself off the windowsill to hang from my fingertips, then dropped the six or seven feet onto a grassy bank. Taking cover by bushes, I made sure I hadn't been seen, then grabbed the bag and ran.

When I reached a road, I realised it was best I didn't look suspicious, so began walking normally. As I kept away from the main roads and well-lit areas, I sent messages to make them think I was still there: Like I said, come back with my money and this can all be over.

Her: my pimps gunna fuk u up lol u silly cunt

Me: You're the one who's been silly. You don't know who you're dealing with.

I enjoyed the journey back to my flat and kept smiling at the thought of them too scared to go home. And then, when they had the balls to, they'd either have to kick the door in, or get a ladder to go through the window.

As I passed the glued coin on the pavement, I remembered the hammer I'd put in the bag. It only took one well-placed hit to free it, and it skimmed across the road like an ice-hockey puck. Retrieving it, I put it in my pocket.

About an hour later, Charlie and her 'pimp' must've managed to get in; I received a barrage of messages: wtf cum bak wiv my stuff!!!!

Then: u fuked my tv ur gunna get fuked!!!

Then: giv me my shit bak or we gunna play a game!!!

I'd written, 'You don't know who you're dealing with', but after the adrenaline had dissipated, I worried I didn't know who *I* was dealing with. I knew they were stupid, and stupidity can be dangerous. The threat of guns was probably just talk; they were likely just small-time scammers. But they could've been wannabe gangsters.

I wasn't interested in playing their game; I'd been playing my own and had got caught up in it. It had been fun, but I'd been lucky. What if they *had* been in another room, or had come in while I was still there? Would I have used the knife? What the fuck was I doing carrying a knife?!

I responded: You shouldn't have taken my money and left me alone in your flat. I could've done a lot worse.

Her: ur sick and ill tell cops u raped me so ur gunna get nicked!!!!

Me: Yeah, good luck proving that. I didn't even touch you!

Her: The emails u sent is proof

Me: How do you figure that? They just show what we agreed to do. If you want to talk about proof, these texts you're sending pretty much prove I didn't.

Her: u wot

I wished I'd never booked her; this wasn't how I'd wanted or expected the evening to go. It was time to end it.

Me: Your stuff is safe and I just want my money. I'll give it back, but I'm not doing anything tonight. I'll sort it tomorrow. X

Her: u betta or this is gunna be anuva leval

Not long after, she sent another text: u took my dildos! Cant sleep wivout my dildos ;(lol x

That *did* make me 'lol'.

34

A man was sitting on my chest. The weight of him was making it difficult to get a breath, and I couldn't move. I tried to lift my arms but it didn't feel like I had arms to lift. I tried to tell him to get off but couldn't find my voice. Barely able to breathe, I panicked. I thought I was going to die.

Why was he doing this? Was it a joke or was he actually trying to hurt me? Summoning all my energy I attempted to shift him, and suddenly, as if my body had been switched back on, I was able to move. I pushed him away.

In a cold sweat and breathing rapidly, I sat upright. Casting my eyes around the semi-darkness of the room I expected to see him on the floor, but there was no one. For a few seconds I couldn't be sure if it had been real or not, but it must have been a kind of sleep paralysis that had translated itself into a dream, into a nightmare. I'd never experienced anything like it before. Calming myself, I tentatively lay down.

I turned onto my side and tried to get back to sleep. I became aware of my ear and was sure I'd never noticed it as much before. How did I normally sleep on it – folded over, or flat to my head? Either way it felt strange – hot and alien, like it wasn't part of me. I rolled onto my back. But I can never fall asleep on my back.

I got out of bed and went to the window. Opening the curtains, I saw it was still dark outside. It was raining, and the street lights blurred through the droplets on the glass. Some drops had formed most of the constellation of Orion, and I watched Betelgeuse supernova into a rivulet and collide with the middle star of Orion's belt. I closed the curtains and went back to the bed. The ear was mine again, and I drifted off to sleep.

I dreamt I was running a race through a forest along a narrow, tarmac path. Usually if I try to run in a dream I don't make much headway, but this time I easily caught and passed the other competitors and knew I could win.

We stopped at a row of fridges to stack yoghurt pots that had pictures of anthropomorphic raspberries riding on camels. But the bottoms of the pots were rounded and most of them fell out and spilled over the floor. Abandoning the task, we continued the race.

The path split into two, long, brightly-lit corridors, and I was unsure of which route to take. A small group ran past me down the corridor on the right, so I followed them, and we soon came to an escalator going up. Travelling to the top, we found ourselves in a clothes shop dressing room with curtained-off cubicles along two of the walls. With no obvious way onwards, I investigated behind the curtains and discovered a winding, wooden staircase leading to a closed trapdoor. I could hear a swishing noise and somehow knew there'd be a blade swinging over the opening to cut off my head. I backed down the stairs.

At the escalator, I attempted to descend, but the faster I tried, the more it sped up until it had delivered me back into the dressing room. The other runners were no longer there – they'd all gone through the trapdoor – and I could hear screams and heavy bangs through the ceiling. I sprinted up the staircase to help them. The hatch was open, but there was only darkness and silence …

I was woken by a text: wots goin on need my stuff 2day!!! need my underwear and remotes

Me: I can't do anything about it until later – I'm at work.

I wasn't, but telling her that would buy me a bit of time.

Her: I want my bear!!!

She was sounding like a child.

Me: Just have my money ready and I'll be in touch.

Having had enough of crazy dreams, I got up and went to the kitchen for something to eat.

There wasn't much food in the flat, so I picked up a lone satsuma and peeled it. Not thinking clearly, I threw it away and took the peel with me into the living room. Sitting on the sofa, I swore at the contents of my hand and headed back to the kitchen to retrieve the fruit from the bin.

The rucksack was on the floor in the hallway where I'd left it. Remembering something I'd put in there, I dug out the Nutella and fetched a spoon.

Taking a long bath, I ate the Nutella from the jar. I stared at my feet placed either side of the overflow; sticking halfway out of the water and mirrored in the reflection, they looked like Cornish pasties – my toes forming the crimped edges. I thought about the bathtub painting by Frida Kahlo that was in the book Holly had bought me: images from Kahlo's life, floating on the surface of the water above her submerged legs.

In the afternoon I sent a message: Hi Mikaela. (That was the name on her paperwork – her real name – and I used it to show I knew who she was.) This is what's going to happen: I'll drop your bag off somewhere then text you the location. You'll pick it up, put the money in the same place, and leave. X

Her: wot time x

Me: Later today. X

So that was the plan. But it wasn't the plan. Long before this point I'd given up on my money. While I was in the bath, I'd gone through every possible scenario to see if I could get it back without exposing myself to danger. If they paid it into my bank or sent it through the post, they'd know my name and where I lived, and if they left it somewhere, they could be waiting when I picked it up.

So why give the stuff back at all? Although I didn't think I could be traced through the escort website, and probably wouldn't be recognised if she saw me again, I didn't want to risk it, or have the fear of comeback hanging over me. The only way to conclude this was for both parties to win. Or if not win, be somehow satisfied.

But how would *I* feel satisfied?

The contents of the rucksack were on the living room floor. Beginning with her clothes (which I folded carefully), I began placing it back in the bag. But I wasn't going to give it *all* back – just the personal items, and the things she'd specifically mentioned; I was keeping the food, the knife, the DVDs, a couple of bits of underwear, a photo, and a few other things. Before I put the remote controls in, I took down my jeans and pants, lifted my balls, and from front to back, wiped my arse with them. I did the same with the teddy bear.

The perfect place to leave the bag was in the play park near her flat. Wearing a hat to disguise myself, I went after dark, careful not to be seen.

Safely back at my flat, I sent a message: Hi Mikaela. Your bag is in the park at the end of your road – in the bushes behind the roundabout. Leave the money there and don't contact me again.

She didn't ever contact me. I don't know if they found the bag or left the money, if they went with back-up and waited.

I don't know if she noticed the spare keys to her flat had gone from the drawer in the kitchen, and whether she realised it was me that had taken them. I don't know if she was frightened I'd come back, and had to change the locks. Perhaps she had to move.

35

Someone famous came into the shop. I didn't know his name but recognised his face; he'd been in a sitcom I hadn't watched. He wasn't *that* famous, but even so, there was a noticeable buzz amongst the other customers who whispered and watched as he bought a set of copper pans.

The second he left the shop, a middle-aged woman excitedly came up to the desk. "Do you know who that was?"

"Yeah."

Obviously disappointed not to be able to tell me, she said, "You were so calm when you served him though."

"I suppose."

"What was he like?"

"Uh, he seemed nice … he said 'thank you'."

The woman nodded in approval of my answer. She bought something – a glass inkpot for four pounds. I got the impression she was only buying it because it connected her to him; she was someone who'd been served by someone who'd just served a famous person. I was sure she'd be telling the story to whoever would listen.

It was a strange morning and not long afterwards, a man went past with his son of around two or three sitting on top of his shoulders. The florist's next door had an awning overhanging their shop window, and the man didn't take his increased height into account. I could see it was going to happen before it did, but there was nothing I could do to stop it: the boy's head smacked into the metal bar at the side of the awning.

I'd already made it over to the door by the time the dad had set his son down on the pavement. Blood was streaming down the boy's face from his forehead near his hairline. He was screaming and screaming. The man was saying, "I'm sorry, I'm sorry."

Rushing them inside, we went straight to the back room. Using a damp paper towel to stem the blood, I reassured them the wound wasn't as bad is it seemed. I was just saying that to calm them down, but when I took the towel away to have another look, it turned out I was telling the truth, and we agreed it probably wouldn't need stitches. The man took over and cleaned the boy's face, and the boy finally stopped crying.

After they'd gone, I had to clear up spots of blood that had dripped onto the floor. I'd just finished when Keith came in, and I filled him in on all that had been happening.

"Busy day!" He glanced at a table near to the desk. "And you've sold the flask too."

There was a space where an ornate, brass powder flask had been. "Uh ... no."

It had been stolen.

Thinking back, I remembered a man with long, greasy hair was in while I was helping with the injured kid. He was the likely culprit.

"Will you report it?" I asked.

"No point – a waste of everyone's time."

"I'm so sorry, Keith." I was gutted it had happened on my watch.

"Not your fault. But I hope that was all he nicked."

We both did a quick scan to see if anything else was missing: nothing obvious.

Keith said, "I see someone's bought your pineapple. That's good."

"No, I'm just making people think that so they'll want it." I hadn't made any sales of my items in a couple of weeks, so I was trying out the 'SOLD' sticker thing on the ice bucket. "I don't know why no one's bought it yet though – I quite like it."

"Well, *I* think it's hideous," he said. "But everyone has different tastes."

"Do you reckon there's anything in the shop that's *so* hideous, no one will ever buy it?"

"Apart from your pineapple?" he joked. "No. Some of it stays around for a while, but it all goes eventually. I remember I had a stuffed rat in a glass case once. It was badly done – who would bother to stuff a rat anyway? – and dressed in a pinafore and straw bonnet. I thought I'd get stuck with that, but the woman who bought it was thrilled."

"Yeah," I said. "There's something for everyone."

Keith spent some time in his workshop before he left again. I went on the laptop to browse escorts; I was determined not to let one bad experience stop me.

Got to get back on the whores.

'Roxy XXX' was Romanian, nineteen, and a 36DD. She loved 'sucking cock', would 'give a GFE or PSE', and was 'eager to please and fulfil your every fantasy'. In her profile picture, her face was pretty and her tits, amazing. I paid to see her private gallery, then paid to see a video of her giving a blow job (although I had to turn it off before the money shot because Mrs Valensis came in).

She seemed perfect, definitely the one I should choose. I messaged to see if she could do that evening, and this time I'd book an incall at my flat so I couldn't be ripped off again. I asked if she'd do role-play, but didn't specify; her profile led me to believe she'd be fine with anything.

Roxy *was* available that evening and could be there at nine o'clock. It would be a hundred pounds. But I didn't have a hundred pounds: I'd overspent while Marcus was staying, had lost money to Charlie/Mikaela, and had direct debits due out of my account.

I'd have to postpone for a week or two.

I didn't want to postpone …

A man who'd been in half an hour earlier had bought a piece of Japanese netsuke – a carved, wooden dragon – for a hundred pounds. He wasn't a regular customer, had paid cash, and hadn't asked for a receipt. I took the money out of the till and put it in my pocket. Destroying the top page of the notebook, I re-wrote the day's transactions with that one omission. If Keith noticed the dragon gone, he'd assume it had been stolen along with the flask.

Roxy was late; I found the anticipation of her arrival wasn't as exciting as going to someone's place. In fact it was irritating, and as I smoothed out the creases on my duvet, I doubted she'd turn up at all. But she arrived at twenty past, letting herself through the unlocked gate as I'd told her to. Hearing her coming up the stairs – heels on metal – I opened the door before she'd reached the top.

Roxy had brown, shoulder-length hair and was as good as her photos. She was dressed in a black, short skirt and a denim jacket. We went to my room, and she stood next to the bed and stared at me.

"Oh, money." I gave her the cash, and she deposited it in her black handbag.

She still stared; she hadn't spoken at all yet.

I said, "Uh … so, I need to tell you about the kind of role-play I'd like–"

She interrupted in halting English, "Excuse me. Where is … the bathroom?"

I showed her. She took her bag with her, and I saw her eyes dart towards the front door as we passed it.

Don't even think about running out on me.

I stood like a guard in the hallway between the front door and the bathroom. She was in there for a long time, but I knew there was no window for her to climb out of. I was thinking about knocking on the door, when she came out.

Back in my room, she put her bag on the floor, took off her jacket, and timidly began to undress.

Moving towards her, I said, "Let me do that."

But she backed away and said, "No."

It annoyed me – I'd paid my money, so I should get to do what I wanted – but I left her to it, and took off my own clothes. As I did, I tried to talk to her about how I wanted it all to go.

"So, about the role-play …"

"Huh?"

"Role-play? Uh … acting?"

She shook her head, but not because she didn't do it, it was because she didn't understand what I was saying. Was this going to be another waste of money?

Roxy was fully naked. Her tits were big and shapely, but my eyes were drawn to her belly which was saggy and covered in silvery-purple stretch marks like she'd recently been pregnant. Crouching down, she took a condom out of her bag, and tore the side off the foil square.

"Not yet," I said. "Can I get a bit of a blow job first?"

She looked at me quizzically.

I gestured to my dick and her mouth. She understood.

It wasn't very good – not what I'd expected after seeing her video. She wasn't doing it very deeply and kept coming off. I put my hand on the back of her head but she pushed it away. I went to touch her tits but she crossed her arm over them.

It wasn't worth continuing, so I got her to lie on the bed. I put the condom on, and as I went on top, she turned her head to the side and faced the wall. I tried to put my mouth to her nipples but she brought her arms up to cover herself again. She just lay there, looking away, hardly moving.

In a way, she was giving me the experience I would have asked for. But this was different – we hadn't discussed it. This wasn't role-play. She wasn't acting. She wasn't enjoying it, and neither was I.

I kept going, but it felt wrong. I wanted it over with, but didn't think I'd be able to come quickly – maybe not at all.

So I faked it.

"Thank you," I said.

She didn't say anything.

With my back to her, I took off the condom and wrapped it in a tissue so she wouldn't see it was empty. When I turned around, she'd pulled the duvet up over her body.

Gathering my clothes from the floor, I made it clear I intended to leave the room to give her some privacy. She smiled in gratitude.

Her phone rang while I was dressing in the hallway. She spoke Romanian (I assumed), and although I didn't know what she was saying, her tone was subdued.

The call ended. She came out of the room, and exited quickly through the front door. I followed her out but she was already halfway down the stairs. Standing at the top of the staircase, I watched her go through the gate and get into a silver BMW that was waiting for her. They drove away.

Back in my bedroom, I saw the disturbed sheets on the bed.

Taking my keys, I left the flat.

36

Ten o'clock at the tomb in the churchyard. Tilting my head back, the branches and leaves of the oak tree above me were dark silhouettes against the moonlit sky. The lowest bough was around three metres from the ground, sturdy and strong – a good place to hang a noose from. Not that I'd ever do that. No, jumping in front of a train probably *would* be my preferred option. And if I got to that point, I wouldn't care if people were inconvenienced, in fact I'd like them to be.

Roxy hadn't wanted me touching her, hadn't wanted me fucking her; even though she hadn't said as much, her body language shouted it. So, she was just doing it for the money – fair enough – but couldn't she have *pretended* to enjoy it, or at least not shown how much she hated it? I imagined it would be horrible to be with unattractive men from time to time, but there was nothing wrong with me. If she didn't like doing it with me, presumably she didn't like doing it with anyone. And if she didn't like doing it at all, she should find another vocation.

It hadn't been an issue with the others. Marina in Amsterdam seemed to have had fun – she'd even mentioned her boyfriend who was supportive of her work, and how *they* did things like that together. And what about Kristal, Sasha, and Candy? I was sure they'd all enjoyed it … or maybe they were just better at acting than Roxy.

Why couldn't you just pretend?

If she *had* pretended, I'd have been able to ignore the other things: the car, the phone call, and the fact she hardly spoke any English. She couldn't have written her profile by herself, so was the person in the car – the expensive BMW – helping her? And were they *helping* her do it, or *making* her do it? What had I paid for? What had I been party to?

The website was supposed to be a place where women independently advertised their services; I imagined bored housewives, students, and horny sluts doing it for the extra cash and/or excitement. But was the reality that some, or many, of the profiles were a front for pimping?

I didn't know anything about Roxy's situation, but suspected it wasn't good. The stretch marks – signs of a pregnancy – meant there must also be a baby somewhere. Had she been trafficked? If I reported my suspicions to the police, could they do anything? Would they care? She was here from a different country under circumstances I didn't know, so if I reported it, I might be making life worse for her. And would it create problems for me? I hadn't *forced* her to have sex, and she hadn't told me to stop, but it had still been against her will – technically – and I'd known that. I shouldn't have done it. What I should've done was give her the money and let her leave.

But it wasn't even *my* money – I'd stolen it. No, not stolen, just *borrowed* … hadn't I? Thinking about it, I honestly didn't know if the intention had been to give it back. But I *would* be giving it back – and as soon as possible. I'd drop the price on the pineapple and other things to make some quick sales.

Leaving the churchyard, I walked through the park, through the industrial estate, past houses and into the city centre. Bubble bath had been poured into the fountain, and the empty bottle was on the wall. The churning water created a thick layer of white foam that overflowed the fountain like the magic porridge pot. A few students were excitedly watching as the wind caught and blew lumps of foam around the square.

I headed away from the centre down roads I'd never been before, choosing any I came across with interesting names:

Blackberry Lane, Seven Sisters Street, Zig Zag Road, Butts Close. A narrow passageway called The Thrunge sounded like some kind of sexually-transmitted disease, and in Shiny Bricks Lane the bricks on the houses were matt and it wasn't even a lane.

I didn't know where I was, or where I was going. I passed a blue plaque on a house where a scientist I'd never heard of had lived, and a front garden decorated with dozens of owls instead of gnomes. I saw a house with a round tower and tall conical roof that could have been the sort of place Rapunzel was kept. I thought of Kristal with her long black hair. What was *her* story? She was with an agency, but did that make it more or less likely that it was all her own choice. She was also from a different country – Slovakia – another Eastern European. Did she need saving too? Was she a damsel in distress? Why was it that no one ever said 'damsel' unless they followed it with 'in distress'?

At the end of roads and houses, I came to a footpath and a stile. I climbed over and ascended a hill over rough ground and dewy grass. The only sounds were my uneven footsteps and my heavy breathing.

At the top of the hill, I turned around to face the direction I'd come. It wasn't very high so I didn't have a great view of the city, but I got a sense of its size from the spread of street lights, and it was vast.

It was dark around me; everything was black and grey and blue. I could just about make out the Milky Way above and it was like seeing an old friend. I looked at the sky until I began to get cold, then headed back down the hill.

In the field to my right, a plot of small trees were attached to wooden stakes to help them grow. Seeing them triggered a memory of Elspeth.

Being older, Elspeth was trusted to take me to school – she even took me in on my first day – and our route passed a field with similar trees. There was a sign on the gate which read

'Trespassers will be Prosecuted'. I knew what 'trespass' meant because we'd learned *The Lord's Prayer* at school, but I'd mixed up 'prosecuted' with 'executed', so to me, those stakes and trees were to mark the graves of the people who'd strayed in there. One day, to catch a grasshopper that had jumped away from her, Elspeth put her arms through the fence into the field. When I saw what she'd done, I became hysterical thinking she'd be killed. I was truly terrified I'd lose her until she calmed me enough to find out what was wrong, and explained what the sign really meant.

Attempting to get back a different way, I skirted the city before picking a road leading in. As I walked through a memorial garden for the locals who'd died in the World Wars, a short man came towards me wearing a T-shirt so tight I could see his nipples from quite far away.

People are always friendly in the early morning, when it's five or six and the sun is up. But in the dark, at three o'clock, people are suspicious. The short man glared at me as if questioning why I was out.

Well, what the fuck are YOU doing out at this time?

It made me angry that he'd looked at me, that I'd been seen. I almost wanted to turn around and follow him and get into a fight. I almost chose to be crazy … but if you feel you can choose, then you aren't really crazy.

I left him to his direction and continued on mine.

Dawn broke and I was back at the fountain; most of the foam had dispersed, but some remained in cloud-like clumps on the water. As I perched on the wall there, the pencil in my back pocket dug into me. I took it out.

My usual pencil had been sharpened too many times, so I carried a new one that I'd acquired from Charlie/Mikaela's; it had a light-blue, hexagonal casing, and a white rubber.

Nothing came to mind to write, so I just made marks on the stone beside me. It was the first time I'd used her pencil, and it wrote differently – more like charcoal. I checked its grade, written in silver lettering along the side: 2B. I didn't know what my old one had been, but assumed a standard HB.

I knew graphite was graded in 'H's and 'B's along with numbers. I thought H meant harder, but wasn't sure what the B stood for – why wasn't it 'S' for softer?:

2B OR NOT 2B? THAT IS THE QUESTION

No, 2B definitely wasn't as hard as the lead in *my* pencil. Smirking at the double entendre, and in homage to what I'd written at St Paul's the day we'd hired Kristal, I wrote:

MY BONER PENCIL LEAD

I thought it could be a metaphor for the vastly different things that men got off on; what would be high on the hardness scale for a foot fetishist – say a 5 or 6H – might not even register for someone who favoured BDSM.

Amongst other things, what seemed to do it for me was the *idea* of a girl not being into it. But I didn't want the *reality* of that – they were two very different things. Although I thought I knew that before, now I *knew* it ... but should I feel bad for entertaining the fantasy in the first place? Surely you can't help what turns you on?

Deciding I didn't like the line I'd written, I rubbed it out. But I *did* want to continue that Surrealist idea of writing seemingly unrelated things. My pencil was poised, but what could I write that meant something to me?

My foot a Cornish pasty? No, that's crap.

I was used to giving up when the words won't flow easily. At university my tutor praised me for having potential, but he also said he was disappointed by my lack of effort. He knew I could do it if I tried. But he knew I didn't try.

But this time I would. I wasn't going to leave until I'd come up with three good lines.

And they were:

MY VIEW A PYRAMID

MY SHAME A DRAGON

MY SALVATION A PINEAPPLE

Why was I doing this anyway – writing on walls? What *was* the point? And why was I waiting for inspiration for the 'big story'? I could be noting down snippets of conversation, descriptions, unusual details, and characters I saw all the time; the shop was a goldmine.

I resolved to make more of an effort to write – on paper and on my laptop. I had to work at it because it would never happen by itself.

But not just writing, more effort had to be made with everything. That week I'd robbed a flat, been threatened with guns by a pimp, had sex with a prostitute whose consent seemed dubious, and had stolen money from my employer – my *friend.*

This wasn't me. This wasn't the person I wanted to be.

Like Holly had said – I make bad choices. And it was time I made better ones.

PART 4

2B OR NOT 2B?

37

As I wrapped a set of cups and saucers using the local newspaper, a picture of Mr Stephenson caught my attention: it was alongside his obituary. I put the page to one side to read when the shop was quiet.

Victor Stephenson had been ninety. He'd recently celebrated his seventieth wedding anniversary with his wife, Kathleen, and their five children, fifteen grandchildren, and nine great-grandchildren. He'd taken part in the D-Day landings and had been awarded the George Cross – which I was pretty sure was a big deal. He'd worked most of his life in the railways and was a former councillor and mayor of the city. It had been his idea to install the fountain in the square. The article, which had been from three weeks ago, stated the funeral was to be held in Oldchurch. Thinking back, I realised it must have been him in the coffin the day I climbed over the wall.

You don't get much of a clue about the life a person's led just by looking at them. Mr Stephenson was a little old man, and it was hard to imagine him as anything other than that. But we all start off as young.

Before I got the chance to return the money to the till, Keith noticed the dragon gone. He asked me about it.

"Lyle, did you sell the netsuke?"

My insides jumped and I felt my face flush. "Uh, no?" I hadn't meant it to be a question.

"It's not there – I think it's been nicked as well."

"Really? Oh no." I tried to sound natural, but could hear the guilt in my voice.

I knew he'd heard it too, or had seen it in my face. But he misinterpreted.

"It's not your fault," he reassured. "It could've happened any time – when I was here, or Maggie. Don't blame yourself."

That I'd sold it and kept the money hadn't occurred to him – he trusted me – and by trying to make me feel better, he made me feel much worse than I did already.

How could I have stolen from this man who'd done nothing but help me? And if he'd found out, I'd have lost everything – my job, my home, our friendship, the faith he had in me. I'd been stupid to risk it all. But I was going to do my best to make it up to him. And I'd pay the money back somehow.

With my focus on the shop, I tried to make it look as good as possible. I cleaned the brass and dusted the furniture. I rearranged a few things and switched long-standing stock to the selling spots. I spent a few days listing items on eBay for Keith, getting good sales from that. If there was a quiet moment, instead of looking out of the window, I leafed through the reference books, learning about antiques – in particular mid 20th century glass and ceramics.

I started going to boot sales again and checked the local charity shops every couple of days. I found many things to buy, including a boxed *Guess Who* game. Going through the cards, I reacquainted myself with the characters: Susan who resembled 'Hot Lips' from *M*A*S*H*, and Alfred with his long hair and moustache like a '70s porn star (although I wouldn't have thought that when I was a kid). And there was Bill with his egg-shaped head, Paul, Sam, Philip and Charles.

How did I forget you all?

Each time I sold one of my items through the shop, I gave Keith his twenty percent. But I exaggerated the prices they went for so as to add extra money onto his cut. After a few weeks of this gradual payment, my debt – the monetary one at least – was settled.

Because I was doing well and my stock was turning over

quickly, Keith let me have a bigger space to use. I created a new display which was quite different from the rest of the shop and got a lot of attention. Keith referred to it as my 'Retro Corner' and the name started to catch on with the customers too. One afternoon, a man who'd seen my collection, brought in a box of things he wanted to sell. Keith was in his workshop so I fetched him.

After a brief rummage, he said, "This is more up *your* street, Lyle. Why don't you handle this."

So I went through the box containing Midwinter plates, an orange fibreglass lampshade, decorated shot glasses, and plastic egg cups. I offered twenty-five pounds for the lot, which was accepted, and as I made my first deal, Keith watched on like a proud father.

Later, he said, "It's good to see you buying and selling – you've got an instinct for it – but I know this isn't your ideal job."

"It's fine," I told him. "I enjoy working here." And I realised I meant it.

For the first time in a long time, I wasn't doing too badly for money. And then to top it off, I had two 'Lovejoy moments' which gave me a buzz better than gambling, perhaps even close to sex.

Firstly, at the boot sale, I found an ashtray in the shape of a whale on a table amongst DVDs, old paperbacks, make-up, and other crap. Made from wood and Bakelite, and marked 'YZ', it was slightly damaged – an eye was missing and part of the tail had broken off – but I liked it anyway and bought it. I'd seen something similar in a Miller's guide and, although I couldn't remember how much it was worth, knew it would be more than the two pounds they were asking at the stall. I didn't even haggle. It went straight on eBay and sold a week later for a hundred and thirty pounds.

Secondly, I happened to be in the Age UK charity shop just

as they were putting a glass vase out onto the shelf. I immediately claimed it. It was a heavy, faceted vase of red glass encased in clear – a technique I knew from the books as *sommerso.* Eight pounds was on the ticket, so eight pounds was what I paid. But as the lady volunteer wrapped it, commenting how pretty it was with its pink edging, I worried I was being deceitful.

From online research, I identified it as 1960s, by a well-known designer for a factory in Czechoslovakia (as it was back then). When it sold for two-hundred and twenty pounds, I donated a quarter of the money to Age UK.

38

Louisa had finally sorted out the things she wanted to sell, and invited me round to her place – a big house overlooking the park – on one of my days off. I only got to see part of the downstairs, but it was unlike any other old-lady house I'd ever been in.

Through the front door, an Art Deco hall stand was the first thing I saw. Next to it, a tall, large-leafed plant stood in a jade-green pot on a real parquet floor the colour of honey.

In the living room, art adorned much of the brightly-papered walls – canvases of abstract images and figures, framed landscapes and sketches. Just about everything was beautiful and stylish and colourful – the red leather sofa, the chrome and glass coffee table, and the mushroom-shaped lamps. It was like it had been carefully assembled from the pages of an interiors magazine … apart from the oxygen cylinder next to the armchair.

I was drawn to a collection of photographs displayed on a long, walnut sideboard. In one picture, a woman wearing a headscarf and oversized sunglasses stood in-between two men, her arms hooked inside theirs. She looked like a film star.

"Is this … you?" I ventured.

"Yes, that's me."

Although she'd changed so much, enough of Louisa's younger self remained in her smile to see that it was.

"Is that your husband?" I pointed to the taller, more attractive man.

"No, that's Yves Montand." Seeing I didn't know who she

meant, she added, "He acted in the film *Grand Prix* that Jack worked on."

I remembered the film. He played a racing driver.

She indicated the other man. "*That's* Jack."

He was a bit short and balding, and didn't look like he belonged with the stunning woman standing next to him. Unlike Yves Montand.

"People were surprised when we got together," Louisa said, as if she knew what I was thinking. "But he was a wonderful person and I was lucky to find him. We were very happy."

Further along, she was in a photo next to a man who had a distinctive moustache – the long ends curled up towards his eyebrows.

"Wow, is that–"

"Salvador Dali," she confirmed.

"How did you know him?"

"Oh, just the circles Jack and I moved in. We knew many artists – Picasso, Man Ray, Alexander Calder, Max Ernst and Dorothea Tanning ... have you heard of them all?"

"Yeah!" Thanks to Holly's book, I had.

"Well, I'll tell you *those* stories sometime if you like."

"That'd be great." Scrutinising the pictures on the walls around us, I said, "You don't happen to have any of their work, do you?"

Louisa laughed, "Sadly, no."

Her laugh turned into a cough which continued for a longer time than I'd ever known it. As she held a tissue over her mouth, I tried hard not to visibly recoil.

"I'm so sorry," she said when it was over.

"Are you OK. Do you need ... " I gestured to the oxygen.

"I'm fine," she wheezed unconvincingly.

She took a few moments for her breathing to become steadier, before guiding me through an archway where the living room transitioned to a dining area. Covering a large table and another sideboard were the items she wanted to sell. There were more than I'd expected, and I didn't know where to begin.

"Are you sure you want to get rid of all this?" I said.

"Absolutely. The house is up for sale and I can't take it."

"What about your children? Won't they want some of it?"

"We didn't have children."

"Oh. Sorry." I should have known from the absence of photographs, and that she'd never mentioned any.

"Don't be," she said. "It just didn't work out that way. Besides, if we'd had children we wouldn't have been able to do half the things we did. I've no regrets. I'm not sure I would've taken to motherhood anyway – I like my freedom and my own company."

"So you haven't felt lonely then – not having kids or getting married again?" The question came out before I had a chance to realise it was insensitive.

"Lonely? No, I've had good friends. And I told you I never remarried, I didn't say I hadn't had … companionship." She had a mischievous look in her eyes. "It's been a wonderful life all in all – I've had careers as a model and an artist, and travelled to every continent several times over. I would've liked Jack to have been around for more of it, but I'm grateful for the time we had."

By the way she'd talked about her husband before, I'd assumed Louisa had spent the last few decades mourning him. But it seemed she'd been getting on with her life.

Approaching the table, I scanned the array of objects, recognising a couple of glass vases as Mdina and Riihimäki. Some items looked to be souvenirs from her travels. I wondered what memories they contained for her.

"It sounds like you've done a lot in your life," I said. "I haven't really done anything yet."

"How old are you – twenty? Twenty-five?"

"Twenty-three."

"Well, I'm *eighty*-three so I've got sixty years on you. Your journey is just beginning."

"Maybe," I said. "But sometimes I feel like it's already over."

"Do you?" she asked, amazed. "Why? At your age you should be having adventures, experiences. You're just finding out about yourself and the world."

I absently picked up a pewter box and opened it – it was empty. "I don't know. I kind of feel like ... like I'm waiting for something to happen." I put the box back on the table and faced her. "Did you ever worry that you'd made the wrong choices?"

She stared at me thoughtfully before answering. "I did make some along the way. We all make mistakes. Sometimes though, you'll find that mistakes lead you to places that you might not have gone to otherwise. And some choices you make aren't forever."

"Yeah," I said, "but important choices – like what degree to study at university – have a huge impact on your future. I had to decide that at *seventeen* ... or earlier even when I chose my A-Levels and GCSEs. And no one knows what they want to do at seventeen. I reckon I'd choose differently now if I could."

"Would you? What would you do?"

"Uh ... I don't know," I smiled, aware at how ridiculous I probably sounded.

She smiled back in sympathy. "But if you *did* know, why couldn't you do it now?"

"Money, I suppose."

"Yes, but if it was something you *really* wanted to do, you could make it happen."

"That's the thing, though – I don't have a plan, and I feel I should have one."

"You're thinking too much," she said. "Just be happy – that should always be the plan. And if you're not happy, then change something. You'll work it out."

That seemed simple. But I wasn't going to work it out right now; I needed to concentrate on the reason for my visit.

I didn't know how much to offer Louisa. I was confident about some of the items, but there were others whose value I couldn't even guess at – programmes from shows on Broadway, African tribal masks, sheet music for 'Moon River' signed by Henry Mancini. I worried I wouldn't come up with a fair price and she might be offended.

She could see I was struggling. "Let me make this easy for you. I want a hundred pounds for the lot."

"What? No! That's not enough."

"It's fine by me. I'll be pleased if you make a good profit from it."

"But some of this might be worth a fortune – Henry Mancini ..." I said, holding up the music.

"A hundred is fine," she insisted.

But I couldn't just give her that; it wouldn't have been right – even though it was she who'd named the price.

"No, this is what we'll do," I said, suddenly sure of myself. "I'll buy all of this for a hundred ..." I moved away what I thought were the more valuable items, "... and I'll put these up for auction for you on eBay and take a commission. I do twenty percent with Keith – how about that?"

She considered it. "Yes, but I won't agree to anything less than fifty-fifty."

I argued, but she wouldn't give in. "OK. Fifty percent."

Under entirely different circumstances than the times before, I counted out the cash and handed it over.

Louisa gave me boxes to pack everything up in. I said she should keep hold of the auction items until they sold.

She disagreed. "No, take them. I trust you."

"That's not the way most people do business, you know."

"I'm not most people."

"No," I said, "you're not."

It took me several trips to move the boxes back to the flat, and as I carried them through the streets, I thought about

Louisa's life. There was at least a book's worth of good stories there – someone should write them down. Then it occurred to me that *I* could write them down … perhaps as a kind of memoir. I had the beginnings of a plan.

As I climbed the stairs to the flat with the final box, sweating and arms aching, I heard the melody from the phone in my pocket that a text had come through. After placing the load on the coffee table, I checked the message, assuming it would be from Marcus.

But the text was from Holly: Are you free this weekend? I've found cheap flights to Prague. Want to come? x

39

I'd like to say that I didn't go, that all of the stuff with prostitutes was behind me ... but I went to Prague with Holly. Besides, the Universe had provided me with the money – some of it from a *Czech* vase: it wanted me to go.

When we met in the departure lounge at Heathrow, Holly seemed guarded; although she greeted me with a hug, it was a cautious one, and it didn't feel the same as before. Our conversation was mostly about what was around us. Neither of us spoke about how she'd left, or mentioned anything that had happened in the weeks since.

During the flight of an hour and three quarters, she read the airline magazine. We were sitting closely together and every time our arms or legs accidentally connected, she broke the contact and moved away as if I were a stranger. On our descent, as we emerged beneath the layer of cloud, she leaned over me to point out the orange-red roofs of Prague, and the meandering Vltava river and its bridges. But she kept a space between us.

Holly had done the groundwork this time – she'd come prepared. She'd brought a guide book with a map, and an A6 notebook with the addresses of some clubs.

We had reservations at a four-star hotel near to the east bank of the river; it was another cheap internet deal – two nights for the price of one. It was half past seven (local time) when the taxi dropped us there.

In our room, Holly went straight to the mini bar without stopping to check the price list. We started to make our way through the alcohol, me sitting on the bed, and her in a chair by the window.

"Why don't you come over here?" I said.

"I'm comfortable where I am, thanks." Hearing a bell outside, she parted the net curtains to watch a tram pass down the street below. The sun was beginning to set and the light she let in illuminated her in orange.

I drained my glass and began to ask the obvious question, "So ... do you want to–"

But she cut me off. "Let's go out."

"What, now?"

"Yep. Let's go to a club."

Holly said there was a strip club nearby that offered sex. She'd memorised the way but took the map just in case. As she led us down a maze of streets, I had a feeling in my insides that I couldn't decipher – was it excitement, or doubt and apprehension? Probably a combination ... or maybe it was the aeroplane food.

When she stopped, I thought we'd reached the club and the internal soup that had been simmering reached a rolling boil. But we were outside a casino. She wanted to go in there first, and I was happy with that.

We ordered drinks at the bar – beer for me and gin for her (a double) – and sat in two free seats at a roulette table. Holly opened her purse and put down a five-hundred koruna note for the male croupier to exchange.

Not confident she'd remember all the rules, she wanted my help. So we both played with her chips, winning some bets and losing others, but we never dropped to less than we started with.

Holly finished her drink before I'd even had half of mine.

"Play on if you like," she said, "I'm going to the bar. Do you want another beer?"

"No, but you stay, I'll go. What do you want?"

"Really?!" She seemed surprised that I'd offered. "Thanks,

I'll have another gin, please … um, can it be a double?"

When I returned to the table, she'd had some good wins; in front of her were two-thousand korunas of chips in four neat stacks.

"Wow, you've done well," I said. "You didn't need me then."

"Nope," she smiled. "How much is this anyway? It doesn't even seem like real money when it's in a different currency."

I made the calculation. "About seventy quid I think."

Like the claw in a soft-toy arcade machine, her hand closed around a stack of chips and lifted it.

"I'm going to put everything on black."

"All of it?!" I said. "Don't get carried away. Quit while you're ahead, remember?"

"Yes, but it's been red five times in a row, so it's got to be black now."

"That doesn't make sense."

"Of course it does." She placed the chips in her hand on 'Black' and picked up some more. "It can't be red a sixth time."

I tried to explain. "The odds of red coming up six times in a row *before* any of it's happened is not the same as the odds of it being red given it's *already* happened five times." I watched her reach for a third stack. "Will you just wait a minute?!"

She didn't wait. "What do you mean?"

"I mean if something's happened, it's happened. And it doesn't have any influence on what happens next."

As she added the last chips, she said, "Oh, I suppose so. I get it."

"Good. Take some off then."

She shook her head. "Nah, let's do it anyway – all or nothing."

And then it was too late to change her mind. The croupier began to spin the white ball around the wheel. It slowed, dropped down, and hopped around before coming to a stop within the boundaries of number thirteen.

Black.

Holly showed no sign of triumph or relief, and I got the impression it would've been the same to her whether she'd won or lost.

Ending it there, we exchanged the chips for real money.

Outside, Holly said, "Right, let's find this club then."

"Are you sure you want to? We don't have to do anything tonight – we could just have a wander around."

She laughed at me and started walking away. "Come on, it's down here. Let's go fuck some hookers." Then she half-shouted, "Woooo!" which had a tone to it almost like sarcasm.

I jogged the few paces to catch her up.

Through two tuxedoed doormen, we descended stairs into the club. I had to pay an entrance fee, but they allowed Holly in for free.

It was a large room with a bar along one side and a raised stage opposite. On our way to the bar, a semi-naked dwarf passed us. I tried not to stare at her body but couldn't help it – it was something you don't see every day.

Hi ho, hi ho.

As Holly waited for the drinks, I turned around to observe the room.

It was like any other nightclub I'd been to with loud music, black-painted walls, mirror balls, and flashing lights … but then there were the women – dozens of them, dressed in underwear or topless.

Two girls cavorted and contorted on poles on the stage. Wearing only thongs and dangerously high heels, they effortlessly span upside down with their gravity-defying, spherical tits. On sofas and chairs around the room, girls were giving lap dances, or were just sitting and talking to men.

A blonde girl stood up from a sofa near to us, followed by the man she'd been with. His friend patted him on the back before the couple walked towards the far end of the room and disappeared through a curtain. As I watched them go I couldn't help thinking about Roxy, and wondered if the blonde girl was happy to be doing what she was presumably about to do. She *looked* happy enough, smiling and laughing and entertaining – they all did – but how many were?

But maybe they were. Maybe my bad experience with Roxy had been a one-off. I had to forget about it … just like I was trying to forget about what happened with Charlie/Mikaela.

So, my last *two* experiences had been bad, but I reasoned that meant the next one was bound to be fine. And then it occurred to me that I was contradicting myself from earlier; did different rules apply to prostitutes than roulette?

Holly handed me my drink. "Who do you want then?"

"Uh, I don't know." I hadn't been thinking about who to choose.

"What about her?" She pointed out a girl barely wearing shiny gold underwear.

"Yeah, she's OK."

"Alright. I'll ask how much."

Before I had a chance to argue, Holly had gone over to her. She spoke to the girl, the girl nodded, and they both looked over at me.

Holly was coming back; I took a deep breath thinking it had all been agreed. But when she got to me, she said, "I need to get out of here," and started moving quickly through the crowd towards the exit.

I caught up to her on the stairs. "What's wrong?"

She didn't answer and continued up and out of the door. I followed, past the doormen, and into the street.

"Holly, what's wrong?" I grabbed her arm to stop her.

"I feel sick. I – I've drunk too much."

That was all it was? I let go of her arm. "Well, you *were* going for it with the gin."

She furtively glanced back to the club as a group of six men were going in. "Can we get out of here?"

"Sure." Fine by me. "Do you want to go back to the hotel?"

"No, lets just walk."

We walked in step, and in unspoken agreement of the way. We soon found ourselves on a wide street, busy with four lanes of traffic, and moved in the direction of flow.

Holly spoke. "Sorry I made you leave the club."

"That's OK," I said. "I didn't like it in there anyway."

"What, you didn't like wall-to-wall tits and arse?"

Taking it as a joke, I laughed. But she didn't look amused.

"Actually, I didn't," I said. "It was too much of a meat market."

"Yes, it was. And all those letchy men were looking at me. It made me feel … weird."

"Were they?" I hadn't been aware of it. "They probably weren't. Not with wall-to-wall tits and arse."

I was trying to be funny, but it was a wrong move.

"Why? Don't you think they'd notice me?" she said confrontationally.

"That's not what I'm saying–"

"Don't you think I'm worth looking at? Fuck you!"

"Of course you are."

"Whatever. You're a cunt."

I'd forgotten that Holly wasn't a good drunk; she was emotional and unreasonable … and sweary.

I said, "Come on, you know I didn't mean it like that."

"Oh, just shut the fuck up." Glancing around as if suddenly aware of her surroundings, she said, "Why are we going down this shit road? Let's get off it."

We took the next junction on the right down a quieter street. At the end of that, on the left, the tarmac transitioned to a cobbled surface.

"This is more like I thought Prague would be," she said.

We passed by a pastel-pink church that looked like an elaborately iced cake. It put me in mind of the witch's cottage from Hansel and Gretel, and maybe we should've laid a breadcrumb trail because Holly insisted we were getting closer to the city centre, and I thought we were going farther away. And then we saw the bridge.

The busy road we'd been on previously had converged with another to make a huge bridge which spanned a low valley. It was so high that even though the buildings below were five or six storeys, the structure, with its massive slanted supports, still towered above them.

Holly voiced what I'd been thinking: "I bet a few people have jumped off there."

A path traversed the slope of the valley, and we followed it until we were standing directly under the top of the bridge. We could hear the cars clearly overhead.

Graffiti had been sprayed on to the concrete bank there, and in what looked like marker pen was written:

DANNY IS A WANKER

And underneath:

MANCHESTER UNITED

Seeing the word 'united' I noticed how close it was to 'untied', how the reversal of two letters also reversed the meaning of the word.

I said, "British football twats have been here, then."

"Yep, stag weekends," Holly decided. "More men cheating on their girlfriends with hookers."

"Probably. I hate this kind of graffiti."

"But what you write is fine, though?"

"Well, yeah … kind of," I said, "but you were right."

"What about?"

"About it being half-arsed. I've started writing again – properly."

She shrugged. "Do whatever you want."

I thought she'd be pleased – she liked being right – but then she hadn't been acting the way I thought she would, not like herself, not since I'd met her at the airport.

I said, "Are you OK?"

"Yes, I don't feel so sick now."

But I didn't mean that. "No, are you *OK*?"

She looked at me. "Why wouldn't I be?"

"I don't know, you seem a bit … strange. Are you still angry with me … from before … when you left."

"No." She faced away, down into the valley. "It's fine. I'm just drunk."

Realising I didn't know anything about her life since I last saw her, I said, "Where are you working now anyway?"

"Nowhere."

"What have you been doing then?"

"Not a lot."

I might've continued the conversation had I not needed a piss so badly.

She stayed facing the other way while I went against a blank patch on the slope of the concrete. As I started going, it formed an 'L' shape. I decided to try and write my name.

When I'd finished, I zipped up my jeans and called Holly over. "What do you reckon to *this* graffiti?"

Folding her arms, she considered it. "Quite impressive. Possibly the best thing you've ever done."

"I know. You can actually read it!"

"You can," she agreed. "I wish *I* could do that … but it'd end up all over my shoes."

"Yeah," I said. "I always suspected you had penis envy."

She laughed, "Thanks, Freud! Come on, let's get back to the hotel."

40

I was awake before Holly. She lay beside me in the double bed with her long hair fanned around her head as if she were underwater. On her side with her back towards me, her shoulders and arms were exposed, and a thin strap was twisted on the white vest she wore. I watched her back expand and contract with deep and steady breaths.

I might have woken her; I might have slid my hand under the covers and over her body. But despite our proximity, there was a distance, and I didn't feel I could touch her without an invitation. I got up to take a shower.

In the bathroom, her clothes were on the floor from last night. She'd changed in there and then gone straight to bed and to sleep; I didn't remember her ever not changing in front of me before.

When I returned to the room, Holly had rolled over but was still sleeping. After quietly dressing, and for something to do, I sat in the chair by the window and started reading her guide book.

As she began to stir, I checked the time – half ten. She peered out at me under half-closed eyelids, her face scrunched up.

"Morning," I said gently. "How are you feeling?"

She groaned.

"That good, eh?"

"Hmm." She closed her eyes.

"I've been looking in your guide," I said. "It's a beautiful city."

"It didn't look that great last night," she mumbled.

"I think we just went the wrong way." Taking the book, I sat on the bed and flicked through the pages. "It's the 'City of a Hundred Spires'," I quoted. "Look, there's the river, town square, castle … and there's a museum about Kafka – we have to go there."

"Sounds good," she said, not making any attempt to see what I was trying to show her. "But I don't know if I can."

"Yeah, you can. Have a shower and something to eat and you'll feel better."

It took another couple of hours until she was ready to leave the hotel. In that time we watched some TV, and I went out and brought back bread and fruit from a minimarket – the only things she felt like eating.

Using the map, we headed towards the old town. It *was* a beautiful city with a labyrinth of cobbled streets, archways and squares, and spires straight out of a Gothic fairy tale.

We crossed the Charles Bridge, lined with statues of saints, and packed with tourists, traders and musicians. In the streets before, we'd been shaded by the buildings, but here we were unprotected from the blaze of the August sun. Already squinting from the effects of her hangover, Holly felt compelled to buy sunglasses, and I bought a fridge magnet with the slogan 'Prague: Czech it out'.

The Kafka museum wasn't far away from the bridge on the other side. We passed through wooden gates into a courtyard and saw the entrance to the museum next to a large letter 'K'.

In the middle of the courtyard was a fountain. Two life-sized, verdigris men stood in a pool of water, facing each other as if participating in a duel. But instead of weapons, they held their penises.

The statues' legs and upper bodies were fixed, but their mid-sections around their hips swivelled, and the penises moved vertically, arcing streams of water from them.

"What's this about?" Holly said.

"I don't know."

A middle-aged American tourist was taking photos. He heard us and said, "They spell what you want with their pee."

He pointed to a plaque on the ground which read, 'SMS Peeing Men'. There was a number you could text.

"Ha!" said Holly, "Get them to write *your* name, Lyle."

We paid our entrance fees to the museum and went in.

Watching a screen showing old black and white images of Prague set to violin music, I said, "That was strange."

"What?"

"The fountain. That they were doing what I did last night."

"The pissing thing? I suppose it was a bit."

Prague was warping and distorting as if viewed through water or a shattered mirror.

"That happens to me all the time," I said. "Coincidences, I mean."

"Yes, me too. It happens to everyone … urgh, this is making me feel sick."

Moving away from the screen, we went over to a timeline of Kafka's life displayed on the wall.

I said, "Do you ever think they could be more than coincidence though? That someone has *made* them happen?"

"Um, not really." She looked at me sideways. "Who do you think is making them happen – God?!"

"Of course not – you know I'm not religious. The Universe?" I ventured.

"The Universe? What does that even mean?"

"I – I'm not sure." Thinking of stars, I looked up but saw only wooden beams crossing the ceiling. "It just seems like coincidences happen so often there has to be a *reason* for them. Like they're part of a plan or something."

"A reason for writing your name with your wee?"

"That makes it sound stupid when you say it like that."

"Yep."

We'd reached the end of the line, where Kafka died of

tuberculosis at the age of forty: too young.

She said, "Hmm, I don't believe there's a reason for coincidence ... or anything else. I can understand people want that to be true – when bad things happen – but I don't reckon there's some kind of divine plan for us."

"That's a bit depressing, though," I said. "If there's no plan or point to anything, then why do we bother? Maybe we should all go and jump in front of trains."

"No – it's the other way round. If there's a plan then we're all following it without knowing, and without free will. *That* makes life pointless. *That's* depressing."

I'd never thought of it like that.

She said, "Maybe you just want there to be a plan so you don't have to make one."

Passing a revolving projection of the significant women in Kafka's life, I came to a screen showing an animation of his drawings. Accompanied by eerie music and the sound of cawing crows, a black figure of a man fell through the air onto a blank page and turned into writing. The page transformed into a table, the ink morphing back to the shape of a man, slumped over it with his head in his hands.

Holly was looking in a perspex case suspended from the ceiling by chains. The case contained passages from Kafka's diaries translated into English. I pointed out an excerpt I liked:

> *You do not need to leave your room.*
> *Remain sitting at your table and listen.*
> *Do not even listen, simply wait, be quiet, still and solitary.*
> *The world will freely offer itself to you to be unmasked,*
> *it has no choice, it will roll in ecstasy at your feet.*

Holly said, "Actually, I saw something else he wrote, which kind of contradicts that." She found it in a different case and read it to me: "'Paths are made by walking.'"

We descended a flight of wooden stairs that creaked with

every step. The walls were lined with planks and, as if reliving a memory from a previous life, I got a sense of the trenches of the First World War. At the bottom of the stairs we found ourselves in a corridor of shiny black filing cabinets.

Holly said, "It's not surprising your ego finds it easy to believe the 'Universe' is making coincidences happen for you … because you've got to admit – you *are* a bit of a narcissist."

I was about to defend myself but, with all this talk, I remembered something. "Well, you can't blame me for being narcissistic when I find out someone went out of their way to see me, then pretended it was a coincidence."

She was silent; I was sure she knew what I was getting at.

"I saw Marcus," I said.

"Did you?" she asked innocently.

"Yeah. He said that he saw *you* and told you where I lived … you knew I'd be there!"

"Um, yes. But I didn't *know*–"

"You said you went to the park because you used to go there."

"Well, I *did* use to go there." She opened one of the cabinet drawers and closed it again. "I didn't know if you were still in Oldchurch – nor did Marcus – and I didn't know you were working in the antiques shop. I just walked around and hoped to bump into you, and when that didn't happen, I thought I'd go into the shop and see if they knew if you still lived there … and there you were."

"So you didn't come in for the music box then?"

"Not exactly," she said. "I mean, I saw it in the window and liked it … but I was coming in to ask about you."

"Why didn't you just tell me that?"

"I don't know."

We came to a room with mirrored walls reflecting images of barbed wire and staring eyes.

Holly said, "Do you want to get out of here? I'm not really in the mood. It's all a bit weird – kind of claustrophobic and …"

"Kafkaesque?" I offered.

"Exactly!"

"OK," I said, "we can go."

Outside, I was surprised to see it was daylight; there was so much darkness in the museum I'd forgotten it wasn't night.

Holly said, "I'm feeling hungry now."

"Yeah, me too. Let's find a restaurant."

"It's OK, we can just grab a sandwich or something."

"No. It'll be nicer to eat in somewhere."

There were lots of things Holly claimed she wouldn't be able to stomach, but she inexplicably had a craving for greasy Chinese food. We found a place.

The menu in English had small pictures of the dishes next to the names. One was, 'Chicken with Strange Flavour'. In the picture it looked like sweet and sour, and something had probably just gone wrong with the translation, but neither of us were prepared to risk it.

We both had noodles, and after we'd eaten, were given a fortune cookie each. I opened mine, sure it would reveal something significant. But it was 'Do not be the singer when you can be the song'.

Holly said, "What does *that* mean?"

"Uh ... not sure. Maybe it's lost in translation again."

"It could be a Czech proverb that we've never heard of? Or a Chinese one?"

"Could be. What does yours say?"

She cracked hers, pulled out the slip of paper and read, "'You must still applaud the good actors in a bad play'." It seemed equally enigmatic.

"So," I said, "what shall we do now?"

She placed the broken cookie, uneaten, on her plate. "What we came here to do, I suppose."

41

Checking her notes, Holly thought we should go to a place described as a 'small, intimate club'. It wasn't far away.

When we got to the address it didn't look like any kind of club at all; there wasn't a big sign or a doorman, just a closed wooden door with a black, graffiti tag sprayed on it. But underneath a plastic doorbell, a badly-handwritten label with the name of the club showed it *was* the right place.

Unconvinced, I said, "Shall we try somewhere else?"

"No, let's ring the bell and see what happens."

She pressed it.

We waited.

"I don't think anyone's here." I half-hoped that was true.

But as Holly reached forward to ring the bell again, the door opened and a man appeared. He must have been at least seventy, and had a bushy, grey moustache that covered the entirety of his top lip and most of the bottom.

"Hello," I said.

The man nodded a greeting.

"Uh, can we … come in?"

Staring at us, I didn't think he'd understood the English, but he said, "You want to come in? You know what is here?"

"Yeah," I confirmed, without being sure if he meant what I thought he meant.

"Her?" he motioned to Holly, sceptically.

"Yes," she said. "We want to come in together."

The man raised his eyebrows (also grey and bushy) and then smiled. "Sure. Come in."

Letting us through the door, he ushered us before him down

a long passageway and into a lounge area. There was a bar in one corner and the man went to stand behind it. Three girls were sitting on tall barstools watching us.

"You want drinks?" the man offered.

Holly asked for a gin and tonic. I went for the same.

As they were poured, I avoided the girls' stares by surveying the room. There were cream-coloured sofas, lamps with frilly shades, and figurines of elephants and horses on the windowsill; it was less like a club than someone's nan's front room converted to a home-bar. Music was playing from an old stereo, wires trailing along the walls to the speakers mounted on high brackets. It was 'The Power of Love' by Frankie Goes to Hollywood.

The man handed us our drinks and we sipped them awkwardly.

"So," he said, "what you want to do?"

I didn't know how to answer. Did he need specifics? "Uh …"

"You want private room?"

"Yes," Holly said. "How much?"

He handed us a laminated tariff as if we were choosing bar snacks. The prices were based on the time in the room, not by the services, and were in quarter hour increments. Holly leaned over and quietly told me that it was half the price she'd been quoted in the place the night before. I studied the tariff for longer than was necessary.

The man said, "Who you like?"

Looking at the girls, I saw them properly. They were all wearing short dresses, and their legs were crossed in identical poses. Two of them were older – in their mid thirties – and were both quite rough; one had black permed hair reminiscent of Brian May from Queen, and the other looked like her eyebrows and the line of her lips had been drawn on with felt tip pens in the dark. I was thankful to see that the third was in her twenties and was pretty. It was obvious we didn't need to discuss it, so I indicated the younger girl who started giggling in what seemed to be a mixture of amusement and embarrassment. The rejected ugly sisters glared at me.

"Ah, very good," the man said. "Her name is Marta and she is Czech – from Prague. She does not speak English, but she understands." He said a few words to her in their own language, and she nodded and got off her stool.

He said, "You want hour?"

"No," Holly decided. "Forty-five minutes."

We paid the man the money – for the drinks and for Marta – and she beckoned us to follow her.

Through a door, padded in white leather, we entered a peach-coloured room. The furniture was all white melamine, and grey, plastic Venetian blinds hung at the window. Red-framed pictures of women's legs in high heels decorated the walls, and the towel draped over the screen of the corner shower had a wolf design. It was a room from the 1980s, and something about it reminded me of the bedroom Elspeth used to have. I could well believe the old guy had been running the club since then.

Marta pulled her dress up and over her head; she hadn't been wearing anything else. She picked up a folded sheet from the bedside table and bent over as she spread it on top of the bed. Although while we'd been in Prague my mind had been conflicted about how I felt about hiring another girl, at that moment my dick knew exactly how *it* felt about the situation. And it wasn't the first time I'd realised the two aren't necessarily in sync.

Out of the corner of my eye, I noticed Holly taking off her top.

"What are you doing?" I said.

"Getting undressed."

She unhooked her bra.

"Why?"

"Because that's what you want, isn't it? You want to see me with another girl?"

I was stunned. "Well, yeah … but I didn't think you were into it."

"I can get into it."

Holly took off the rest of her clothes. It was the first time I'd seen her naked during our holiday which I found more exciting than anything else.

When she lay on her back on the bed, the escort understood what she was meant to do and went down on her. Holly closed her eyes. I undid my jeans, put my hand down my pants and got into it too.

After a while, Holly opened her eyes. She frowned when she saw what I was doing and halted the escort. "That's all you're getting," she said to me. "Your turn now."

So, I got ready for my turn.

I began with Marta on all fours. "OK like this, Holly?"

She didn't reply.

"Holly?" Looking back over my shoulder, I saw her step back into her skirt and pull it up.

"What are you doing?" I said.

"Getting dressed."

She picked up her bra, put it around her, and fastened it.

"Why?"

"Because I want to."

Her top went on.

"OK," I said, disappointed. "Tell me what you'd like me to do though."

"Just do what *you* want."

So I did what I wanted, which were the things I thought Holly wanted to see, because I was doing it for *her*. I tried to put on a good show, and I was sure I did.

Afterwards, Holly said, "Get dressed then, and we'll go."

"Now?" I estimated we'd only been there twenty minutes or so. "We've still got time haven't we? I can do it again."

"I'm good … but you go for it if you want."

But I said, "No, let's go."

So I dressed, and Marta dressed, and we all went back to the lounge. The other two women were still on their stools at the bar and they glared at me again. The music that was playing was by a female singer whose name I didn't know, but I knew the song was also called 'The Power of Love'. I was sure there was a third song with the same title in *Back to the Future* and I wondered if that was on the playlist too.

The man seemed surprised to see us back and asked, "You have good time?"

"Uh, yeah … thanks."

"You like another drink?"

"No." Holly edged towards the door. "We just want to leave."

The man nodded, stepped out from the bar, and showed us the way out.

42

As we walked away from the club, to break the silence, I said, "That was good."

"Hmm. Forty-five minutes is still too long."

We paused at the kerb as a tram rattled past, then crossed the road.

On the other side, I said, "Strange place. What was with that old guy? And the music ... and the rooms?!"

"Hmm."

"And those women at the bar!"

Holly didn't comment.

"We were lucky there was a decent one," I continued. "If there hadn't been, we couldn't really have walked away – it would've been a bit rude."

A short burst of laughter exploded from Holly.

"What?" I was unsure why that was so funny.

"Nothing."

"Come on – what?"

She shook her head. "Don't worry about it."

As we headed back in the direction of the Old Town – the Staré Město – I was thinking about what we'd just done, what I'd just watched.

"So, how was it," I grinned, "...when she went down on you?"

"It was alright."

"Just alright?"

She sighed impatiently. "Do we have to talk about it?"

We *always* talked about it – she liked to. "Don't you want to?"

"Not really."

"Why not?"

"Can you just drop it, Lyle!" she snapped, her pace quickening as if trying to get away from me.

I kept up. "What's the matter?" I said, confused by her tone.

"I knew I shouldn't have come here! This whole thing was a stupid idea – I'm over it." She spoke with hostility as if she was accusing me of making her.

"Hang on a minute. It was *your* idea to come to Prague … it was your idea to do *any* of this."

When Holly had come to stay at the flat that first weekend, we'd had a conversation about the first time we'd each had sex. As I told Holly my story, she discovered she liked hearing it. She liked it a lot and asked to hear other stories; it turned her on to think of me with other girls. *That* was why we'd gone to Rotterdam – Holly had wanted to watch me with someone else.

"Yes," she said, "I thought it would be *fun*."

"So did I!"

We rounded a corner as two girls came from the opposite direction. I stepped off the narrow pavement to give them room to pass, and smiled.

After they'd gone, Holly said, "Do you always have to do that?!"

"Do what?"

"Check out every woman that goes by?"

"I didn't," I said innocently.

"Yes, you did. You were subtle, but I knew what you were doing."

She was right. It wasn't as if I turned around and blatantly looked at their arses, but my eyes *had* strayed to the tits of the girl in the low-cut top.

She said, "Can I ask you something?" But she didn't wait for my consent. "Do you even see women as equals?"

"Of course I do!"

"Do you?" she challenged. "No, honestly … do you?"

"What are you talking about?! So, I look at women. What's that got to with *equality*? I'm sure you check out men."

"Not really."

"Really?"

"Well, maybe *some* men. But just their faces or their hair or their clothes … I'm not looking at their bodies. I'm not constantly thinking I want to fuck them."

"I'm not *constantly* thinking that."

Her expression showed she didn't believe me.

I said, "Yeah, but I bet if men walked around with their shirts off you'd be looking. It's difficult *not* to look at women's bodies – especially in the summer. Anyway, when we were in Amsterdam you admitted *you* were checking out women too. And you're not even into women … are you?"

"You know I'm not."

"So why are you having a go at me? You're not being fair."

"Maybe," she admitted. "But don't do it so much – especially when you're with me."

Finding ourselves in the Old Town Square, we sat down on one of the benches that surrounded the huge monument in the centre. I looked at the church to our left. Lit from below, eerie shadows were cast upwards like a torch shone on a face from the chin. Windows on the symmetrical towers appeared as eyes, and an elongated central window was the mouth, gaping in shock or song.

Holly said, "I meant what I said before though, I *am* over all this. It's starting to feel a bit … *wrong* or something."

"I know what you're saying – I've been thinking that too."

"Have you?" She was surprised. "What have you been thinking?"

"Uh … that you don't know who you're getting and what their story is. It could involve drugs or abuse, or they could've been trafficked. You never know if the girl is doing it for the right reasons."

"And what are the right reasons?"

"That it's their choice and they enjoy it, I suppose." I decided to tell Holly about Roxy. "A few weeks ago, I got someone – an escort – to come to the flat, and–"

"You did what?! Why? It was meant to be *our* thing!" She seemed hurt, as if I'd told her I'd been cheating. I thought we were going to have another argument, but she quickly shook it off. "Sorry, it doesn't matter. Go on – what were you going to say?"

So I cautiously told her what had happened, how it had made me question why Roxy was doing it, why they were *all* doing it. How it had made me feel guilty and sleazy.

Holly listened without interrupting. When I'd finished, all she said was, "We're not going to do this again, are we?" But it was perhaps more of a statement than a question.

"I don't think so. Not unless we find someone we know who'd be cool with it."

"Hmm, that would be an interesting conversation ... but you know I wouldn't want that though. It was good it was anonymous. If it was someone we knew, it would get too weird."

"Yeah, I wasn't serious. It's about time they invented realistic sex-robots."

"Ha! I'm sure that will happen one day."

I was sad it was our last night. There was a lot more of the city I wanted to explore – art galleries, the castle, maybe one of the black light theatres – but our flight was in the morning and we wouldn't get the chance. Even though it hadn't been the best time with her, I was sad I'd be leaving Holly too. I didn't know what was going to happen between us when we got back. Would we see each other again? Would she want to?

I broached the subject. "You know when you said at the restaurant, about it being what we came here for?"

"Yes?"

"Well, it's not the reason I'm here."

"Isn't it? Why *are* you then?"

"I think it's so I can spend time with you."

She bowed her head and didn't say anything, which wasn't the reaction I'd anticipated. And then I saw the tense expression on her face, like she was about to cry.

"Holly?"

She took a deep breath. "Lyle, you know when we put up my escort profile and you said everyone has a price?"

"Yeah?"

"You were right," she said. "I did."

43

Five-hundred pounds. A lot of money, but not much at all. Just five-hundred: not enough. Perhaps everyone *did* have a price ... but this wasn't about the money. Not really.

Gregory – the man she'd messaged on the escort site – *had* gone to London on business, and booked her to spend the night with him at his hotel. She kept the appointment.

"Was he violent?" I asked anxiously. "Did he hurt you?"

"No, it wasn't like that – he was a nice guy. He didn't make me feel scared or threatened ... although ..." She trailed off.

"What?!"

Staring at her feet, she tapped her heels together. "Well, after I got there I realised I hadn't told anyone where I was."

"Holly, what the fuck were you thinking?!"

"I know. It was stupid."

"You should have called *me*," I said. "I'd have come and got you if you'd needed me to."

She studied my face for a few seconds. "Would you?"

"Of course."

She returned her focus to her feet. "It was OK. Like I said, he was a nice guy ... just not what I was expecting."

"What do you mean?"

"Oh, just that I built up a picture of who he was and how it would all be."

"Yeah," I said, "fantasy and reality are two different things."

I waited for Holly to say more, but she didn't. So I prompted her. "What *was* it like?"

"Um, it was kind of awkward. And once I saw him, I didn't really want to do it anymore."

"Why didn't you just walk away then?"

"I couldn't. It wasn't … polite." She looked pointedly at me and I understood why she'd laughed before.

"What was he like then?"

She bit her lip. "Kind of short, bald, businessy. He was forty-three – which I knew anyway – but from the things he wrote, I thought he'd look a lot different."

"Did you tell him it was your first time – it was your first time wasn't it?"

"Of course it was. First and last!"

I was relieved. "OK, but did you *tell* him?"

"No. I thought that would make it even more awkward."

Again she seemed reluctant to continue. Again I prompted. "So, what happened?"

"We went for dinner first. He took me to a restaurant by the river."

"Did you talk about what you were going to do?"

"No. We just talked about the food and London and stuff."

"And then you went back to the hotel?"

"No. We walked by the river for a bit."

But I didn't want to hear about dinner and walking and whatever else. I wanted her to get to the point. "But what happened when you got back to his *room*?"

She shifted uncomfortably. "Well, I had to – I had to suck him off in front of the mirror …"

Whoa!

My stomach lurched. Was it disgust? Jealousy? Something else?

"Maybe I don't need to hear the details."

A picture had formed in my head of a short, bald, ugly businessman with his penis in Holly's mouth. It wasn't an image I wanted to see. It wasn't turning me on – far from it. But although I didn't want to know, I *had* to know something.

"Did you actually f … *sleep* with him?" I couldn't bring myself to say the word. It was too real.

"I thought you didn't want to hear the details."

"I don't. Just tell me that."

"Yes," she confirmed.

My stomach lurched again and he was on top of her, thrusting. I shook my head to dislodge the image and said, "I don't get why you even went in the first place."

Holly gathered her hair and brought it forward to settle over one shoulder. "I don't know ... it was exciting – getting the emails – and after what happened with us, it was good to have the attention. I never really had *your* attention ... well, except when sex was involved."

"That's not true."

"Hmm. It *did* feel like you'd just been using me for sex the whole time."

I could see how it would. "I'm sorry I made you feel that way. It wasn't ever *just* about sex, I enjoyed other stuff too – boot sales, going to the Tate, watching TV. But having you there at the flat all the time ... I wasn't used to it."

"And I'm sorry you thought I was trying to run your life. But I was honestly just trying to help."

"I know you were ... anyway, so let me get this right: you felt hurt by me using you for sex, and made yourself feel better by meeting a man who was just using you – *paying* you – for sex?" Slowly, mockingly, I nodded my head. "That makes sense."

"If you say it like that, it *doesn't* make sense. But that's not how it was. When we were messaging, he said lots of nice things about me."

Having seen some of the early emails, I said, "Yeah, about how much he wanted to fuck you!"

"Not just that. He was saying how intelligent and interesting I was. It wasn't just about sex, he liked me for me."

"What, you told him about yourself?"

"Well, no ... maybe a couple of things. I made up most of it because I was playing a role really – I was Suki."

"OK ... so you liked him ... because he liked you for you ... even though you were pretending to be someone else?"

She laughed. "Pretty fucked-up isn't it?"

"Yeah," I agreed, "pretty fucked-up."

A group of men emerged from a bar directly opposite and began loudly singing some kind of football chant; they were English. As they headed out of the square down a side street, I listened as their song grew fainter. Instead of the usual disdain, it made me feel strangely nostalgic.

"So if you thought you only got my attention from sex, is that why you've been doing all of this? Why we've been hiring escorts?"

"Are you analysing me?" she said in amusement. "Ha! You *do* think you're Freud don't you?"

"No, but you're always going on about *my* motives. Do you ever consider your own? Seriously, is that why we've been doing this – because you wanted my attention?"

She immediately shook her head. "No. I wanted to do it; I *liked* doing it. I mean, yes, I did like that I was doing it *with* you, that we were both into it, but I'm not actually *that* pathetic that I was doing it all for your attention."

"What about coming to Prague though? And what was that just now in the room? Was that something you wanted to do – because you seemed to be saying *that* was for me."

She took a little time to respond. "I don't know ... yes? ... no? You tell me, Freud!"

But she didn't want me to tell her; she meant that to be the end of the conversation, because she stood up and said, "Let's go somewhere else."

44

Standing in front of the Old Town Hall clock, Holly took out her guide book. "It's an astronomical clock," she read. "There's a legend that after it was made, the maker was blinded by the city councillors so it would be the only one."

"Harsh."

His eyes a clock.

She scanned the page. "It doesn't mention how it works though."

Examining the clock face, I tried to figure it out. On the outer dial were gold numbers up to twenty-four, and inside was a ring of Roman numerals also up to twenty-four; they did not correspond. On a smaller inner dial were the signs of the zodiac, and on two of its hands were representations of the sun and moon.

Pointing to them, I said, "I think they're meant to show the position of the sun and moon in relation to the stars." I glanced to the sky to see if I was right. I couldn't see the moon, but I was surprised to see that, even in the city centre, some stars – the brightest – were visible overhead. "Do you know any constellations?"

Holly didn't.

Indicating a group of four stars that formed an almost-square, I said, "That's Pegasus. And the ones up there ... those ones that look like a cross ... that's Cygnus the swan."

"I see them."

"The bright star at the top of the cross is called Deneb. It's one of the stars in the 'Summer Triangle'." I'd bent down to her height and our heads were almost touching as we both looked along the line of my arm, raised to the sky. I was fifteen again, experiencing the expectation of first-time closeness. "If you go across, you'll see another bright one ... that's Vega in the constellation of Lyra. And the last one in the triangle ... yeah, there ... that's Altair, part of Aquila the eagle."

Holly moved away. "I didn't know you knew that."

I slowly stood up straight. "Yeah, my sister taught me."

We left the Old Town Square down another cobbled street flanked by more old buildings; the beauty of this part of the city was getting repetitive. We stopped briefly to peer in the window of an antiques shop, and saw items of glassware I knew Ian Cognito would like. But even if the shop had been open, they'd be too heavy to take back on the plane.

As we walked in silence, I couldn't help thinking about what Holly had told me. It wasn't disgust or jealousy even: what I felt was guilt. Had she decided to meet him because of me? Was it my fault? I wanted to talk to her about it again, but would she want to?

The silence became uncomfortable; I should say something – anything!

But Holly was the one who spoke. "You've never talked much about your sister. She's older than you, isn't she?"

"Uh, yeah. Eight years."

"You're not very close then?"

"We used to be," I said, "before she went to university. Before she got a boyfriend."

"Have you tried to get close to her again?"

It was an idea I'd never considered. I hadn't made an attempt to see Elspeth's new house, couldn't remember the last time I phoned her, and the only times I saw her were at Mum and Dad's at Christmas.

"No," I said. "She'd be too busy."

"Surely she wouldn't be too busy for her brother. What does she do?"

"She's an astrophysicist."

"Oh, stars," Holly smiled. "I bet that's an interesting job."

"Yeah, probably. I might've wanted to do something like that … but she got there first."

"Why did that matter? You still could've."

"I know," I said, "but I didn't want to follow in her footsteps – there would've always been a comparison. And I'd never have achieved what Elspeth has. It takes hard work."

Holly nodded as if agreeing I wasn't capable of that. I was disappointed she wasn't prepared to reassure me – not that I would've expected her too – but then she said, "It would've been OK – you don't need to work hard because you're clever. You're lucky. I wish I was like you."

She wasn't stupid – far from it – but she *had* worked hard on her degree and in the end got a grade no better than mine. Had everything been more difficult for Holly than it had for me? I'd never felt particularly lucky, but was I?

"Maybe I'm lucky to be an only child, though," she said. "No footsteps to follow … or avoid." She smoothed her hair with both her hands. "I've got no idea what I'm going to do when I get home."

"About what?"

"About everything. Just … everything. I remember sitting in Annabel's room at the beginning of the first year, and thinking this was it, this was the beginning of my life and I could do anything I wanted. I really believed it then. But I haven't felt that since and I don't feel it now. It's like there's nothing for me anymore. Absolutely nothing."

"That's not true," I asserted. "Of course there is."

She raised her gaze towards the sky. "Oh … anyway. So, which was Pegasus and …" she stopped abruptly. "What's that man doing?!"

From a pole jutting out over the street from the roof of a three storey building, a man casually dangled by one hand. The other was in his trouser pocket.

"I don't think it's a man," I said, and as we got closer it was apparent he was a statue.

"I'll see if there's anything about it in the book. Where are we?"

I pointed to a plaque on the wall that read 'Husova'.

Holly turned to the index in the back, found it, and flicked through until she reached the right page. She laughed.

"What?"

"It's by David Černý – the same guy who did the pissing men – and guess who it's meant to be?"

"Kafka?" I ventured.

"No, Sigmund Freud!"

"Ha!" I said. "See what I mean – coincidences."

"Hmm, coincidences."

As we contemplated the dangling Freud, Holly said, "Lyle, after we graduated I tried to call you but your number was disconnected."

"Yeah – I changed my phone."

"I checked Facebook a few times just in case … and I looked for Marcus on there too – I thought *he'd* know where you were."

"He's not on there either."

"I know – he's not … but the weird thing was, then I saw him in the street! Out of all the people I could see – and I don't think I've *ever* seen anyone I know in London – I saw *him*."

"That's strange," I said.

"It really was! At the time I was thinking about you, and how I could get in touch, and there he was. If you want to talk about coincidences, that was a big one … but don't start thinking it means anything. It was just weird."

"Yeah," I smiled. "Just … weird."

"You know, I don't really like Marcus," she said. "He wasn't that nice to you. I feel sorry for Nina having a baby with him – she always seemed alright."

"I feel sorry for her too."

We continued on and came to a wide street with a lot more people and traffic. A grand building was at the end of the street – possibly a museum or a gallery – and we headed, slightly uphill, in that direction.

We passed a woman standing in an unlit doorway. Dressed like a street hooker in a tiny skirt and high-heeled boots, I assumed that was what she was. She gave me a look as if to say it was a shame I had a girlfriend. I turned away.

Holly said, "I suppose we should go back to the hotel – it's getting late. I wish we had more time." But I wasn't sure if she meant more time in Prague or more time together.

I said, "So, what happens now? With me and you I mean."

"Um, what do you want to happen?"

"I don't know … for things to go back the way they were before. Well, not *exactly* the way they were," I backtracked. "Not that. But you could … you know … come and stay? We could see how it goes?"

She said, "I don't think that's a good idea."

"But I thought that was what you wanted."

"I do, I did … but it won't work. We don't bring out the best in each other."

"But I reckon we *could* if we tried …"

"No – we're too different."

"You're wrong," I said, "We're not that different."

"But what I did though … doesn't that change things? Doesn't that change the way you see me?"

I shook my head. "No, not at all. Why would it?"

We'd reached the end of the street by a large statue of a man sitting on a horse. He was holding a staff and a flag, and surrounded by less-important figures.

Holly said, "I don't like these *old* statues much." She was changing the subject, but I decided to let her – for the time being.

"No, nor do I."

"Who's this guy supposed to be anyway?" She took out her book and found the right page. "It's St Wenceslas."

"As in *Good King* Wenceslas?"

"I think so … hey, do you know how he liked his pizza?"

"Does it say that in there?!"

"No. Did they even have pizza back then?" She closed the book and returned it to her bag. "Come on, how did Good King Wenceslas like his pizza?"

Realising she was attempting a joke, I played along and said my line. "I don't know, how *did* Good King Wenceslas like his pizza?"

She smiled, pleased with herself at the punchline to come.

"Deep pan, crisp and even."

It was a good joke – a great pun. I never liked her as much as I did then. It may even have been the point that I started to love her, or began to realise that I already did.

I put my hand in hers and she didn't let it go.

45

As I sat at the desk and looked out of the window, 'Mr Walker' was passing the spot where the pound coin used to be. He momentarily focused on the pavement as if marking its absence.

It's strange how some people get your attention and others don't. It was Keith who had made me aware of Mr Walker. I hadn't seen him before that (although Keith said I must have), but once I *had* seen him, I saw him everywhere – in the park, in town, passing the shop. He just seemed to be around all day, walking. He was a man in his forties who wore a brown zip-up jacket with red stripes down the sleeves. I don't know why I hadn't noticed him before – he wasn't particularly inconspicuous – but, for whatever reason, I hadn't.

Mrs Stephenson came out of the newsagent's carrying a paper in the crook of her arm. I didn't recognise her at first because she was on her own, and her yellow coat had been replaced by a black one. How must it feel to suddenly be by yourself after seventy years? It can't be easy when you've spent a lifetime with one person. I thought about Louisa and the comparatively short time she'd had with *her* husband, and was sad for them both – the long-time alone and the recently alone.

Stepping up to her crossing point by the kerb just outside was the girl-with-the–

No, her name's Carla.

As if sensing me there, Carla looked behind her and gave me a small wave. She sometimes did that. And we always said hello if we saw each other, which was often as I no longer avoided the café when she was there. I raised my hand in greeting, then turned away from the window.

A man and his two children were in the shop. The kids were standing by the table in front of the desk, quietly looking at the items displayed there. The older girl whispered to the younger boy not to touch anything, but as he pointed to a cast iron elephant, his finger accidentally connected. He glanced up at me with eyes wide in fear of my reaction.

"It's a money bank," I said. "Do you want me to show you how it works?"

The boy nodded shyly.

I pressed one of the buttons on the till and it opened with a 'ding'. I took a few pennies from their compartment and leaned over to place one of the coins in the elephant's trunk. As I lifted its tail, the trunk rose upwards and the money dropped into the slot behind the elephant's head. The kids liked that and I gave them each a turn with a coin. The boy wanted his sister to go first and he followed.

I said, "Do you want to see something else?"

They both nodded enthusiastically. I reached for a long wooden box, the top decorated with painted flowers.

"This piece ..."

Piece?!

"... is a Victorian pencil box – you might've had something like this at school a hundred and fifty years ago." I demonstrated how it opened. "The lid slides out and then turns like this."

The children were listening intently, so I picked up another object and carried on.

"And this is a perpetual calendar. That means you can keep using it year after year." Moving the small wheels on the side, I showed them how the number of days, days of the week, and months could be changed. "It's made out of Bakelite – an old type of plastic."

Their dad came over and stood behind them, placing a hand on each of their shoulders. He'd heard what I'd been telling them and said to me, "You know a lot about antiques."

"Some things," I said. "I'm learning all the time."

"Well, it's a great shop to learn in – it's just like an Aladdin's cave."

"Yeah, it *is* like that." I smiled – genuinely – then covertly added another line to the tally.

Later, Mrs Valensis came in. I thought she'd want Keith (who was working in the yard), but she didn't ask for him. Instead she went over to 'Retro Corner' and found a set of blue and white Cornishware jars to buy. She knocked the price down – of course – and as she was paying, told me how well her new furniture fitted into her house. Then she thanked me for delivering it.

* * *

A few days after returning from Prague, I thought more about Roxy and what I could do to help her. I considered going to the police, but decided it would be best if I talked to her first to see if she'd tell me what her story was.

If other people were in control of Roxy's profile it would be pointless to message her, so we had to speak face to face, and the only way was to book another incall. By doing that I knew I'd have to give her money, and by having her come to the flat again I might be putting myself in danger. But after last time I felt I owed her.

I logged on to the escort website, and typed what I remembered her profile name to be. It came back with no results. Had I got it wrong? Had she changed her name? I tried just typing 'Roxy'. There were a few, but not her. I made a search of all the escorts in the area. She wasn't amongst them. A wider search also revealed nothing.

I didn't have a phone number for her – we'd just been in

touch through the site – so there was no way I could get in contact. I wanted to believe she wasn't on there because she'd stopped doing that kind of thing, that she'd got away from whatever situation she'd been in. But I didn't know. And probably would never know.

I'd psyched myself up to helping her. I was going to buy an English-Romanian dictionary so we'd be able to communicate, and came up with elaborate plans of how, if it came to it, I'd implement her escape and let her stay in the small room ... for a little while. But I felt impotent, unsatisfied. I paced the flat between the kitchen and the bedroom and the living room. I thought about distracting myself with porn, but the timing was inappropriate, and anyway, I'd been finding it difficult to just see the fantasy.

My phone was lying on the sofa. Picking it up, I wanted to ring Holly ... but should I? I scrolled through the names on my contact list (which wasn't very long), then stopped and pressed 'call'.

"Hello?" A female voice.

"Hi."

"Lyle, is that you?" Elspeth's voice.

"Yeah, it's me."

The conversation began like a chore – like phoning your Great Aunt to thank her for the birthday present. Elspeth spoke about her job, Alex's job, and what work they'd done on their house. She asked me what I was doing, and I told her I still lived in the flat, still worked in the antiques shop. Partly to close a subject I couldn't be bothered to talk about, I added, "But I know that's not as interesting as what you're up to."

She was quiet for a few seconds and then said, "Why did you do that, Lyle?"

"Do what?"

"Put yourself down."

I hadn't expected the question, nor did I expect my reaction to it. "Uh, well, why not?" I said. "I know Mum and Dad think

I'm a fuck-up … you all do." My voice quavered slightly with the last three words, giving away what I was suddenly feeling. But it wasn't just about my family, it was everything.

"Who cares what Mum and Dad think!" she said. "And don't put that on me too."

I tried to compose myself before I spoke again, but Elspeth continued. She had a softer tone to her voice. "Look, they just want the best for you – for both of us – but you know what they're like."

"Yeah, right," I said. "You've got no idea what they've been like to me. *Your* life is always so perfect." I knew I was sounding like a whiny and unreasonable little boy, but couldn't help it.

"Ha! My life isn't perfect," she scoffed, "far from it. And do you think they never put their expectations on me too – to keep getting As, to get a first, to get my PhD? Why do you think I never went back to live there?"

It hadn't occurred to me that she'd been under pressure. She hadn't gone through the huge rows and slammed doors that I had as a teenager, so I'd thought it had all been fine.

"Seriously, don't worry about what they expect, Lyle," she said. "You've got to live your own life. Do what's right for you."

"I know," I said, all feelings of injustice gone. "I'm coming to that conclusion."

We talked some more – properly. I told her about Holly and our few days in Prague (not all of it), and Elspeth invited me to visit her soon, which I would.

The conversation ended, and I realised I'd been staring at the wallpaper – at the drawing of the two people in the boat. My gaze shifted to the music box in the centre of the mantelpiece. I went over to it, lifted the roof and took out the pound coin I'd put in there. Running my thumb over the side of the coin, smooth with dried glue, it reminded me of a Toffee Penny from a tin of Quality Street.

I planned to write inside the box, and as I thought about it, remembered something Holly had said to me. She said I wrote on things because I wanted to be seen. Maybe that was true. But *she'd* seen me and, although I hadn't realised it, that was enough. But I don't think I'd really seen *her*. Not until Prague. Not until after I'd fucked it all up.

I'd wanted Holly to move in with me, but she'd been clear – she needed to get her head together. And I understood that. After all, I was still working on mine.

I knew what to write:

OUR HOME A MUSIC BOX

That night, after dark, I re-glued the pound coin in its place on the pavement.

46

I spoke to Keith about my concerns over the safety of the gas fires, and explained how cold it was in the flat in winter; he responded in his usual kind, generous way by having central heating installed. He also replaced the lino in the hallway with carpet, and paid for the materials for any redecoration I wanted. But I was keeping the living room the way it was.

I painted over the clown-face wallpaper in the small room, and swapped the bed for a desk – my writing desk. From the top of the shelves that held my books and CDs, my granddad's old typewriter watched my progress with what I started to think of as an encouraging grin. I couldn't write with my own music on – it was too much of a distraction – but somehow hearing Amy's through the wall didn't bother me.

As I sat at the desk with my laptop open in front of me, I was often on Twitter or Facebook. Marcus still wasn't on there, but Nina had accepted my friend request so I got to see the photos she posted of their baby, and of the three of them appearing to be a happy family. Her statuses were frequently along the lines of how lucky she was to have Marcus, and how fantastic he was with his daughter. I didn't know if that was true; I learned quickly that some people falsely represent their lives on Facebook.

Holly had been right about social media: the likes and the retweets satisfied some kind of need for validation. On Twitter – under the username @MyPencilLead – I wrote puns and Kafka quotes, and posted photos of good graffiti, and anything beautiful, unusual or out of place. But I still carried a pencil in my pocket.

I wasn't writing Louisa's memoirs. Instead I'd decided to fictionalise and incorporate her stories into another project. The plan had changed, because that's what plans often do – they adapt and evolve.

I was working on a novel: a series of interconnecting stories following several characters living at different times in a small community. They become connected in many ways – not least because they're buried near each other in the local churchyard – but mainly because at pivotal times, when their lives are at a turning point, they discover etched writing on stone that changes everything. The opening line of the book was: We all die. But first, we all live.

One of the threads of the story is set in the early 1800s and follows Bobby Hickson, a young man of twenty-three with large gambling debts. After accusing someone of cheating, Bobby refuses to apologise and is challenged to a duel. Neither man wants to fight, but both are determined to uphold their honour ...

Then there's Ava Silver, a Victorian girl – the youngest of seven sisters – with ambitions of becoming a teacher. Unmarried and pregnant, she brings shame on her family, and the baby is taken away. Self-destructing, Ava turns to prostitution, and intends to throw herself in front of a train ...

In the 1970s, Louisa is the muse and model for her Surrealist-painter husband. They have a lavish and happy life together full of holidays, film premieres, and celebrity parties. When her husband dies suddenly, Louisa confines herself to her house, only leaving to buy groceries. She never cleans and begins to hoard newspapers and food packaging ...

There's also Stephen, the son of an antiques dealer who becomes a hero during the occupation of Amsterdam in World War II; Edward, who tends the graves in the churchyard in the present day; and an unnamed stonemason who adds hidden details to his work. I almost included a magician who gets framed for his assistant's murder, but decided against it.

I liked that I was creating a world where coincidence had reason – and they weren't the *Universe's* reasons, they were *mine*. But the story was as much about cause and effect as it was coincidence, how one thing leads to another. Not every character has a happy ending – because it doesn't always work out that way – but there's the common theme of taking control over their lives, and realising they can't deny or hide from their problems.

I thought back to everything that had happened while *I'd* been hiding. It seemed like such a long time ago, like it was a different life and I was a different person. It had been a crazy time, but a lot of it had been fun. And part of me missed it.

* * *

I brushed the brown, desiccated oak leaves from the top of the tomb, and sat in my place next to Robert and Sylvia, next to the words which now read:

LYLE McNORTON

AGED 24

LIVING NOT EXISTING

Looking up, I saw the stars through the bare branches of the tree; even the Pleiades were easy to see in the clear sky.

The stone of the tomb was cold, and my jeans didn't offer much protection for my legs. Knowing it wouldn't be comfortable to sit there for long, I checked the time, but it was still a while to go until my appointment.

We'd messaged a few times through the website before I made the booking, and I was pleased her grammar and spelling were nearly perfect. On her profile, her pictures were self-taken and didn't include head shots, but I was impressed by the photos of her body in a range of outfits and poses.

We wrote dirty to each other – good-dirty – and I discovered that messaging could be as important a part of the experience as the actual sex. But I made sure to ask (on more than one occasion) whether she was *really* OK to meet me, and stressed that I didn't want to do it if it meant a bad time for her. She assured me that it would be as fun for her as it was for me, and I didn't get the impression she was pretending. By the time I made the booking and it was confirmed, I was more than eager.

At the door, I was exactly on time. My heart beat faster. Composing myself, I knocked, and through the illuminated rectangle of the sandblasted glass panel, I saw the indistinct shape of a figure approaching. The door opened, and I went inside.

As I lay on the bed recovering my breath, I took in my surroundings. On the walls were prints by Escher, Magritte, Klee and Hundertwasser, and over the bed, draped with a string of electric blue, star-shaped lights was a *Moonraker* film poster. It had taken three coats to fully cover the brown wallpaper underneath and I could still smell the paint. Along the windowsill were brightly-coloured glass vases and my phone that I'd positioned there to film us. On a teak G Plan chest of drawers opposite was the unsold plastic pineapple and the music box.

It finally looked like a home – *our* home.

"So," I said, "role-play worked for me. How about you?"

"Definitely," Holly agreed. "Let's watch it back."

ACKNOWLEDGEMENTS

Many thanks to those who read, commented and encouraged during the various stages of this book. Notably: John Cattle, Lisa Jolliffe, John Clarke, Lucy Blanchard, Rachel Swyers, James Nye, Jim Willis, Emily Heath, Felicity Fair Thompson, Glenys Lloyd-Williams, Ellen Weeks and all at Wight Writers.

Thank you J&S, BB, MR and AW for the answers to awkward questions.

Thanks to Holly Jenkins (Holly Cade Photography) for the cover photo.

I'm extremely grateful to Sir Roland Penrose's estate for permission to reproduce the lines from his painting *Portrait,* and to Graham Gouldman and EMI Music Publishing LTD for permission to use the lyrics from 'Love's Not For Me'.

ABOUT THE AUTHOR

Fran Heath was born in 1974 and lives on the Isle of Wight with her two children.

After graduating from the University of Greenwich (with a BSc in Environmental Earth Science), and a brief stint on the dole, she worked in her parents' antiques shop for eight years.

Pencil Lead is Fran's debut novel. She's also written and illustrated a children's picture book: *How We Choose to Play.*

Facebook/Instagram/Twitter: @franheathwriter

If you've enjoyed this book, please leave an online review (Amazon, Goodreads etc.) and tell your friends.
Thank you!

Made in the USA
Charleston, SC
07 September 2016